New to Santa Clara

Kenneth Crowther

Published by Kenneth Crowther, 2024.

NEW TO SANTA CLARA

First edition. January 2, 2024.

Copyright © 2024 Kenneth Crowther.

ISBN: 979-8224323142

Written by Kenneth Crowther.

"The most interesting information comes from children, for they tell all they know and then stop." Mark Twain

CHAPTER 1

---

*S*ummer 1957

Lyle and I had been out of school just three days and were about to shed the warmth of our well-worn Utah jackets for California short-sleeves. Lyle's mind was all about entering a high school full of strangers next fall and forever leaving his home and life in Utah behind, and he let us all know about it with his silence. I was presently happy enough having survived Liberty Elementary first grade and the disapproval of Mrs. G. I may have worn only a few of Lyle's hand-me-down clothes, but even they didn't fit very well in the eyes of Mrs. G. "Why can't you be more like your brother?" In first grade I mostly learned about failing other people's expectations. Something new had to be better.

My mother's mission—Lyle and I tagging along—was to meet up with Aunt Clara and Uncle Mac in San Bruno, a hillside town just south of San Francisco to find a new house in the bay area. We had ten days to do so before the orange and silver California Zephyr for which we had return tickets raced back along the Feather River rails to Utah. My mother reassured Lyle and me the family would be settled in California so we could start our new schools by September.

I suspect the deadline had more to do with my father getting his vending machines up and running by fall, which meant first having a garage ready in time for September delivery of two hundred yellow and blue metal Rite Master ball point pen-dispensing machines and three-foot tall black iron stands, and box after box of colorful "Click It Rite" ballpoint pens and cardboard tube packaging for each, which he had already ordered on credit. This new and, in my mother's view, risky business venture was the unending topic of chatter between her and Aunt Clara on our visit. My Uncle Mac didn't say much.

During my goodbyes to my friends and schoolmates, I was asked several times, "Aren't you afraid of earthquakes?" That wasn't anymore of a threat to me than the atomic bomb dropping on Liberty School, and we practiced for that in first grade with duck and cover drills. But the tentacles of fear were reaching for me now in the sight of someone sitting directly in front of me as I clung to my mother's side on a cold white painted steel bench on a Western Pacific-operated Bay ferry from Oakland to San Francisco.

With the chill of the San Francisco Bay blowing in our faces in the open-sided ship's cabin, we still wore our jackets zipped tightly to our necks. My mother would try to excite our interest in new sights:

"And that's the Golden Gate Bridge. And there's Alcatraz Prison. What do you think of the ocean?"

I was fully fixed on this apparition robed in black, her saucer-round chocolate face visible between white head splints and the bib of a nun's habit. I hadn't really learned much about Catholics or "nuns," especially black ones, but I am told I was born in Holy Cross Hospital, a Catholic hospital in Salt Lake City. Later, I would reveal that fact as a badge of honor when people assumed I was a Mormon because I was born in Utah. Just before we reached the ferry building in San Francisco, my steadfast stare became too much for even a disciplined woman of the cloth. She momentarily stopped playing with her beaded necklace and with a soft smile and treats in hand, she offered two short sticks of Dentine gum she pulled from her tunic pocket as a peace offering, one for me and one for my brother. With some hesitancy, I accepted after my mother's okay. I nudged Lyle, stubbornly sitting next to me, out of his muted anger for this trip he did not want to take and move he did not want to make, and he too took the gum. The nice lady in the black and white costume waved goodbye to me as we disembarked. I should have told her I was born in a Catholic hospital.

My Aunt Clara and Uncle Mac greeted us with open arms and hugs and welcomed the three of us to California, though my mother was actually born in California, in the San Joaquin Valley, forty years ago and had escaped the town of Sanger, most of her family, her Methodist upbringing, and this state, long ago.

Clara and Mac's San Bruno house perched on a street corner on a hill, in a row of dozens of other boxed shaped, mostly white, stucco structures that sat in what seemed to be a never-ending blanket of grey clouds and crawling white fog, not exactly Salt Lake City, but I was easily distracted by the nearby shopping center pet store which contained an array of parakeets, canaries, tropical fish, and snakes, and the Brentwood Bowl that we learned to love as much for its oily grilled cheese sandwiches and fountain as for its fifteen cent bowling lines when I got a little older.

We would begin our new journey the next day. The search was on for a new house. My mother was born for things "new." She was forever disposing of perfectly good stuff—chairs, dishes, clothes, even good toys, to clean the slate, to start anew. Later, mother would throw out Lyle's priceless collection of baseball cards—because he "never used them." She was ready for change and not sentimental, as she would be first to tell you. She had acquired these traits from her mother Ada Inskip, who at sixteen had left England and old things behind, and with her best friend headed for America. My mother would defend her practical actions as "spring cleaning." In her cleaning efforts, mother had left the San Joaquin Valley many years before where she had had a steady job as counter waitress at the Giant Orange restaurant in Tulare. It was there she met my father passing through town. Together they would dispose of the old and acquire new things for many, many years.

The Santa Clara Valley itself was doing spring cleaning, and the orchards, crops, the small towns, and even the waterways, were rapidly being filled by newness—suburbs, industry, cities, and land-fill. Local families turned politicians and fortune-seeking newcomers all claimed to know what was best and fought each other to sell, buy, reinvent, and annex the freshly plowed acreage in the "valley of hearts delight." It was not like the valley of California my mother had left years ago. It was the crossroad of change.

The five of us loaded into Uncle Mac's glade green and white '57 Cadillac coupe Seville, with push-button everything, shark fin fenders, air suspension, wraparound front and rear windshields, power seats, cruise control, and even air conditioning. For some curious reason his soft green leather and ripple silk seats were permanently sealed beneath the stiffness of Sears's clear plastic fitted covers. Uncle Mac was a quiet but imposing kind of guy, and his wide plaid Pendleton shirts of muted beiges, greens, and yellows, his smelly cigars, swollen belly, fat ruddy nose, and flashy Cadillacs always said that. He owned a sheet metal shop, meaning he built tin gas stations, as he called them. He had more business than he could handle. Patriotic Chevron bars, yellow Shell scallops, and red Texaco stars were lighting up shiny sheet metal houses of gas on the roadway corners, overnight, especially along the new and retread streets off El Camino Real.

We began our journey seeking new housing tracts down the peninsula. My mother had already decided she wanted to live between the City and San Jose. I don't know what she didn't like about San Jose, but the feeling has rubbed off on me for no good reason. One truth then was housing was cheaper and more plentiful the farther south we headed on The Kings Highway. We tromped through subdivision after subdivision, from San Bruno, to Millbrae, to Burlingame, to Hillsborough, to San Mateo, to Belmont, to San Carlos, to Redwood City, to Palo Alto, to Los Altos, to Mountain View, even aside to Cupertino, Saratoga, Campbell, Los Gatos, and back to Sunnyvale, and eventually to Santa Clara.

Every day began early morning with my mom and Aunt Clara searching the *San Francisco Chronicle* or the *San Mateo Times* or the *San Jose Mercury,* sitting in Aunt Clara's bright yellow kitchen diner booth, slurping freshly perked coffee, my aunt puffing away at Salem after Salem, the two of them circling ads for new homes, studying brochures picked up the previous day at builder sites for other developments owned further south, and then the five of us driving a little bit farther down El Camino on the hunt. The further south we drove the sunnier the day seemed to get.

To Lyle and me, most of El Camino was a blur of trees, fields, businesses, shopping centers, and houses. The further we'd drive east or west from El Camino, the more housing developments appeared, all with descriptive names to market them as idyllic. You could live in an estate, a place, a meadow, a park, a woods, even a manor. At the day's end we returned to the greying skies south of San Francisco. I learned to measure how far we had to go to get back to Aunt Clara's home by the bleachers of the Tanforan Race Track and the white and black checkered walls of the See's Candy Factory, just up the street from my aunt's house. My Aunt Clara actually worked at See's for a while. I could imagine her at work as Lucy Ricardo, losing the battle with the candy conveyor belt. Aunt Clara always had a dish of chocolate "seconds" on her living room coffee table.

By the time we reached Mountain View on our house hunt, on Thursday, the tree-covered hillsides were giving way to flatter land and more farms and orchard ranches as we moved into the south end of the valley. Fewer storefronts hid the orchards of apricots, cherries, pears, peaches, and prunes or the family plots of corn, beans, strawberries, tomatoes, and onions. Their sweet and pungent aromas mixed and sometimes confused our noses. Of course many of these farms were rudely interrupted by the rooftops of tract homes.

"Homes here are too expensive," my mother would complain after leaving yet another set of model homes sandwiched among orchards. I could tell, secretly, my mom was delighted there were so many new houses to shop. It was all so new.

On Sunday, we reached the western edge of Santa Clara at the crossroads of El Camino Real and Lawrence Station Road. Orchards and crops ran along Lawrence Station Road, a two-lane roadway, running north and south from El Camino, bordering Sunnyvale. Even then you could see housing invading in the distance—Darvon Park, Bowers Park, Briarwood Park, Westwood Oaks, Junipero Gardens, Killarney Farms, Greenvale Manor—a frenzy of construction. We went through them all. In various stages of completion, they were mostly single-story stucco "ranch" homes, and all were built since I was born. To me, the houses looked pretty much the same. I could never understand what was "ranch" about these nondescript houses. Only Killarney Farms stood out in my mind because the developers hosted a couple of donkeys kids could pet in a corral with a barn, and some of the garages had rooflines that looked like barns.

Recently staked lots on acres of vacant dirt would become some 200 houses beginning at the intersection of Lawrence Station Road and newly constructed Cabrillo Avenue. The three models at the west end of Cabrillo were open for viewing, complete with white ranch fencing and manicured green lawns. When we arrived, all the marked lots were sold, and two of the three showroom homes were all that was left for sale. Fresh stick frames like a gigantic toothpick village outlined houses-to-be down both sides of the new avenue. Empty sold lots behind Cabrillo stood awaiting construction. We were almost too late. The first model house on the block and nearest to the highway was a flamingo pink stucco structure with white-enameled wood trim. It was the premier model, complete with pink built-in Tappan kitchen appliances and pink porcelain fixtures throughout to match the exterior. Its latest technology included hi-fidelity speakers built into the hall walls to pipe in music from the hi-fi system in the sales garage.

We men waited what seemed like hours in the Seville for my mother and aunt to come out. Every fifteen minutes or so Uncle Mac would impress us once again by closing the push-button windows, running the engine, and turning on the air conditioning for a "cool down." By now we had lost all interest in the hunt and mostly listened to KGO radio—"one of the good things about San Francisco"—to while away the hours. But eventually my mother came out of the garage office, waving for us to come in. She had found our home.

What impressed me the most was the mammoth permanent sign that stood in the middle and diagonally on our soon-to-be new front lawn. It stood five-foot high by twenty-foot wide on two huge dark brown wooden slats, held between a pair of even taller three-foot square red-brick pillars and surrounded by a brick flower box of flourishing red and pink geraniums. The sign spelled out L-A-W-R-E-N-C-E M-E-A-D-O-W-S, in giant white-enameled wood script lettering for anyone traveling up or down Lawrence Station Road to see. We had arrived. The sign and the three model homes would distract drivers and passengers along this two-lane road from the blur of orchards surrounding the newest tract in the area. They announced more than a housing development. Our move, the houses, the neighborhood were promises of newness.

Endless hours of paperwork and a large deposit—*the largest check my mother ever wrote, she said*—made the house ours, *almost*. The plan was for my father to see the house only after we drove as a family across country to take possession. Letting my mother pick out a house without his even seeing it was his concession to my mother for uprooting us to California for a vending machine business. My father would remind her everything in Santa Clara was brand new, and he could use his CalVet loan, which somehow meant cheap money to buy the house since he had lived in California when he fought in the war.

Four days before final papers were signed, the bank had decided his new business venture, CalVet loan, and deposit were not enough to buy a $16,000 house on credit. He would need a second job. One

Friday night after driving truck all day for Garrett Freight-lines, his best friend Merle drove him to Salt Lake City Municipal Airport. My dad would spend the next four days in the south bay searching for a second job to qualify for the loan. Success! As a teamster, he would drive for Willig Freight Lines, a new trucking company only five miles from our new home. My dad would have a garage for all those vending machines and pens after all. The bright yellow and blue Willig trucks would coincidentally match all those pen machines.

CHAPTER 2

all 1957

F   *In the days before my dad returned to Salt Lake, Lyle was more like his old self.* "We might not be going after all," he cheerfully told Phillip and Billy and Richard. They were all on their way to South High in the fall. But it didn't turn out that way for Lyle, and we made the 766-mile trip in our two-tone green '53 Pontiac Chieftain in two days.

Mayflower Movers had left our empty Salt Lake house two days before us, loaded with everything the family owned in an immense yellow and green semi-trailer. Its metal sides adorned in huge painted drawings of the original *Mayflower.*

Rough sailing, our belongings didn't arrive for another seven days. Unprepared for an empty house, the four of us spent the nights camping on the living room floor on newly-laid golden shag carpet, wrapped in sun-faded army-green wool blankets dug out of the Pontiac's trunk and padded by scraps of shag that had been left in the garage by the builder. It was a suburban adventure.

Paul Ruffino was twelve, but he commanded a small band of neighborhood kids who were all three and four years younger. That made him even bigger in the eyes of other kids. He was a modern Dickens character. He was the roughest kid in the neighborhood. A thick dark crop of hair on his head rolled back on either side in a pompadour, meticulously combed and coiffed and always kind of greasy looking. His dilated black eyes were scary. Cheeks that were pre-maturely pockmarked from bobby pin picked blackheads dominated his angular face. Volcanic pimples in multiple stages of activity added color to his skin, altogether splotchy like a McIntosh apple. He had that "Scarface" kind of look at twelve. The first time he spoke to me face-to-face was in front of the pear orchard directly across the street from our house.

The tract builders had leveled the farmland on which our block and neighborhood were built but left two lots empty across the street, and now the land hosted only weeds. Nobody seemed to know why. Houses of Lawrence Meadows now stand where tomatoes and seed crops once grew, but I never saw them. To the left of the double lot in front of our house was a perpendicular fully paved but short street complete with sidewalks that ended at the pear orchard. The street sign read Fairbanks. We called it the "street to nowhere," but it was headed directly into Frank's orchard. There were many streets to nowhere in Santa Clara at the time. A yellow road sign marked "END" hung on a white ranch fence where the orchard began. Lawrence Meadow homes, now just finished, ran along the left side of the nowhere street, completing our block.

The vacant double lot across from us made a vast world of entertainment for boys. In mid-August, the lot was fully yellow and bristling with weeds towering high enough to hide in for ambushes or war games of air rifles or slingshots or dirt clods. It was dry, dusty and dirty, the perfect place to play. No trace of a city or suburb if you did not look behind you at the houses going up.

Frank Musso's pear orchard began on the back edge of the lots in front of our house and spread toward El Camino until dense rows of apricot trees began behind it. A small school bus yard and Arne's Sign shop dented trees along the Santa Clara side of Lawrence Station Road and disturbed the orchards' flow. From our front windows, we could also see several rows of bing cherry trees on the Sunnyvale side of Lawrence, though most of the cherry orchard sat out of our sight, deep into Sunnyvale. An extensive tomato field beyond the visible cherry trees reached the rest of the half mile to El Camino, where seemingly little cars moved along the highway.

A forty acre orchard of mostly prunes running deep into Sunnyvale grew at our immediate right across Lawrence, less than two hundred feet from our house. Single rows of black walnut trees on each side of the highway separated orchard, crops, and now houses, from the highway. Behind our house lay another forty acres of noisy fields, now defined as lots, in various stages of stick, concrete, and stucco construction. The frenetic construction of houses behind ours and the new cast of houses that enclosed Cabrillo were an explosive contrast to the three solitary model homes that sat on Cabrillo Avenue just two months ago. Deeper south and west of our new neighborhood, you could reach acres of cherry, pear, apricot, prune, peach, and walnut orchards without much of a walk or bike ride, but more trees were being plowed over almost daily.

A five-foot high, vertical concrete culvert stood in the right corner of the Musso pear orchard near the highway edge. An always-locked, dilapidated wooden pump shed leaned about four feet in from the tank. Inside the culvert was a rusty half-buried pipe; in its middle a steering wheel-sized helm to open and close the water flow to the turned dirt below the trees. That of course was chained and padlocked to guard the water flow, I guess, but that didn't stop people like me from imagining all this to be some sort of seagoing equipment in the tree landscapes before them.

Having just moved to the "Meadows," I was busy investigating these genuine meadows, the tall weeds of the vacant lot, plotting how far to dash into the next sticker blind I would tamper down for hidden surveillance. This was pretty cool, plenty dirty and unruly. Suddenly, a blur of some other kids caught my eye just yards in front of me dodging between the pear trees. Three potential combatants. Then, much like me, they began darting from blind to blind across the field, and, like a combat reconnaissance team, headed toward the empty water tank near the highway just a dozen yards from me.

I hadn't been spotted yet, or so I thought. I kept low-lying and my eyes sharp, peeking from among the weeds. Now nearing the tank, the tallest boy made a quick leap up, over and actually into the empty concrete cylinder. In a flash, he was up, over and out, a black metal rod in his right hand, then all hidden from view in the weeds again.

It was forever before I saw any movement. Then it started. Ping, ping, ping, ping, ping. The sound was unmistakable to a seven-year-old. It was a BB gun. I could see spits of dust fan about when a BB hit a pear tree branch or a bunch of weeds near me. Paul was shooting unpredictably. I didn't want to get shot my first week in California. I lay face down, stone still. I would wait them out.

"You are not getting a BB gun, and that's that. Do you want to lose an eye?" responded my mother to the worn-out question Lyle had had for years. It was Lyle's question but she was looking at us both. My dad nodded in agreement with my mother from behind his forkful of chuck roast at the dinner table, but said nothing himself. It was an old declaration brought to mind.

The next thing I knew I was smothered by two assailants who pounced on my back and twisted my arms behind me before I could wrestle free from their weight and the weed-splattering dust and scratchy stickers. They had pinned me to the ground. Their knees compressed my back and legs. My hands held at the wrists by four. On my belly, with my head crooked upward, I made out Paul towering over me, the morning sun spotlighting his pimply face, the pistol muzzle inches from my forehead. But randomly I only thought to myself that close up his zits were even worse than I had imagined from a distance.

"What are you doing in our field?" he demanded. I explained to him that I was the new guy on the block that I lived in the pink house across the street.

"I already knew that. We saw you move in, even been in your house before you. You need to learn to stay in your own yard. This lot belongs to us," he said, waving his gun toward his two amigos who still had me pinned. "You want to use this field, you pay me first," he threatened me, jamming the gun into my forehead, and then he worked up a big hanging loogie, leaned his head inches from mine, and let it slowly drop by a gooey mucus string, just missing my nose and chin. In the distance, I could hear a man's voice yelling out:

"Paul. Holler, Paul. Where are you? Holler, Paul." Paul looked up and adjusted his focus to the distant call. He was someone else when he spoke again.

"I'm down the street. I'll be right there," he yelled in return, as was the duty of any kid when his dad called out for him. Instantly back in character, Paul looked down on me and pointed the gun at my head one more time. "You know what happens to squealers?"

I nodded. They were gone.

Paul put his weapon back in its hiding place as quickly as he had retrieved it, and the three of them sprinted off toward Paul's, four houses down from mine. I lay in the dry dirt for a while, recovering in my new neighborhood.

I stayed out of Paul's way for the rest of the summer. I would occasionally see Paul and his followers shuffling along the street, heading to I don't know where. He was headed off to junior high next month.

Art and I did manage to retrieve the gun from the water tank a couple months later, wrapped in a rag and buried directly under the water helm. It disappeared from our own hiding place near the shed shortly after that. I've always wondered why Paul didn't come after me for the gun or why it disappeared.

While I didn't have much say in the course my life was taking at the moment, I also didn't give it much thought, or at least not as much thought as Lyle did. He spent most of his time in his room, occupying himself with his Topps and APBA baseball cards or listening to Buddy Holly, Little Richard, or Elvis Presley on his new transistor radio, a consolation gift for the big move. "It's not fair" was his first line and last line of defense when I asked him why he was so mad at everything. His war against moving to California was not over, nor would it be for many years.

I saw the promise of things ahead of me. Second grade started Monday. Briarwood school was only two years old itself. It was one of at least a half dozen new schools built in Santa Clara within the last five years. Rather than looking back at what I had left in Salt Lake City, I was looking forward to being out of the clutches of Mrs. G, my first grade teacher. Anyone else would be an improvement. At least I didn't carry the baggage of having an older brother precede me at this school. New was good.

Everyone was excited about the first day of school. Kids were everywhere, on the playground, in the outdoor halls, hanging out at the quad by the flagpole. I was seven, and old enough not to be taken to school my first day by my mother, but she insisted on walking with me anyway, at least as far as the alley on Nobili. That was the backdoor to the school grounds on the far end of the field. My mother and I had gone to Briarwood together to register and get the lay of the land the week before. Once I got to the buildings alone this morning, all the kids clustered here and there, a sudden creepiness came over me. I didn't know anybody. I weaved my way through the knots of kids who were too busy getting reacquainted to notice me make my way to #6, Mrs. Fay's room. And then I saw her, Lorraine Jackson.

Although we hadn't met, I had seen her and her several smaller brothers and sisters making furtive glances our way from three doors down in their driveway as we unpacked, and they pretended to play some kind of kick ball. We had exchanged glances but that was that. Now she was standing along the wall before Mrs. Fay's door, along with about five other kids. Her brown freckles stood out against her sunbaked cheeks on a face framed by disheveled dirty blonde hair. Her speckled green eyes and long eyelashes gave her smile a sparkle. When I spoke to her, I realized that she was actually "in line" for class to begin. She giggled when I told her who I was, and, without telling me her name, she told me I should get in line.

At the right wall of Mrs. Fay's door stood an unattended, very tall metallic blue trike, white and red plastic streamers hanging from the translucent blue handlebars, a metal basket between the two rear wheels. The trike became a customary fixture outside Mrs. Fay's classroom. When the first bell rang, kids came charging up to their rooms throughout the school, pushing to get into lines.

Lorraine and I, along with twenty-six other second-graders, were assigned to newly hired second grade teacher, Mrs. Evelyn Fay. Twenty-seven of us stood along the back wall of the room until, one by one, Mrs. Fay read out our name from a sheet of paper in one hand and ordered with a pointy red pencil in the other to the desk where each person was to sit, alphabetically, of course. The owner of the blue trike, Susan Molloy, was already at her assigned seat when we arrived. It was one of the few times she was treated any differently than the rest of us. We filled every desk.

On cue, as if he had personally witnessed our execution of Mrs. Fay's directions, Principal George Boyko welcomed us to the new school year and announced to the student body on a whistling, erratic public address system piped into the classrooms that Jefferson District had added one hundred new classrooms in Santa Clara this year.

"The city's population has . . . oubled to over 32,000 in only three years. This accounts for the larger class . . . *hiss.* . . . notice this year, but we . . . *hiss.* . . of the progress and . . . our city, which is liter. . . *hiss.* . . ing at the seams. We know as responsible youngsters in . . . *hiss.* . . will help us make this a rewarding year." We would hear *more* or less the same speech in an all-school assembly in the cafeteria later that week.

I thought about how many orchards and fields had been bulldozed to make room for all these classrooms, houses and people, myself included. My mother had already told me that the Santa Clara schools were desperate for new teachers. Just how desperate, I soon found out. Turns out Mrs. Fay wasn't that new. We were told she had been a parochial school teacher for the past twenty-five years and had even retired from that line of work. At the time, I did not know what a parochial school teacher was anyhow. Playground rumors went round that she had also been a nun once, but nobody I know ever verified that. I had met a nun once.

Mrs. Fay was nearly six feet tall and built of solid oak. We second graders were her little people, but it was no happy Munchkin Land. Her iron-gray hair, parted down the middle of her head, was pinned in a bun against the back of her scalp. We never saw just how long it really was because she never let her hair down in front of us. She wore cats-eye glasses with black plastic pointy temples and silver wire frames either low across the bridge of her nose from always looking down at us or on a silver serpentine necklace hanging around her neck. In the groove above her right ear she wore a bright red marking pencil. It was as much a part of her wardrobe as the plain black leather, heel-less pumps she wore everyday. Her mid-calf-length nylon dresses were usually a boring, solid color, blue or black or of small checked or striped patterns and always with a high round neckline, occasionally trimmed with a doily white collar that looked like something off the back of my grandma's overstuffed chair. Most of the time, she would hang above us in class as we sat orderly at our small beige metal desks, but when she sat up front at her reigning teacher's desk, her pointy red pencil reminded you she was around. Her pencil, always at the ready for marking up our offerings, when not on her head or busy correcting, was in her right hand balanced between thumb and index finger, tapping on her oak desk at a speed and volume that increased with her impatience, which usually meant it was moving rather rapidly and getting louder.

I wondered if things were going any better for Lyle. His first day was more complicated than just going to a new school. Lyle would be in the Class of '61 of a high school yet-to-be built. Buchser High School was still on paper when Lyle started school this fall. He had to catch a school bus two blocks down the street from our house and temporarily attend Santa Clara High School on the far side of town on a double session schedule. His classes started way too early. The bus left at just after six, and he was taking starting over harder than I was.

When the morning recess bell rang our first day at Briarwood, most kids were already into the swing of things. In the big freshly poured sand and rubber chip-covered playground there were lines of mostly first, second, and third-grade boys and girls waiting to take a turn on the cold metal slide, push go-round, chin-up bars, steel rings, monkey bars, and belt seat swings. Other kids stood on the dark black asphalt, waiting for an opening at foursquare played in one of the six painted white geometric boxes on the freshly slurried surface or a chance to be challenger to the next tetherball winner. Bunches of girls jumped hopscotch on the permanent courts painted on the black surface. The smells of tar, sand, and rubber filled the fall air. The sounds and commotion of kids took off the chill. The older boys congregated at the south end of the campus and hogged the basketball court and area in front of the taller chin-up bars. The older girls huddled or sat on the green wooden benches by the porcelain water fountains at the end of each hall or at the wooden picnic tables between the halls, gossiping to one another. Toward the front of the school, you could get a glimpse of the kindergarten playground surrounded with its low cyclone fence, little kids at their own games, corralled. It was a community.

I had noticed Carlotta O'Reilly in class, a couple of rows over. She had a healthy tan and two full front teeth that were always evident. I could identify with that and was forever told to hide my own when class pictures were taken. Carlotta was husky for a seven-year-old girl and didn't look comfortable in the dress she had to wear to school. "Quit fidgeting, Carlotta," Mrs. Fay had scolded her at least four times the first day. Her sun-streaked brown hair was pulled back into a perfect braid and tightly held with knotted thick rubber bands, and she would wrap her braid around her fingers again and again. I liked watching her distractions from across the room until Mrs. Fay told me to pay attention.

Carlotta was about to step up to the metal starting platform of the steel rings at recess. A couple of her friends shouted, "Go, Carlotta. Go!" That got my attention. Apparently, she was the only girl in 2nd grade who could actually skip two loops at once as she swung. Four-eight-twelve, she did it effortlessly. Carlotta was a favorite with most of the boys. On the softball field she'd hit as far as any other kid, boy or girl. In dodge ball she was a deadeye, and her whip-like throws could sting you with a ball. Some boys didn't like her for those talents.

While all the action was going on at the rings, another commotion was taking place at a foursquare court on the asphalt. I had just walked over after Carlotta's feat and was bumped in the shoulder by a kid being picked on.

"Who said you could play, PUDLOW?" demanded Hubie Leaper. He looked tough with his white rolled-sleeved shirt unbuttoned to expose his bare neck. His shock of unruly blond hair blew over his eyes as he moved. He pushed Reginald Pudlow out of line for foursquare, but Reginald quietly skirted back in.

"Go somewhere else, you sissy," Hubie said and he pushed him back again, this time right into me as I faced them. The kids playing continued their game. The others in line said nothing. There were yard-duty mothers on the playground, but with so many kids outside, this incident went unnoticed for the moment. The bump jolted me off balance momentarily.

"Watch it!" I yelled, at the both of them. Hubie took my remark personally and directed his wrath at me.

"Who do you think *you* are, telling me what to do? Punk. Want to make something of it? Come on. I'll pound you right now," he said, his face in mine, and then he stepped back and put his fists up to fight.

Suddenly, the game stopped. Everyone circled us like hungry cats gathering around a fresh bowl of tuna. We were surrounded. All was quiet. The lull caught the attention of the nearest yard-duty lady. She blew a silver coach's whistle that had hung from her neck until that instant and, with fresh purpose, headed our way.

I had said two words on the playground, and I was already in trouble. Hubie pressed toward me. With his right index finger threatening forward at me, he managed to utter before the distressed yard supervisor could pry her way to the center of the small people crowd, "After school, in the alley, punk!"

"Break it up! Who's fighting? It's the first day of school. Let's not spoil it," the woman pealed in, not actually knowing who the offenders were. Then the bell rang for class. Then it was over, but it wasn't.

By lunch I was a celebrity. The boys wanted to see a fight after school. I was cajoled by a handful of faces from my class, all with arguments about why I needed to show up.

"You aren't chicken, are you?"

"Hubie bullies everyone."

"He deserves to get pounded."

"Don't let him scare you."

A group of girls watched from the table area as they ate their packed lunches. Carlotta O'Reilly marched over to me and grabbed my attention.

"It's time somebody took him on. Everyone else is afraid of him. He's picked on Reggie since kindergarten and nobody stands up for him."

Somehow I had become Reginald's defender. Trying to figure that out, I said nothing. Her words didn't exactly inspire confidence in me, but what could I do? Bolstered by my peers, I had to make an appearance. Allan Callahan, a bespectacled kid with a sticky butch wax flattop who sat right across from me in class, became my fight promoter in class the rest of the afternoon, encouraging the bout.

To tell the truth, I had never hit anyone in my life, other than horsing around with Lyle. I was all butterflies, but shoulder-clapped by Allan and three or four newfound friends, I was shepherded after school to the alley.

Hubie was pacing the gravel alley alone awaiting the fight. The swarm of second-graders propelled me across the forty yards of playing field toward him. As the space between us narrowed and the others withdrew to watch, he unbuttoned the rest of his white shirt, pulled the tails from his trousers, and tossed the shirt to the ground beside him for effect. He rocked on his heels, spit on the ground at my feet, then rushed at me. He charged his face right into my unready open left hand. I couldn't believe it myself.

The loud smack of my hand making contact amplified as I cupped both his nose and mouth with my palm. Bright red blood shot out instantly from his nose and lip. He was stunned, and terror stalked his face when he realized he was a bloody mess. He covered his injured face with the hollow of his hands to stanch the flow but blood quickly seeped through his fingers. He never said a word.

The fight was over. Frantically, he grabbed at the ground for his abandoned shirt and brought it up to his blood-spattered face. It took on the appearance of a bloodied Civil War bandage. Hubie turned and ran home, bandage in place. The spectators got the blood they wanted to see the first day at school and lingered about re-describing the event they had just witnessed to each other. I felt kind of queasy. Only this morning my mother had stood with me in the alley. Maybe new wasn't so good, after all.

• • • •

I WANTED TO BE PART of Allan Callahan's family. He had it all, except for good eyesight. He wore bottle-bottom-looking glasses in big black horn-rimmed frames. He was constantly wiping them off with his shirtsleeves or untucking his pants to get hold of a fresh chunk of plaid shirttail to rub his lenses clean. The only times I saw him without his glasses, other than cleaning them, were during class photos and when we went swimming. Despite that, he turned out to be an excellent third-baseman in little league.

Allan's parents were very hip. They had an actual bar set up right inside the living room. Their house was decorated in modern blonde furniture with floral rugs and curtains. Even their hi-fidelity record player cabinet was blonde. Allan's dad had recently retired from the Navy. The family had lived all over the world. We made our way around his house, sipping bottles of coke and landed in big rattan chairs padded with exotic red and yellow flowered cushions surrounding a glass-topped table on the back patio. Allan told me these items came from Hawaii, where he was born.

Allan's father and mother now owned a tow shop on El Camino and had three tow trucks. My favorite was a black 1955 GMC. It was a life-size Tonka truck. It had red bumpers and a massive red towing rig. The door panels were streaked with yellow flames and chrome details were everywhere. There were even two little "red" corrugated trashcans secured to the truck bed. Cars and trucks were the family's thing. They were always on call for an accident to cleanup and tow, and Allan and his brother had free run of the neighborhood.

Allan's brother Alex was in high school, and he was into hot rods and speed. He was a "cool" brother. His styled wavy brown hair was a cross between James Dean and Fabian. He was always getting pulled over by the cops for something in his '41 Plymouth Special Deluxe convertible. It was Sumac red with black tuck 'n roll leather seats, and of course bright orange and yellow flames on the side panels. Under the center dash, below the radio, Alex had fitted a portable Highway Hi-Fi 45rpm record player, the only car phonograph I've ever seen.

• • • •

EVEN THOUGH MANY OF my friends' parents were born in other countries, the sameness of our new neighborhoods hid many of our differences behind identical front doors. We Americanized everything different, even the way we spoke. I lived on Cabrillo Avenue, but everyone called it Cab-rill-o, like the "Brillo" scouring pads. It was not until we learned about the California missions in school and sometime after Cabrillo Middle School was built that we were told it was not Cab-rill-o, but ask anyone who's been here awhile, and you'll still hear it called Cab-rill-o. We called the road *the* El Camino, not El Camino Real, and so on.

I never thought about what life in Mexico was like until I met Arturo Contreras, and even after that, only for a minute. It was kinda like meeting a nun for the first time. Art, as everyone outside of his family and me called him, was the only kid in my class directly from Mexico. It seemed even then that he was very good at hiding that fact. I spent so much time around his family, it seemed natural to call him by his given name at times, but he answered to either name. It was like family calling me Benny instead of Ben or Benjamin. In the neighborhood Art was just another kid, whose skin color proved he spent a lot of time outside, always dressed in blue jeans and a carefully ironed plaid shirt buttoned to the neck. He was always much neater in appearance than I so it was a good thing Art sat directly in front of me in Mrs. Fay's class so she could look at him, not me. It was inevitable that Art and I become friends because we both loved playing baseball and riding bikes.

Among the advantages of Art's friendship was his backyard, part of the Briarwood housing tract, which backed up to the northeast corner of Frank's pear orchard. Cutting through the vacant lot and the pear trees to Art's yard was definitely a more adventurous way to go to school than taking the sidewalks. Once you were to the edge of the orchard and found Art's back fence, if you knew where to look, you'd locate one worn redwood slat that was conveniently but inconspicuously hanging by a single 16-penny nail so it could be swung out of the way enough for a kid to sidle through. Loose fence slats were common backdoors throughout the neighborhood. Some led to orchards. Some led to schools. In later years, everybody's friend, Gary Flinch, had a back fence that faced Moonlite Drive-in. We would use his fence's swinging access to sneak into the rear of the drive-in at dusk and turn up the hanging aluminum car speakers in the almost-always empty rear rows of the drive-in so we could hear the movie better, which we watched from plastic chaise lounges on a four-foot high platform his dad built along the inside of the backyard fence. Later, the drive-in people blocked the wooden fence with a cyclone one, but we simply climbed up and back.

But besides the benefits of an early morning orchard trek and having someone to hang out with for the remaining two blocks to school, best of all, cutting through Art's yard meant his mom feeding us each a freshly hand-made flour tortilla before we were out the front door. Señora Contreras spoiled me every morning I cut through their yard and picked up Arturo for school, which was regularly until the Roman Catholics built their chapel which blocked the way.

Señora Contreras got up at 4:30 every morning, long before everyone else in the family, to make burritos for his father and his dad's "unmarried" friends on his construction jobs. His dad would be long gone to work in his old beat-up Watts red pickup truck by the time we were even awake. The smells of cooking beans, onions, tomatoes, and garlic permeated Arturo's house. There were always *olla de frijoles* simmering on the stove. Arturo and his sister Esther refused to take any burritos from home to school. His mom seemed to understand their unwillingness. Like most of us at school, they packed sandwiches or ate in the cafeteria on hotdog and pizza days.

Tortillas were new and exotic to me. Señora Contreras would skillfully and rapidly, and in various directions, roll out a perfectly round and ever-so-thin tortilla on her flour-dusted wood block, lightly fling it onto the sizzling cast-iron *comal*, flip it once with her thick fingers, and, at precisely the right moment, gently toss it onto a gingham checked dish towel, where she would brush it with melted butter and then roll it hot in a white paper napkin. All this done within a couple of short minutes. One for me, one for "Arturo," and one for his big sister Esther.

"Donde estas Esther?"

"Estaré allí en un minuto," Esther would yell back from down the hall. Without fail, Esther would be ratting and spraying her hair at the bathroom mirror, and her mother from the kitchen would scold her in Spanish for being so vain and insist she get into the kitchen to eat her tortilla before she left the house. Señora Contreras's inflection provided all the translation I needed though I did learn some Spanish hanging around the Contreras house.

Then it was off to Briarwood for Art and me. Heading down Santa Barbara Avenue, we would often see Susan Molloy and her mother leave their house ahead of us. Sometimes we would catch up and talk with them as we cut through the alley to the school grounds.

Susan Molloy was born with multiple sclerosis and many other complications of that disease I never understood. She'd been dealt a bad hand. She was different from us, but she was our friend. Her frail-looking body couldn't get her very far, but she and her mom persevered. She had a "Casper" paleness about her being but lacked the robustness of even a ghost. Susan's patchy thin blonde hair couldn't hide all of her scalp despite her mother's efforts at permanents for her. She had a very foggy voice, but with great effort she could speak to you. She would puff syllables from her small white lips, but her sunken cheeks refused to billow in her efforts. Everything about her was rickety. We learned to understand her better than our teachers did. During oral reading time, Susan read as quickly as any of us until she ran out of wind and she would rasp for more air. Just listening, you really couldn't follow her nasal utterances, lacking air enough to enrich the words, unless you also followed along carefully in the reader. We would silently read with her, catch our own breaths in stiff cadence, and quietly root for her as she read her part. Yet Susan was smarter than the rest of us, or so it seemed, especially in math. We used to go to her house for help in arithmetic. It wasn't until much later that I realized her mother had had a hand in encouraging us to get this help. It kept Susan in the loop of other kids.

Mrs. Molloy, grayer than the other mothers in our neighborhood and always plainly dressed, accompanied Susan everywhere, and she was as much our friend as Susan. She fitted Susan with a big blue trike so she could get distances. She would walk beside Susan as Susan slowly pedaled along the sidewalk or pavement edge. Outside, regardless of the weather, Susan wore her favorite cornflower blue hand-knitted cardigan over her matchstick frame. On their journeys, her mother usually pulled a two-wheeled wire grocery cart with one hand and occasionally helped Susan steer with her other hand. I don't remember seeing Susan in a wheelchair, ever. Susan would quietly ride right up to the door of the classroom every morning. If you happened to be in front of her, she would flick her handlebar bell lever and "ring" up your attention. Her top lip would purse slightly, suggesting two big front teeth and a smile. Her bike, and her mom, would be outside the door when school was out every afternoon.

I met Michael McClintock, not at school, even though he was in Mrs. Fay's second grade class with me, but a week after school started at the Killarney Farms stable one afternoon. I had ridden my bike to see the two donkeys the Killarney Farms tract builders had housed in a barn and corral area built just for them to lure prospective homebuyers. Lyle and I had been here before when my Uncle Mac had driven my mom and Aunt Clara to the area in search of a new house back in June.

We had petted the donkeys Grace and Morris and had fed them some hay pellets out of an old gum vending machine located outside the rail fencing. The donkeys seemed happy to see you when you approached the corral and would hurry toward you, but they were smart enough to know with people came pellet treats. They spent a large part of their day eating barely straw, often in the barn, and grooming each other with their teeth. When I got there, the vending machine was empty. So I leaned on the rails, calling the donkeys by name, trying to coax them from the barn. Their names were machine-carved on a wooden sign that hung over the lintel of the wide barn door, but they knew there was no reward waiting in my hand. Michael had seen me approach the donkeys from his house across the street.

"Hey," he said as he came up from behind me.

"Hi. Michael, right?" He joined me hanging on the fence railing.

"Yeah. I saw you pound Hubie Leaper after school the other day." I didn't respond. I still wasn't so happy about that. I had even thought about apologizing to Hubie.

"Do you live around here?" he asked to change the subject.

"I live on the corner of Cabrillo and Lawrence."

"I live just across the street, there," he said, pointing at the perfectly manicured green yard that framed a gunmetal grey and white single story house with a suburban barn garage. His bicycle stood at near attention, kickstand down, in the driveway.

"I guess they ran out of treats for the donkeys," I said, pointing at the empty machine next to me.

"Oh, they limit the amount of stuff the donkeys eat so they don't get too fat. But at least you got here before the end of the month. They're going to take the donkeys away. There aren't anymore houses to sell in this tract."

"Where are they taking them?

"They're starting another Killarney Farms tract about six miles down Lawrence beyond the El Camino. There's lots of prune orchards to build houses on in that direction. Miguel, the guy who runs the stable, told me that they are going to take the corral and barn apart, board-by-board, and put it back up just like it was. They do it all the time. When the new tract office is ready, they'll rent the donkeys again. The donkeys come from a farm in Modesto. Miguel says even though the donkeys have never stayed anywhere very long, they always take a while to get comfortable in a new place. He says they can sense they are about to move again and they're mad. They've been hee-hawing a lot and not cooperating with anyone. That's half the reason they won't come out to you. He says they'll do that after the move, too. Miguel says it's self-preservation."

"I think I know what they feel," I said, thinking more about Lyle than myself.

"Tell me about it. We've been here six months, and that's the longest I've ever lived anywhere. My dad's a captain in the Marines. We've lived all over the country. But he says this time we're putting down roots. He's going to work for NASA and the space program."

Michael and I would become good friends. I would learn a lot about the military and aeronautics through him. His dad took us to a Moffett Field open house that year, and we got to climb up to the cockpit of an A-4 Skyhawk in Hanger 1 and see the Blue Angels F-11s up close.

His dad's military life rubbed off on Michael. Michael was always soap-scrubbed clean. He even filed his nails. I can't say either of those things about myself. His blond hair cut short, square and trim, he was his dad's duplicate. His bedroom was a tribute to his father. The white walls displayed framed Marine citations and photos of his dad at Marine functions. It was Michael's room, but it was his dad's life on the walls. There were very few traces that Michael spent any time there.

Michael always addressed his father as sir and answered to him when there was trouble, never to his mother. Michael was probably the most competitive friend I have ever had. That got him into a lot of fights. He told me once his dad didn't mind his fighting, as long as he won. His gorgeous sister Michelle, four years older than Michael, soft-spoken and fragile, seemed contained in her bedroom when not at school. Michael's dad was obsessed with the threat of boys to Michelle and was constantly yelling at her for her excesses on her pink princess phone. I could picture the day when Michael would be sent out by his father to defend his sister's honor.

The first week of November, everybody in Mrs. Fay's second-grade class began working on an alphabet penmanship project, which eventually amounted to twenty-six half-sheets of paper, a letter of the alphabet on each half-sheet, a word carefully written in cursive that began with that letter, and a crayon drawing of the object represented by the word. *A* is for *Apricot,* for example, with a bright sunny orange apricot surrounded by deep green leaves filling the rest of the page, but I drew animals when it was practical. Invariably they looked somewhat related, no matter what the animal, but it was the effort that counted. Given you had to draw and then crayon the object, an abundance of colors made up for other shortcomings in my work. The real goal of the project was to show off our cursive penmanship, anyway. The plan was we would take time every few class days and be done by Christmas, and with a decorated construction paper cover front and back, all bound together with brass paper brads, these would make fine Christmas gifts, so we were told. I was already at a disadvantage in Mrs. Fay's class, being left-handed.

From her desk, her pencil loudly tapping, Mrs. Fay critiqued my efforts.

"You're smothering your work. With your hand curled like that, no wonder you write with a backward slant. Straighten up that wrist!" tap, tap, tap.

Much of the joy of writing was missing in my schoolwork, especially when her pointy pencil starting tapping for my sake.

Every day we worked on the project we would put our completed work in our Formica lift-top desks until the next workday. Some people spend their entire lives trying to stay organized, my mother would say. I guess I was on the way to becoming one of those people. We were on the letter "z" the Wednesday before school was out for Christmas break. Of course I had drawn, colored, and labeled a fine looking, though somewhat of a lopsided variety of zebra, complete with pink ears, green eyes, and black and white stripes against a patchy blue sky and brown turf backdrop for my final page. At the end of the session I tossed my work into my desk amongst every other sheet of paper I owned.

Thursday and Friday before Christmas break, we were to finish the covers, bind the booklet, and wrap the project for someone in our family. Thursday came like any other day and we were all busy chatting away while we worked on our covers, the noise level increasing. Mrs. Fay's red pencil was tapping faster and louder for everyone's benefit.

Then came time to bind our work. Panic. I was missing almost half the alphabet from my desk. Somewhere a dog, an elephant, a fox, a goat, a hyena and about a half dozen other alphabetical animals and objects were on the loose! I had such a mess in there I could hardly blame anyone else, but suspicion of Lorraine Jackson crossed my mind for a minute.

Mrs. Fay saw my dismay. Her red pencil was drumming out everything else going on in the room. Then silence. She headed my way. By the time she reached my desk, her face had reddened to the color of her pencil jammed back into her ear groove in the two broad steps it took her to get to me. She screamed at me for being so careless, so disrespectful of my work and her lesson.

"What kind of a mess do you have here? Do I have to monitor your every move? Just what do you plan to do now?" she demanded, but the planning would be all hers.

The rest of the class was dead silent. It was not the first time since September a second-grader in her class had been on the hot seat. I had much to say, but I was speechless, red-faced but speechless. I truly expected to get rapped on the knuckles with a ruler or pointer. After a long minute, she gathered her composure and told me in an unusually calm voice but with the firmness of a Gestapo officer that I would stay in for recess and lunch and after school to re-do my work.

She began to walk away from me to stew on what she said, then turned to me and asked, "What do you think your mother will say when she hears about this?" I had ruined her lesson plan and there would be hell to pay. I had the unspoken sympathy of my classmates who now had their own heads bent down looking at their own work.

I did my time at school Thursday afternoon in solitude and silence and spent the rest of the evening at the kitchen table completing my drawings before I went to class on Friday. My mother, uninformed of the events, even praised me on my sudden interest in my schoolwork.

"See what you can do if you put your mind to it."

The next day Mrs. Fay, at least somewhat impressed, said nothing about my accomplishment, which I knew from her was the closest sign of approval I was going to get. However, it didn't stop her from calling my mother that afternoon before Christmas break began. So much for new teachers.

CHAPTER 3

Winter 1957

  By the time Christmas vacation rolled around, I had pronounced my dislike for Lorraine Jackson to the world. She had forced the issue. Last November all was well with us. We had even become friends, at least friendly classmates. During one of our bike adventures around the neighborhood, Art and I came across Lorraine playing mumbly peg out front with her younger brother Loy. I hadn't seen too many girls playing with a knife so I was impressed. Of course I was impressed just as much with the knife as with Lorraine. It was a stacked-leather handled bowie knife, almost identical to one Uncle Mike had given Lyle on a fishing trip we took with him in Utah. It had made the trip extra special for Lyle and very memorable. That's because a forest ranger caught Lyle throwing the knife at a pine tree and lectured him about it. That knife had a history to it from then on. Anyway, Art and I struck up a conversation with Loy and Lorraine and eventually got in the game. I learned a lot about Lorraine that day.

It turns out Lorraine was the oldest of five kids. Everyone in her family had a first name starting with the letter L, even their parents. There was Lorraine, Loy, Leo, Lars, and Lilly. Their dad was Leroy and their mom Laberta. I can only remember seeing Mrs. Jackson outside once, standing on the porch, one hand pulling her fingers through her straggly brown hair, the other holding a cigarette to her lips, but I would frequently hear her yelling out from inside the house to Lorraine to do something or get one of the other kids. Their dad was never home, but every so often he would leave a fairly recent issue of the *Salt Lake Tribune* on our front porch for my dad. Mr. Jackson traveled a lot on business.

As a matter of fact, Lorraine, although only eight years old, worked around the house as if she were the hired help. As the oldest child, she was the babysitter and housekeeper. Most of the time I saw her outside school, she was in the garage putting in or taking out another load of wash to hang on the line either out back or on lines strung across the inside of their cluttered garage, and the other four kids were always there demanding her attention or care. Leo and Lars were just toddlers. Lilly was just a baby, arms flailing about, in a blue stroller, and usually not far from Lorraine. I think Lorraine's burden was why her brothers and sisters always looked kind of wrinkly. I'm sure that what ironing there was to be done Lorraine did. I felt kind of sorry for her. There was an untidiness about the whole family and their house.

But Lorraine was always nice to me, especially at school, always offering me help or binder paper or a pencil. So seeing Lorraine outside her house actually playing was unusual. Loy and Lorraine were home alone. That alone made it a weird day. Lorraine beat all three of us at mumbly peg. Tired of that, she suggested we play Hide and Go Seek. She made her yard the boundaries, front and back. Art and I thought that wouldn't provide many hiding places, but after seeing Lorraine's backyard, we changed our minds. It was a jungle of weeds, bushes, boxes, and junk, as in an old water heater, an abandoned, rusting table saw on end, and even a trunk lid of a '49 Chevy. It wasn't the safest-looking place for little kids, so of course Art and I liked it.

It was the third round of the game, and I had made it to the free pole out front every time. Loy was counting to a hundred. I cut through the garage and headed for the long cardboard box lying on its side in the far corner of the yard. It had obviously been used for play before this. It wasn't so much that the box was the best hiding place, but I figured I could exit either end and beat Loy back to the starting light pole. Art and Lorraine had headed out the opposite direction. When I got inside the box, I was startled to find Lorraine was there. She had cut through the other side of the house and beat me there.

"Come on in. There's room enough for both of us," she said, an inviting grin on her face.

There was no time to go elsewhere. Loy would be on the hunt any second so I decided I'd have to take my chances with only one exit. I crawled in, let the box flaps drop and waited, crouched down with Lorraine next to me. She started to talk, but I shushed her with my finger between her face and mine. She pulled my hand away by the wrist and kissed me on the lips. I was dumfounded, and I could hear Loy approaching the area. Without any regard for Lorraine or anything else, I ripped out of the box and got a lead on Loy as I ran and beat him back to the light post in the front yard. I was safe for the moment.

Art and Lorraine managed to avoid Loy, and I avoided Lorraine. I made up an excuse about having to get home, and the day was done.

Monday, Mrs. Fay's class was torturous. I didn't really want to talk to Lorraine about last Saturday. In my mind I hoped it was just some girl thing, kissing a boy. But the more I thought about it, the more sinister it seemed. I had been too stupid to see that Lorraine had had a crush on me all along. No wonder she was so obliging at school. No wonder she had come up with playing Hide and Go Seek. Was I wrong?

By recess, I knew the answer. Lorraine had told Carlotta, Sarah and the rest of the girls in our classroom out on the yard that I was her boyfriend, and who knows what else? As I walked by them, they were giggling and carrying on about Lorraine and me in mumbles. I could just make out "k i s s . . . , sitting in a tree."

By lunch, word had gotten out to most of the guys, even Art had heard. I told them it wasn't true, that I couldn't stand Lorraine, and that's the way my relationship with Lorraine "Cooties" Jackson ended.

By the spring, Mrs. Fay's class was a pretty close group, in spite of her reign of terror at times. Even Hubie Leaper came around. One afternoon on the playground, he approached me and said he was sorry about the fight, and he tried to get along with the rest of us by dropping the tough guy act. He even said he was sorry to Reginald Pudlow.

CHAPTER 4

Summer 1958

Summer arrived and I was pretty much into a routine with Allan and Art, and sometimes Michael, when his dad would let him out of the house. We usually spent our early mornings at the Briarwood school field behind Allan's house looking for enough guys to play a few innings of baseball, even if we didn't have enough guys to use the whole field, or we played three flies up against each other until we wore out. Then we headed out on our bikes. Although or because we weren't supposed to go out to El Camino that's where we often ended up. In fact, we made ourselves regular customers at The Red and White Store at Pomeroy along El Camino. The Mulberrys who ran the little white stucco store knew kids were their best customers and so they had the best assortment of penny candy and candy bars in town. We spent our nickels on Big Hunks and Looks and Abba-Zaba bars almost every late morning before we made a trek along the dirt path of the Calabasas creek bank. It was hard to resist buying a Bireley's orange soda even in the morning.

Since there were very few roads crossing the creek, we usually stayed in our own neighborhood between Calabasas Creek, El Camino, Lawrence, and Monroe. Building was still going on at Killarney Farms near Monroe, and watching the workers was one of our favorite activities, but flat tires were a price we often paid for screeching our bikes down yet opened streets lined with building debris. My Firestone patch kit was almost out of rubber patches. The creek path and banks were also treacherous.

Construction scraps and nails, storm debris, and bits of trash seemed to wait for bikes around the creek. Bums sometimes journeyed their way south where the train tracks met the creek on the north side of Monroe just beyond Jefferson Junior High. And the dusty ragged men who rode the rails with their belt-bundled sun-faded grey coats and grubby frayed wool blankets flung over their shoulders or tied to sticks were not always the neatest people after camping the creek bed. Beware a wad of newsprint in the weeds. Our mothers, and probably theirs, warned us to avoid each other, but their discarded bean and beer cans, ragged-edged tin sardine lids, makeshift coffee can stoves, pint liquor bottle shards, and even their dried up poop were common hazards for our bikes after their creek visits until a good rain ran the creek beds clean of everything.

Before it got too late in the day and too hot we would ride up and down the bumpy weedy creek banks looking for items of interest. Sometimes we'd stop and hunt for blue bellies in the creek bed. We were pretty good at spotting them as they warmed themselves on rocks in a morning ritual, and we'd sneak up on them with our bare hands. We learned that if you caught the stare of a male lizard, you could sometimes play bobble head with it. Face to face, you were a challenge to it and it might bob its head and body up and down to your bobbing head stare. It was a kick to see that.

Of course the art of catching a fence lizard is in the stillness of your approach. If you move slowly enough and steady enough you can actually have your hands around the reptile before he realizes the ambush. It's motion that alarms them. Having another guy with you to distract a potential catch also makes the hand grab that much more effective. Do that with an alligator lizard and you risk a nasty bite.

We never really keep the lizards we catch for very long. It's just catching a creature that is so lightning fast and not having it slip away from your hand and leaving you with only its tail. The ultimate success is getting the caught lizard to relax on its back while you rub its fluorescent blue belly. If he is really at ease, his eyes close and you can open your palm flat while he lies on his back. I won't lie and tell you blue bellies and alligator lizards don't make good targets when we have our slingshots or a quarry of rocks within our reach.

Allan suggested the four of us go out to old Lawrence Station today, on the Sunnyvale side of Lawrence Road, beyond Reed Road. (On the Santa Clara side of Lawrence, Reed Road is now called Monroe.) The station was a little beyond our normal territory but there was lots of action out by the rail tracks. Besides penny-flattening trains passing through and distant hoboes making camp and nervous jackrabbits flitting across fields, there was an old quarry where huge gravel and dirt-hauling trucks were always stirring up and down the dusty roads, and tractors and conveyor belts were constantly rotating loads of rock, dirt, and sand. We could watch these events for hours. But the real draw for us was the lizards. There was something about the hot steel train tracks and creosote-oozing railroad ties in a ballast of crushed stone that drew them out in droves. They basked in the sun just waiting for us.

Today we decided to take the creek trail to Lawrence and then head toward Sunnyvale along Monroe, but we were sidetracked. We did some creek bank riding along the way, but I really didn't feel like patching another flat this week, so I stayed to the top trail while Allan, Michael, and Art zigzagged and deliberately brake-skidded the creek bank all the way beyond Cabrillo. From the creek bank at Cabrillo you could look straight up my street, but the pavement ended at a ten-acre field of weeds in front of us, which would someday be more houses. Action-packed construction was taking place between Cabrillo and Monroe. Every day the open landscape shrunk.

By next summer we figure all the Killarney Farms houses will be done and there will be new streets to ride along and beyond the creek. I am not sure it will be as much fun for us once the workers are gone. Maybe someday the city will build a bridge from Cabrillo to the other side of Calabasas Creek and the street will go to Saratoga Creek or even San Tomas Aquino Creek. Those are whole new worlds for us to explore. They've already built Darvon Park houses around them. Machado Avenue is now paved almost to our creek and men like busy carpenter ants are building wood housing frames everywhere in front of us.

We expected to hear sawing, pounding, and buzzing from all the construction, but when we heard the unmistakable ping of glass breaking as we sat astride our bikes watching the builders we knew someone was up to something in the creek bed below us. Sure enough a kid about our age was shooting at bottles and trash with a powerful slingshot just below us.

The four of us were pretty good with slingshots ourselves, and we each had slingshots of some sort lying around our houses. Michael was the best shot, probably a future Marine marksman. I had a couple of Davy Crockett "King" sling shots, made of thick Y-bent wire, but both my slings were on their last legs, meaning the big flat rubber bands are just about exhausted, no more zing to the sling. I need to dig for a couple of good used car-inner tubes from one of the steel barrels behind Stan's Standard station up Lawrence. Inner tubes, even discarded ones, cut up nicely for new sling bands. My sling shots have served me well at targets and birds and fruits in the orchards. But the slingshot the kid in the creek had was different.

"Wow, that's a Wrist Rocket," exclaimed Art to himself for us to hear. "Those suckers can annihilate a bottle from fifty yards out. Its power's all in the wrist." He was right. Part of the shot's frame wrapped around your wrist to give you greater force when you released its enema tube rubber band. We all recognized the slingshot from magazine and comics ads but none of us had ever seen one live until now. This was worth investigating.

"Hey," I said to the shooter from my bike-seat, where I was perched above the creek bed.

"Hey," the messy haired redheaded kid said, startled at our appearance, pivoting toward me and cupping his eyes from the sun as he tried to make out the stranger speaking to him from above him.

The four of us dropped our bikes and headed down to the kid with the Wrist Rocket.

After quick introductions, Carl showed us how to use the Wrist Rocket, and that renewed our interest in slingshots that summer. Carl told us he also had a Daisy air rifle so he had our instant respect. Carl Price was from Chicago, and he laughed when we said something about it not smart to be in the creek alone with the bums who traveled through there.

His family had moved out here just a couple of weeks ago. It was obvious he missed Chicago and his friends, the way he went on about them, but most of all he missed little league and he told us all about it. He was starting to play on something they called a farm team in Illinois. We missed little league with him, even though we had never had the chance to be in it. It gave us one more thing to envy him for. So Carl became a regular on Briarwood field on summer mornings with us. Now we had a catcher.

Everyone in Carl's family wore red hair and freckles. Carl said he was "Welsh through and through." None of the four of us knew exactly what that meant, but we were all eight years old so we had much in common. Unlike our dads, Carl's father wore a suit to work so we assumed his dad was a big shot. He worked at IBM.

That day we rode to Carl's brand new house on Nobili, just three blocks over from my house and not even half a mile north on Allan's street. Carl's mother, who was busy unpacking boxes in the garage, seemed thrilled to see us. We all knew it was parent relief that her kid had found some new friends. We had all been there before and embarrassed by our parents in one way or another. Mrs. Price insisted we come in for a slice of cake. Who were we to refuse?

The house was a disaster inside, so it was a lot like my bedroom, with junk and clothes lying about, and I felt quite at home. The layout of the house was identical to my house, yet we lived in different tracts. Carl's six-year-old sisters, twins, were sitting on the family room sofa amongst the family's laundry, sucking their thumbs and watching *Truth or Consequences*. Their long wavy orange hair made their round freckled faces clown material. The fact that they giggled a lot and whispered to each other the entire time we were there added to their funny routine. Every time I saw the twins at Carl's after that day they were in front of the TV.

Dessert was a priority at Carl's house. There were two home baked cakes on the kitchen table and a row of lemon bars on another plate. Mrs. Price offered us ice cream with our cake. The double-chocolate layer cake was deliciously moist and rich. Carl bragged to us about what a baker his mother was and how the first thing she and the twins did when they moved into their new house was put a cake into the oven. I bet the first thing the twins did was turn on the TV, but I didn't say anything. Carl's mom was all smiles and went back to unpacking. While we were stuffing ourselves, it dawned on me that the four Price family members I had met so far were kinda fat. When I got home that day, I ate lunch and checked out my own waistline in the bathroom mirror before heading out on my bike again.

There were two rumors going around in the neighborhood by the end of summer. The first seemed unlikely but was the topic of a lot of adults on the block. Among all the changes going on around us, the story was those in charge of Santa Clara wanted to tear down the buildings on and around Franklin Street and start over with something called a downtown plaza. Living at the edge of town was not the same as living in Salt Lake City, where downtown State Street was a couple of blocks away from our house, and we knew every storefront and every owner within a two-mile radius, but within a couple of years, I had favorite shops in downtown Santa Clara on Franklin Street, especially Phil's smoke shop, the bike shop, sport shop, and the Santa Clara, the only movie theater in town, and there were tons of other shops I barely knew, like a hobby shop, a couple of variety stores, and the Santa Clara Creamery that some of my friends were experts on. I never went to the Santa Clara Bowl on Franklin Street before it closed, but Allan tells me you could bowl there in your sock feet.

Last September, Mrs. Fay helped everybody in our class start a savings account at the Bank of America on Franklin and Monroe. Every two weeks most everyone would bring at least 25 cents to school. (I tried to deposit 35 cents when I could.) A lady bank teller from Bank of America would come to our class and distribute our personalized, string-tied envelopes for our accounts and we would fill out a new deposit slip. It was fun seeing our money add up in our updated passbooks from each deposit. Our third grade class was supposed to continue what Mrs. Fay started. What would happen to my $12.75 if they closed my bank on Franklin?

"No way are they going to tear out the downtown," proclaimed Allan to the rest of us, but we weren't so sure.

The second rumor this summer was even more important to my friends and me. At the north end of Briarwood school were some empty acres of land where Machado farm once stood, at one time all the way to Monroe. The weed field now ended at Cabrillo. The rest of the land was quickly becoming Killarney Farms houses. Allan's neighbor, an old woman who claimed to know all the history around here, told him that at one time the entire school area was a dairy. We assumed the dirt and weeds that stood in the field north of the school would become more housing soon.

The rumor was that a new baseball park was going into the northeast corner and a city park was going to replace the jungle gym set-up in the weeds now called Killarney Park at the other corner. Now that was a change to cheer about. Almost every boy I knew loved to play baseball, but, as of yet, there was no organized baseball. It was another negative part of living so far from downtown Santa Clara, where Santa Clara Little League already existed. A new ballpark could mean little league coming to this part of town. Our lives could be better. Carl filled us in on little league teams and divisions and got us even more excited about the possibility. The five of us were dreaming about tryouts, teams and baseball uniforms, and that made the upcoming school year more tolerable.

CHAPTER 5

F*all 1958*
School was just around the corner and that meant a trip to Sunnyvale on the city bus with my mom—school shopping. To hear my mother tell it, she has been a walker all her life, mostly out of fear. You would never know she once broke her leg. Growing up in the valley, in Pixley and Sanger, there wasn't much beyond the few houses of the small towns and farms. She did learn to drive on country roads, and at one point in her life her father even sold cars outside their Flying-A filling station. But at sixteen, she gave driving up for good.

Her big family took a camping trip to nearby Yosemite, as they frequently did when she was a kid. She and her Uncle Tommy drove up separately from the rest of the family with all the gear in his 1930 Model A Ford pickup. Somewhere along Highway 41, Uncle Tommy passed out at the wheel. The truck, Uncle Tommy, my mom, and the family camping equipment ended up forty feet down a canyon. Uncle Tommy died of a heart attack. My mother got out with just a broken leg and some bruises, not all of them visible. She has never driven another vehicle since that day. I hear that story every time I ask her why she doesn't drive like my friends' moms—and that is usually when we are hoofing it across town or sitting on a Greyhound or municipal bus to somewhere.

We had only been in Santa Clara a year this fall, but my mother and I had already put many walking miles behind us, and we had taken the yellow and white city bus many times to downtown San Jose and Sunnyvale. Her favorite place to shop was downtown Sunnyvale, though when my dad drove us shopping on a weekend, the new Emporium and Macy's near it at Valley Fair on Stevens Creek were her stores of choice. By sixth grade, I had the floor plan of the Big E mapped in my head for life.

Sunnyvale had a big shopping center on Taaffe Street, complete with Harts and J.C. Penney's department stores, but to get there we had to walk to catch the National city bus at the corner of Lawrence Station Road and El Camino, nearly a mile from Cabrillo. It was a lot shorter distance when I road my bike that far and a lot longer when we walked home from El Camino along the uneven shoulder off Lawrence Station Road overloaded with several big shopping bags to carry home.

On more than one shopping trip we missed the bus for some reason and walked the entire eight miles home, the trip shortened when you cut through the orchards. The highlight of one of those days for me was the two of us helping ourselves to tender ripe orange apricots from an orchard near the road and eating them together as we walked. I love to split the cot like an Oreo cookie, spit the seed from one half and tongue slosh the apricot's sweet flesh. I do not remember ever taking a cab anywhere—too expensive. Cabs were for other people, not us, my mom would say.

It was a yearly tradition for my mother to take Lyle and me school shopping in Salt Lake City. We would walk up State Street, block after block, to get to Sears and nearby Grand Central and then over to Main Street to ZCMI and Penney's to find jeans, shoes, shirts, and underwear. More than once I wandered off down a store aisle and into the universe of one of those huge department stores, my mother reminds me.

I will never forget the big event at ZCMI downtown when I was five. We waited in line so I could say hi to none other than Clarabell the Clown from the Howdy Doody Show. Clarabell as usual didn't do any talking that day, but he honked his horn a lot. (A rich kid could have a photo taken with him for a price.) Clarabell's bright tufts of orange hair, white eye paint, and red nose were somewhat scary in person. Seeing him in color instead of TV black and white just wasn't what I expected, for some reason. Just as I was about to get an animal balloon that he twisted for each kid that made it up to him, Clarabell started squeezing his red rubber ball horn on his Clarabell waist box as two teenage girls walked by. From his bright green and white zebra-striped pajama pocket, he pulled out a quart-sized seltzer bottle and began chasing the girls down a department store aisle, squirting anyone who got in the way. He disappeared in the ZCMI universe. It was funny, but I didn't get a balloon animal, and I doubt he ever caught the girls.

Anyway, those school shopping days with my mom were done for Lyle when we moved to California. Lyle declared he was doing his own shopping now that he was going into high school. The night before my mother and I went to Sunnyvale, there was work to do in the kitchen. From all the junk drawers in the house, my mother's purses, and the Pontiac's glove compartment my mother gathered her loose sheets of Blue Chip Stamps. From her special closet shoebox, she took out her rubber banned already-completed stamp books and her stash of empty ones. She had a second box for her S&H Green Stamps, but that would be for a later time. My job was to fill the empty books with the sheets not yet licked. The goal was fifteen books of stamps. That would get us a pink bathroom scale from the stamp redemption store on Washington Avenue.

For me, the best part of the trip would always be getting a hotdog and a coke at the fountain in Woolworth's, if I behaved and didn't go wandering. The worst part of the trip would be the female elevator operator in Harts announcing, "Second floor, women's wear and lingerie." That would mean pacing up and down aisle after aisle of boredom, not touching anything and staying within voice range while my mother tried on arm loads of dresses, blouses, slacks, and unmentionables.

I would beg to get a pair of genuine Levi's downstairs in the Boys' Department but be told I was too rough on pants and to wait until we got to J.C. Penney's where we would get their cheaper Wrangler brand.

J.C. Penney's had its own excitement that day. Just as we walked in we heard the screaming sounds of a little girl near the escalator. She had apparently decided to sit on the moving stairs in her white chiffon dress and sure enough—as our parents always promised—the escalator grabbed her garment with its silver teeth. The escalator stopped in a loud abrupt thump, scaring everyone anywhere near it and setting off another round of screams from the little girl whose mother by then was working on tearing her free from the jaws of the machine. An ear-numbing alarm bell rang from somewhere beneath the stairwell.

"Why don't people watch their children?" my mother said to no one in particular, and then she grabbed my arm, pinching me at the wrist, dragged me away from the commotion, and told me not to wander off. It was like my getting in trouble because Lyle did something wrong.

After tromping in and out of at least a dozen stores from Youngsters' to J.J. Newberry's to Weinstein's, we finally backtracked to Woolworth's for a well deserved hotdog and chips and then headed for the Blue Chip Stamp store. It was a long trip home after we caught the bus at the end of Murphy Avenue for Santa Clara. Walking Lawrence Station Road home, we were weighed down with weariness, bags of boys and women's clothing, a pair of Keds, and of course a new pink bathroom scale.

By the fall, Lyle had found comfort in high school in books and football. Lyle still took the bus to school, but in September it was heading for the partially completed Buchser High School on Benton, about five miles closer to our house. Despite his anger at my parents for uprooting him from Salt Lake, Lyle spent his energies on school. His freshman report cards were all A's, and this year he had found football. He was small, but he was tough, and he played both ways on the newly created Buchser High football team. He certainly liked the new facilities better than the crowded Santa Clara High, and the bus ride was both later in the morning and shorter to the new school. His new friends were primarily teammates and bus commuters, but he still spent most of his time in his bedroom with the door closed.

• • • •

ON THE WEST SIDE OF our house twenty feet from Lawrence Station Road was a gravel path, protected from the highway by a shelterbelt of black walnut trees, both path and trees paralleling the road north all the way to Reed Road, a mile beyond us. The housing developers put the path there. From the front of our house you could see other walnut trees stretching south along Lawrence Station Road most of the way to El Camino Real on our side, but there was no path, just the pear orchard for which all the walnut trees had been originally planted to protect the orchard from the roadway. Wherever building took place, walnut trees were often the only vestiges of what used to surround fields and orchards along Lawrence Station Road. These leftover city-owned trees were mostly neglected. Every fall my mother laid claim to harvesting the dozen walnut trees that ran along the side of our property and neighbors' back fences. She and my father marched out nearly every Sunday and raked and broomed the fifty-yard stretch clear of roadside litter and debris all year long. That routine paid off for my father who was once ticketed for absent-mindedly tossing a spent Spivey's Restaurant matchbook out his car window at the intersection of Lawrence Station Road and Monroe Street. He argued his case in traffic court to a sympathetic judge familiar with the patch of roadside my mom and dad kept so clean.

When the thick green skins began to blacken, wither, wrinkle, and crack, and walnuts began to fall, Lyle and I were my mother's late afternoon labor. It was a constant battle to beat the blackbirds to the ripe nuts. In the mornings a dark cloud of territorial birds would sit up in the branches and deliberately dislodge nuts onto the asphalt of the highway. If the ten-foot fall didn't crack the shells, exposing the tender nuts inside, the passing cars would. Between the whizzing cars, the merles would "Zero dive" for their spoils. Junior high kids walking to and from Jefferson school along the gravel path were apparently a threat to the birds, and the birds would viciously dive at the many unsuspecting heads bobbling by, even peck one, occasionally. Some kids, their books protecting their heads, would run down bird-guarded sections of the gravel path every school day to avoid the birds' attacks.

In defiance of the blackbirds, my mother would go out after she got us off to school in the mornings, replete with our lunches, mine in my Davy Crocket pail, Lyle's in a plain brown paper lunch sack, apropos to high school, and she would daily collect at least a half of bag of nuts in a big grocery bag while the harvest was in earnest.

Lyle and I would gather fallen nuts from off the flat, raked grey dirt below the trees later after school in the afternoons. Because of Lyle's football practice, it would sometimes be nearly dusk before we made it out there. Being too dark to work would have been just fine with him, and every day we harvested the nuts the days became shorter. He hated having to be out there in the first place. I saw it as an adventure, as long as Lyle was with me.

We were forbidden to climb the trees to get the nuts due to their proximity to the highway. We had a twelve-foot wooden pole with a giant steel hook on one end my dad had acquired, the sort the Kiely farm used to shake prune tree branches. We hung the pole horizontally on the inside of the back fence stringers so it was readily available to help us pry loose more nuts. The sooner all the nuts were down, even the greener ones, the sooner we could stop wasting daylight working, so of course that meant breaking the rule and climbing trees and stretching our bodies on brittle branches above dirt and roadway, pole in hand, to shake loose all we could between increasing afternoon traffic. We only climbed when mother was out of sight. Some nuts would invariably hit the highway and crackle into pieces, and rubber tires of passing cars splattered them on the pavement. This would inevitably bring on another cluster of blackbirds. We learned to fight the persistent birds with flailing arms and clapping hands for the whole nuts and bagged the harvest in more brown paper grocery sacks we brought with us from the garage. Daily, our hands would be stained a sticky yellow-green and black, even before the peeling, cracking, cleaning, and jarring began.

My mother kept an array of silver-plated nut-cracking tools in the kitchen drawer, spring-hinged plier crackers, a handful of dental-looking six-inch picks and even several small silver hammers, all with ornately sketched identical patterns stamped onto their handles. Once we had five or six full grocery sacks of nuts sitting in the garage, several Saturday mornings my mother would set up two rickety wooden-legged card tables inside the garage, tools and nuts at the ready, and get us out of bed and into a dimly lit garage to process the nuts in assembly-line fashion. My dad was always long gone by the time we got up, out collecting quarters from his ballpoint pen machines. We'd tune the old Zenith radio to the newest Bay Area rock and roll stations, KYA, KLIV or KEWB, to keep us company, and Lyle and I would usually argue about which station was best. My mom didn't seem to mind most of the music.

One of us, usually my mother, would first shuck any remaining husks. Barehanded, she'd peel away the black, scabby skin of each nut or pry stubborn or greener skins away with a silver pick. Her hands would be a black mess by the time she was finished. Lyle or I would then crack wrinkly wooden shell casings as they piled on the table using the plier cracker or tap stubborn shells on the concrete floor with a real hammer. The little silver hammers were useless.

Your hands would get sore from the constant pressure of cracking so we would trade jobs frequently. It was an art to crack open the shell without splintering the four-sectioned nut. From the pile of nuts the other of us would separate nut from shell and clean away the thin shavings of the nutshell remaining on the prize with our fingers or another pick and then put the nuts in quart-Mason jars. The shell shards were brushed off the table, swept off the concrete floor, and later dust panned into grocery sacks to be used to kindle fires in the family room fireplace. There were always sacks and sacks of broken shells in our garage. Mason jars of walnuts lined wooden shelves along the garage back wall, along with canned apricots, peaches, and pears, all year long.

At the end of a Saturday stint we'd have to scrub our hands with coarse Lava bar soap and warm water in the deep cement sink in the corner of the garage, then rub them in stinging lemon juice and then filmy vegetable oil, then wash them again in soapy water. Even then, only time worked completely on removing the stains. It was all work we complained about, but we were rewarded. My mother would bake delicious nut breads, cookies, pies, and walnut fudge. Canker sores were all too common at our house.

CHAPTER 6

*W*inter 1958

Every chance he got Carl would compare living in Santa Clara to living in Chicago. But his sad stories were no match for Michael and Allan, who were military brats, and had lived all over the world. Even Art and I were born outside California, and we knew it was different here. For that matter, Arturo was born in another country where people spoke a different language and life was little like what we had now. We all enjoyed hearing about great places in Chicago like Wrigley Field and Lake Michigan, but all of us had left something behind when our families moved to California. We all had a year on Carl living in California. Maybe he would learn to appreciate Santa Clara as we did given more time, but he continued to insist that when he grew up, he was moving back to Chicago.

California winter was harder on Carl than the rest of us. He missed Chicago winters, especially the snow. I had vague memories of Salt Lake City winters. It was all about snow, and I can remember being pulled on a sled by my mom in Liberty Park over a frozen lake and through the snow-covered groves, and the beautiful rainbow feathers of peacocks, iridescent against a snow-filled aviary. I also remember it was cold. Carl told us about minus degree temperatures in Chicago last February. Minus temperatures are something we could not comprehend in California. But I clearly remember Lyle complaining about having to go out in the Salt Lake City cold to shovel snow from the porch and driveway, and the many arguments he would have with my dad about the chore he hadn't completed by the time dad got home from work.

"You're so lazy you stink," my dad would say, first to Lyle and then later on to us both, *"You kids are so lazy you stink,"* when we didn't do as we were told. It became a standing line Lyle and I would use on each other.

The day after New Years is cleanup day after the holidays for many families in Santa Clara and elsewhere. Carl told us many times how traditionally he and his friends in Chicago gathered and re-used Christmas trees in the neighborhood for snow forts and tunnels, how they'd spend hours setting up the trees in the snow or anticipating more winter snow to create elaborate labyrinths in backyards where teams of kids would have endless snowball fights and make sneak attacks and even steal dead trees from one another for their own snow kingdoms, "snow wars" he called them. And he missed them as much as little league.

Carl made the best of his first California winter. As he had done in Chicago, he went around the neighborhood removing discarded Christmas trees from curbs before the dump trucks showed up, pulling them home in his rusty Radio Flyer, but there was no other competition for abandoned Christmas trees in Santa Clara. For a week Carl quietly hauled trees of all sizes and flocks to his backyard. He would be ready for the snow wars of Santa Clara that would never come. We were impressed with Carl's effort and the elaborate maze of trees he had created, arranged as tunnels, bridges, caves, turrets and forts. We were also amazed that his mom let him do it. His backyard was now a little like his house, a mess.

I guess in Chicago the fact that collected trees were already dead and dry didn't matter so much when January forecasts called for high temperatures in the twenties and winter snow, but in Santa Clara, where January temperatures are usually in the sixties and it hasn't snowed for decades, the second life of these trees was ill-fated.

For a month Carl's backyard was a gathering place for boys at war in the neighborhood, and often it was grade-wars, third-graders against fourth-graders or block wars, Cabrillo versus Machado. Tommy guns, air rifles, cap guns, and toy weapons from homemade to Mattel ruled the arid jungle of dead trees. It was fun, but every time you played in the lifeless trees it got more treacherous. Carl would say again and again, "If only we had snow." The web of needle tunnels became torture gauntlets. And it became harder to hide behind barren prickly branches. The limbs and remaining needles were dangerous. You were lucky if you didn't bleed before you headed home. Carl's twin sisters complained they couldn't go out in the backyard to play anymore, but I think that was just an excuse to stay closer to the TV. The snarl of trees gradually became a deserted tinderbox.

In March a Santa Clara fire truck showed up at the Price home. A neighbor had complained about the fire danger, and Carl's unhappy dad paid to have a large flatbed trailer loaded with lifeless trees and taken to the dump. According to Carl, in Chicago at this time of year winter was in full swing. Last year it snowed in April there. So much for "snow wars" in Santa Clara.

CHAPTER 7

S *pring 1959*

I would be off to Art's house Thursday morning and then to school. It was to be a typical March day, still somewhat chilly in the mornings, but the fruit trees all around us were starting to wake up. The apricot trees beyond the pears in the Musso orchard facing our kitchen window were already starting to sprout green nubs. Everyone was looking forward to Easter break next week, except for the Catholic school kids who had to wait an extra week. We were to have a math test in Mrs. Hageman's class in the afternoon, but I was ready for that. I was eating my morning corn flakes, standing at the kitchen window as I usually did, watching the morning traffic on Lawrence Station Road zoom by along the edge of the orchard. The pear trees were about to bloom white. The green weeds and wild mustard were thriving amongst the trees and in the empty lot in front of the orchard.

It was only last month that my mother and I were doing the dinner dishes at the kitchen window when a loud crash, followed by a massive billowing cloud of dirt churned across the orchard and the wide screen of our front row window. A car, tumbling and sliding through the trees, came to rest twenty yards into the orchard. Miraculously, the car missed walnut and pear trees it passed as it somersaulted off the highway and beyond the first row of pear trees. My father, along with half the neighborhood men who heard the horrific sound, ran to the scene before I could even react.

In the righted '56 Olds was a little four-year-old boy crying, curled up on the front seat, his father slouched over the steering wheel, arms hanging through the wheel, his lip bleeding from the cut he got on an open can of Falstaff that lay puddled all over the front seat and floor. The front windshield looked like recycled cellophane. The car's body was rumpled and misshapen but whole. The driver of

55

the sideswiped oncoming car had been able to regain control. He too had rushed to the scene in the orchard. Except for the bleeding lip, both the father and boy, despite the rock-o-plane spin through the dirt, were apparently okay.

My mother had dialed the Santa Clara police, who showed up fifteen minutes later and at the same time as the Sunnyvale cops. The officers argued with each other over whose jurisdiction it was since Lawrence Station Road was the visual boundary between Santa Clara on the east and Sunnyvale on the west and just who should take the report and arrest the drunken father. Before the ambulance arrived, the boy's mother appeared, directed some nasty remarks at her husband, spoke a few words with the cops, and headed for home down the gravel path near our house, the boy in her arms. No one was stopping her.

The scene made by the officious cops, pacing off the car's point of impact and drawing pencil diagrams and halting traffic unnecessarily, lasted at least two hours and was a bigger show to the witnesses than the accident itself. One by one the neighbors lost interest and wandered away from the scene, their heads shaking in disapproval. Lawrence Station Road never did become the boundary between Santa Clara and Sunnyvale. Even today, chunks of land west of Lawrence belong to Santa Clara now. That night Allan's dad showed up to tow the wrecked Olds from the orchard right away but was not allowed to touch the car until the police settled their dispute over jurisdiction. In the dark of night, he winched the banged up sedan through the dirt and trees, his bright tow truck floodlights rudely illuminating the sleeping pear trees.

This morning a big diesel pulling a large flatbed trailer holding a yellow bulldozer turned our corner, turned onto the corner of the vacant lot where the street to nowhere started, and parked. Something was up. Someone was probably going to plow the weeds this year before they got out of hand. I figured it was fire prevention since I did a pretty thorough job last 4th of July burning the entire lot with my errant hot metal sparkler. While the weeds exploded in flames, I remained under my bed as what sounded like the entire Santa Clara fire department descended on the blaze. At least there was no boundary dispute.

More and more, I had begun riding my bike to and from school, always stopping at Art's house, but I walked today to get a close up look at the action across the street. Anyway, after breakfast, I cut by the lot on the street to nowhere, pausing to take a good look at the men unchaining the dozer from its trailer platform, and then made my way through Frank's pear orchard. I headed along the back fence edge until I found Art's yard and his "back door" entrance. As usual, we started the day with a homemade fresh tortilla.

"Donde estas Esther?"

The school day was nothing special, but as I cut through Art's yard at the end of the day between the back fence and the orchard, I could see daylight where there used to be pear trees. A wide swath of Frank's pear orchard had been plowed down; the downed budding trees were shoved into two large piles for burning at the edge of the plowed area. It was an assault. As I reached the nowhere street, the white ranch fence that had once marked the end of the road was gone, along with the trees directly behind it. There was a lot of noisy activity still going on. The dozer was running back and forth flattening and leveling the rich dark dirt where blossoms were trying to bloom just this morning. Wooden stakes marked four corners where it was obvious someone was going to build something. In the weedy vacant lot someone had off loaded a lumberyard full of wood, including large piles of beams and two-by-fours and several eight-foot high stacks of plywood and paneling, directly onto the green weeds.

While we were at school Friday, crews of men built a raised deck foundation for what was to become a chapel in the cleared area just beyond the lot, beyond the street to nowhere. Art and I watched the action after school from my driveway that day. We would have gotten closer, but we had orders from my mother to stay in the yard. I learned from some neighborhood adults talking to one another as they too stood around on the sidewalk watching the action across the street that the chapel was to be only a temporary structure, and that the goal was to be in the meeting hall before Easter week.

By six in the morning, Saturday, the noise of cars, pickups, and people woke us up. By the time we were all out of bed, there were at least thirty men in the lot, working away like bees constructing a hive. Some were foragers; others builders, and yet others overseers. Most of the overseers were priests dressed in black. The sawing, hammering, and drilling went on all day. Men worked in shifts so even during lunch there were still people making the noise of construction. A group of women sat at a long folding table on the pavement of the nowhere street and provided coffee in white paper cups and fresh doughnuts in the morning to the workers. Throughout the day different bunches of women took charge of the table and passed out homemade sandwiches and beers to those who briefly rested on metal folding chairs set up along the curb before going back to hammering, sawing, and hoisting lumber. It was a suburban barn raising, all volunteer work by the Killarney Farms construction workers and members of the parish-to-be.

By ten a.m., Art, Allan, and Michael had joined me on my front lawn, our bikes lying on the driveway, as we watched a piece of Rome being built in a day. By dusk, it was done, a ninety-foot-long building of beige plywood siding and reddish brown shingle roofing. It had an unpainted double front door in the middle of its length, four sets of aluminum-framed windows on the long walls and an eight-foot high white wooden cross on the roof's peak. The uprooted pear trees were still piled for burning, but now they waited behind the new building.

Sunday, various people readied the chapel for mass. A long thick extension cord was stretched from a bedroom window at the Wilson's house across the "Street to Nowhere" into the chapel to light the wooden altar inside that a parishioner had built. One hundred metal folding chairs were neatly arranged inside the structure. Two men unloaded two scary-looking lifelike statues from a white panel van and by hand truck rolled a wounded Jesus and a veiled Virgin Mary made of plaster up the three stairs and into the sanctuary. As we watched the construction Saturday, Arturo had prepared us for their arrival and other things Catholic that Allan, Michael, and I knew nothing about. Even with Arturo's warning, the vividly painted figures were no less frightening to the three of us.

Lyle was embarrassed mowing the lawn Sunday as the parishioners filled the street and parked their cars all along Cabrillo while he worked at his weekly chore, pushing the hand-mower up and down the yard. He shouldn't have waited until Sunday, anyway.

"Can't I wait until they're gone, dad?"

"No. It's not hurting anyone for you to mow the lawn. They aren't looking at you," my dad told him. But of course Lyle saw it differently.

All the before-unidentified Catholics of the neighborhood and beyond came out of their stucco homes to attend the first mass, and Saint Lawrence the Martyr Parish was born. To an overflowing congregation that stood at the doorway and peered through the windows, Father Wilkiemeyer delivered his first sermon from the altar, lit by the generosity of the Wilsons.

Arturo and his family were there among the faithful "three percenters" which Arturo explained to me the next day in his recap of the events meant that his dad and others like him gave a chunk of every paycheck they earned for the new parish. His dad referred to it as his "guilt tax." The Sunday highlight, according to Arturo, came when Father Wilkiemeyer announced the entire "barn" had been built in only thirteen hours, to the irreverent chuckles of the parishioners. Arturo had thought Father Wilkiemeyer had misspoken at the time, but he later heard his mother and father discussing how the chapel was not really a chapel at all, but a barn, and built so quickly because a barn did not require the same permits to build as a chapel. New things came fast in Santa Clara.

It didn't take much time for a few un-catholic neighbors to react to the new church, which in their minds only meant new traffic and parking issues along Cabrillo. For the next three Sundays, Mr. Wiggler, two doors down from us, called the cops to complain. A couple of squad cars began controlling traffic. By the end of the month, the Wiggler house was up for sale. Shortly after, the Kellers, a good "three percenter" Catholic family, moved in and the patrol cars disappeared.

Saturday became Lyle's new day for lawn mowing. It wasn't too long after that that my dad came home one Saturday morning from Sears on San Carlos with a brand new bright red Craftsman power mower. Its tall red Briggs and Stratton motor sat above a potentially threatening powered reel of sharp vertically rotating blades. It was faster and more efficient but louder than the old push-mower, and it would have drawn much more attention to Lyle that first Sunday, but life was getting faster and louder at Lawrence and Cabrillo for everyone.

The neighborhood soon found out there were other plans in the works for this parish across the street. Frank's remaining orchard, all the way to Willow Avenue, was cleared of trees by the beginning of June. For a short time, looking from our kitchen window, we could see glimpses of El Camino, one more orchard left between us and the King's highway. The street to nowhere, officially re-named Lawrence Court from Fairbanks, got more asphalt and extended beyond the front of the chapel. Shortly after, Willow Avenue on the back side of the Musso orchard was renamed St. Lawrence Drive.

Much of where the orchard once stood, behind Art's house, became a paved parking lot. Within two years, a more permanent chapel and an elementary parochial school had been built in the other cleared areas. Across from us now were an empty field and the backsides of stucco buildings of the Catholic complex. Farmer Frank and his family sold their last acre to a townhouse developer and the Musso family, their orchard, and their farmhouse were gone forever.

Two giant flatbed trailers showed up one day transporting two halves of an old red-tiled Spanish style house from somewhere. The halves were planted across the street on the left half of the double lot in front of the temporary chapel, facing Cabrillo. They were set on a new foundation and patched together. Within a month a young couple from India moved into the house, erected redwood fences around the back, sowed a front lawn, and became part of Cabrillo Avenue. The vacant lot across from our house was reduced to a single puny space next to Lawrence. No more trees, no more pears behind it. Worst of all, when construction began on the school, a set of cyclone gates went up at the end of Lawrence Court, to protect the gravel and later asphalt replacing the trees, and it truly became a street to nowhere for me. Arturo's back door was closed most of the time.

The corner of Lawrence and Cabrillo attracted vendors, which always seemed to park across the street in front of the vacant lot or on it, waiting for customers. One of my favorites was Ernie and his Colonial Bread van. If you didn't know better, you would think all Ernie sold was bread. Ernie would show up every Thursday morning without fail in his faded panel van. He was a tall, soft-spoken thin man whose well-worn khaki shirt and pants nearly matched his yellow panel van. He would honk three times as he entered the area. In the summertime I would often go out to his van with my mother to look through the goodies, and he had rows of wide but shallow sliding wooden drawers with glass fronts that he could pull out from the back or side panel of his van to show off fresh pastries and breads. Sometimes the sweet floury smells would waft across the street and draw me outside even if I hadn't heard Ernie's van arrive. The side panel held the breads: white, wheat, raisin, cinnamon, French, and rye. My mom would always buy a loaf from Ernie. We were a white bread family most of the time. The breads were always pillow fresh, baked just hours ago.

Behind the rear doors of the Colonial Bread panel van were drawers always loaded with sugary and fruity pastries. When it was sunny out, Ernie would leave the rear doors opened wide but protected his goods with a green and white striped canvas awning he would crank down over the rear of the van.

"Today we have a special on cinnamon rolls." Ernie would often slice a selected pastry into finger-size bites on a fresh sheet of baker's paper and offer you a free sample to entice you or your mother.

Ernie had fresh mouthwatering doughnuts of every variety; bear claws, cream horns, Danishes, éclairs, strudels, turnovers, rolls, and my favorite, maple bars. I could usually talk my mom into getting me a maple bar which Ernie would hand to me on a square of baker paper, and I would be gone. I would run into the house and down the fresh warm pastry with a cold glass of Edelweiss milk before my mom even finished shopping. Ernie also carried cakes and fresh fruit pies, and you could special order right there at the truck for next week.

On Wednesday afternoons every other week an old hunched-back Portuguese truck farmer would park his produce truck on our street. He wasn't very friendly to kids, a real sourpuss. He had an ancient Model A black pickup with a tall homemade plywood shell painted green in its bed, and he would prop up three hinged wooden side panels to expose a hanging white scale and wood boxes of freshly picked fruits and vegetables, tilted to showoff his goods.

"Don't touch the produce. *I get for you,*" he'd grumble to a too-picky buyer and then choose which peach or onion he wanted you to have.

Since we were only about two hundred yards from the Francia family's Corn Palace, by far the busiest produce stand in our part of town, just up Lawrence Station Road, we seldom bought from the truck farmer, but he would do a steady business each afternoon he was there. My mom would often send Lyle, my dad, or me across the highway for four ears of corn or a bunch of carrots or a couple of yellow onions or a colander of string beans from the Corn Palace for dinner that evening.

Of course we were regular Edelweiss Dairy customers. The milkman delivered Tuesdays, Thursdays and Saturdays on our street. You'd just fan out the color-coded special items you wanted from the cardboard stick menu, set the menu in the top of one of your regular empty milk bottles, and the milkman would leave fresh dairy before you got up in the morning. I loved sneaking a swig from the bottle. Once in a while, I'd request a quart of chocolate milk by pulling out the chocolate milk stick. "I didn't order that," my mother would say when she brought the milk into the house the next morning, but she would let it go. I always thought about ordering ice cream that way, but I didn't want to push my luck with my mother. I didn't know the milkman, who came around too early for me, but I did become friends with Jim Vogt in fourth grade, whose family owned the dairy off Kifer and Coffin roads.

Miss Childrey once took our fifth-grade class out to the Edelweiss Dairy on a fieldtrip. A couple of kids threw up because of the smell. Now that I think of it, the only other fieldtrips we went on at Briarwood involved smells, in one way or another.

We went to the new sewage treatment plant out in Milpitas, where a huge movie poster of the *Cattle Queen of Montana,* featuring movie star Barbara Stanwyck on the shoulder of hired gun Ronald

Reagan hung on the tank room door. It was the most interesting part of the trip.

We had the opportunity to climb the steps into the new San Jose Municipal Airport air traffic tower off Coleman Avenue. It smelled at the airport because onion fields surrounded the runways. At the end of picking season, the airport would allow families to go into the fields surrounding the runways and take any leftover onions. I went once, but I liked going through the tomato fields across Lawrence after their picking better.

Other vendors who peddled to our Cabrillo neighborhood included the ancient Jewish guy who sharpened knives, scissors, and mower blades. His paneled truck bed was crowded with grinding equipment as grey and worn as he was. His bottle-thick glasses magnified his eyes to Peter Lorre proportions (My dad swore by is work), and then there were the tinkers, a weathered-looking gypsy couple who in broken English aggressively begged the chance to repair and sell pots and pans on the spot to you from their metal-rattling pickup bed with its three tall walls of hanging pans of every size and shape.

Of course the ice cream man rang his bell up and down the streets. And we always looked forward to the Fuller Brush man at the front door. While he didn't have a truck for his wares, he would leave us with indestructible plastic oddities like a red shoe horn or black pocket comb. I was always amazed at how much stuff he carried in his oversized brown leather suitcase. The fake ivory hand, lint, and hair brushes we have in the bathrooms have been in the house for years. Likewise, the Avon lady made regular rounds to our neighborhood—"Avon calling"—but my mother conducted those visits alone because I left the room as soon as the sales lady pulled out her Avon Fragrance Demonstrator. After the Avon lady left, the house would smell of an Avon perfume or a new lotion sample my mother tried, but most of her wares were a mystery to me, just a bunch of lady products not even worth looking at in the magazines that she always left with my mom or on the screen door if nobody was home when she made her rounds. They were almost as mysterious as the mom-only "parties" my mother would sometimes go to and then come home with new and trusty tupperware containers and gadgets. My mother threatened to host one but hasn't so far. I did like the Tupperware popsicle makers we filled with strawberry, grape, cherry, or lime Kool-Aid and stuck into the freezer, but the plastic molds didn't last very long before a part went missing or sometimes got chewed up.

By the time I entered sixth grade, only the milkman and ice cream man still came around, and there was talk of Edelweiss stopping home delivery. My dad said shopping centers and big grocery stores were too much competition for the street vendors. We now buy Langendorf or Kilpatricks bread at Safeway, and even some of their breads are more air than bread. We seldom have pastries at our house unless they are cellophane wrapped from the grocery store or my dad makes a special trip to Stan's or Wilson's downtown, which doesn't happen very often. Even the regular ice cream man gave up our area for a while. A new Cable Car ice cream truck, a fully decked out motorized burgundy and gold fake cable car, complete with canned music, sold softies for a little while, but it too stopped coming around.

At least the Corn Palace is still around, but my mother buys more canned and frozen fruits and vegetables at the grocery store as we get older. "They're cheaper and more convenient," she often says. Her big metal waterbath canning pot sits on a shelf in the garage, collecting dust. We eat more Swanson's TV dinners and pot pies and Campbell soups. I guess it's sort of like my grandmother serving Spam and ketchup sandwiches to family as she got older instead of cooking all day, and we have acquired a taste for Spam. As the orchards and crops around our neighborhood have disappeared, so have the street vendors and the fresh tastes and smells, but I will never like canned spinach or canned peas. New isn't always better.

This Friday, Allan, Art and I were the "Spirit of '76 on the first official National Loyalty Day, May 1. President Eisenhower declared that day in Congress, and Principal Boyko officiated at Briarwood as we marched in procession around the playground dressed as patriots in a school-wide costume parade during lunch. I marched and drummed between Art and Allan to the Boston Pops playing "Yankee Doodle " over the loudspeaker system. I held my wooden snare drum looped through my pants belt and my dad's blue bathrobe sash hung around my neck. My mother wrapped a red badge of courage bandage at an angle across my forehead. Across my chest I wore a white three-inch sash that read "SPIRIT OF '76" in red, silver, and blue sparkle glitter glued in place with Elmer's paste.

Art brought a Mexican bamboo flute from home and wore his left arm in a bloody pillowcase sling. His Davy Crockett powder horn hung by a thin rope from his "good" shoulder. Allan wore a black felt three-cornered hat with white edging he got at the Santa Clara fair last year. His name was stitched in white on the brim of one side, and he carried a big 3 x 5 ft. 48-star American flag, even though Alaska was already the forty-ninth state. He had his wounded knee wrapped in gauze splotched dark red with Mecuricome.

I think our mothers enjoyed making our costumes as much as we did wearing them, and the costumes gave us an excuse for wearing shorts to school. We won silk ribbons for our mothers' efforts, and the cafeteria ladies passed out slivers of a white sheet cake decorated with patriotic sugar sprinkles to everybody. Except for the color scheme, the event was a lot like the Halloween costume parades Briarwood has every year, but not as popular and there was no trick-or-treating that night, no parties, no reason to wear the costume again. So far it's the only time Loyalty Day has been mentioned at my schools. I guess it hasn't caught on yet.

CHAPTER 8

Summer 1959

Allan and I had the first morning of summer vacation planned two weeks before school was out. Neither one of us had been officially allowed to ride our bikes down El Camino Real beyond Pomeroy, which kept us pretty close to home some of the time, but the weekend school got out things changed. San Francisco Avenue got a new name, Warburton Avenue, and a new bridge across Calabasas Creek last December. Then the city built a bridge across Saratoga Creek, and now the latest bridge across San Tomas Aquino Creek is opening. Warburton Avenue will run behind El Camino Real all the way from Lawrence to Scott Lane. That will open up a parent-approved new world for us.

Monday we would take Warburton to visit my cousin Bill at his new job working at the Texaco on Scott and El Camino and then ride along the El Camino home before we met up with other neighborhood guys for afternoon baseball at Briarwood. My cousin Bill was nearly as old as my father, the son of my dad's much older brother Ray, who had been killed in an car accident in the forties. Bill grew up in Los Angeles, and I really only knew him from a few visits to Los Angeles when he would appear at Uncle Jack's or Uncle Blaine's, usually when we were horsing around in the swimming pool. But he was a nice guy and always made time to talk to me and my other younger cousins, mostly telling us about his adventures around the country.

"Guess who showed up out of the blue?" my dad asked my mother one evening while he sat at the dinner table eating re-heated tuna casserole. My mom, Lyle, and I had eaten long ago, but that was typical since my dad rarely got home from work before eight in the evening. Sometimes after driving truck all day, he would collect from some of his pen machines at stores and stations, which often made him even later getting home. He would say night after night, "I guess I lost track of time."

My mom would sit and chat with my dad while he ate alone or she'd wash dishes and listen to him tell her about his day. I rarely missed a word of their conversations even though I pretended to be absorbed in some TV show in the family room right off the kitchen. I really wasn't fooling them, and once in a while, if one of them was about to say something I really shouldn't hear, I would also hear: *"Watch out what you say. Big ears is in the next room."*

From what I could gather of this conversation, my cousin Bill was having some hard times. He had left a wife I had never met and was nearly broke when he packed up for the bay area. He had shown up at Willig that morning before my dad drove his route and borrowed some cash from him to get on his feet, and my parents argued about that. My mother's final word, "You know how he is." But I didn't know exactly what that meant. And that didn't stop my father from talking to his friend Chet who owned the Texaco on El Camino about hiring Bill. My Uncle Mac's company actually built that Texaco. Bill told my dad he was an ace mechanic so Chet agreed to try him out.

Three weeks later, Allan and I expected Bill to be in the station garage lubing somebody's Ford or fitting new tires when we arrived on our bikes, but the two uniformed mechanics in the garage were strangers to us.

"We're looking for my cousin Bill. He's a mechanic here," I said to one of the guys who paused from his work under a car on the hydraulic rack to see what we wanted.

"You'll find him around back. He's supposed to be cleaning the restrooms," he said and then he chuckled to himself about it.

Sure enough, we rode around to the far side of the station and there was Bill, leaning his back and one heel against the narrow wall between the two restroom doors, puffing on a nearly finished Camel pinched between his fingers, dressed loosely in his untucked Texaco green khaki shirt and sagging pants, missing his Texaco attendant cap, his thinning blond hair disheveled. An oblong metal water bucket with wooden wringer rollers on wheels stood at his side. With his left hand, he held a wood-handled mop that rested in the bucket's milky grey water.

After he finally realized who I was, he was glad to see us, I think. He twisted out his cigarette butt on the pavement with the toe of his shoe, let go the mop handle, pulled his Texaco cap from his back pocket, and slid it over his hair. As he tucked in his shirt tails and hoisted his pants around his waist and tightened up his leather belt, he told us that this was just a little "shit" job to get him settled in town. He asked how Lyle and my mom were and said he was going to visit us at the house soon. Then he told us he planned to buy a station of his own before the year was up. He was using this job to get a "feel for the business." Although we didn't see any cars waiting to fill up, Bill said he had to get back to pumping gas and gave us a bum's rush goodbye and disappeared around the other side of the station. I guess he'd put away the mop bucket later. Allan and I stopped at Fosters Freeze for a chocolate dipped softie before we headed back along El Camino.

Things were changing. Buddy Holly and the Big Bopper were killed in a plane crash earlier in the year, but their music lived on through Lyle's transistor radio. Superman died of a single bullet to his own head. Space monkeys Able and Baker orbited the earth and made it back alive. Rookie Giants first baseman Willie McCovey went four-for-four and hit two triples that July in his first game at Seals Stadium. But what intrigued me most was the story of the newlyweds who were married in a family fallout shelter a couple of weeks ago. The Santa Clara County fair people promised to have a walk-thru exhibit of fallout shelters in August.

Lyle had made a couple of close friends and was going to play on the newly created Buchser Thirties football team as a junior this fall. The new campus would be completely finished by the time school started this year. He is still upset about leaving his old life behind and spends most of his time in his room listening to music or Giants baseball with his friends, especially Ron Maloney.

One Tuesday in August construction men began clearing away the Nelsons' apricot orchard along El Camino for an 11-acre shopping center at the corner of Lawrence and El Camino that included plans for a big new Safeway. The Nelsons had just a few prune and walnut trees left between Warburton and the Jefferson School District offices. Allan, Art, and I watched dozers knock down trees from a distance on our bikes for an hour or so in the morning. The new shopping center excited my mom, who had relied on the small local Chinese run Bell's Market for immediate grocery needs since she didn't drive but could walk there. The Bell Plaza had been built since we moved to Santa Clara. The Rezzolo apricot orchard and strawberry field used to be there and farmer Rezzolo ran a little store on El Camino. With all the houses being built in the area, Bell's Market was already too small for shoppers by the time it opened. My mom said Bell's Market had a good butcher shop but lacked in grocery basics. My mom would put off the big shopping for Saturdays when my dad could drive us to Littleman's Market on Scott or the Safeway on Franklin downtown.

The Santa Clara Theatre was showing a double-matinee Saturday, The Return of the Fly and The Alligator People. It would be the highlight of my summer before fourth grade. Saturday matinees were the best. My friends and I went to the movies about once a month and alternated between the Sunnyvale and Santa Clara theaters. It was a day of hundreds of screaming kids who mobbed Murphy Avenue in Sunnyvale or Franklin Street in downtown Santa Clara from 9 a.m. to 4 p.m. Clusters of boys and girls would be ceremoniously dropped off in packs in front of the theater by a parent a good hour or so before show time to wait in line for the feature matinee start. Boys were usually more adventurous than girls during the wait and typically left one of their group in line to "save places" so the rest could wander around town.

This Saturday was no different for my friends and me. One of my favorite stops on Franklin was Phil's University Smoke Shop right next to Santa Clara Cyclery and three doors down from the theater. You could find newspapers and magazines from all over the world overflowing from this caboose-size store. Kids would pack in there to read the latest *The Flash* DC comic or *Mad Magazine* or stock up on Milk Duds, Dots, or Jujyfruits before going into the show. It was kind of funny that most of the business done in Phil's during the rest of the week was selling cigarettes, tobacco, and imported cigars. The store glass display cases, crowded by wire news racks, were loaded with opened cigar boxes, showing off Phil's fine Cuban cigars, Belinda, Romeo y Julieta, Partaga, or Montecristo.

Phil was a great guy to talk with. He'd ask us about school, baseball, our bikes, what kind of work our dads did, or discuss what was playing next door at the Santa Clara. He was never mean to kids who came into his shop, who, ninety percent of the time, didn't buy anything, just wanted to look. We would chat with Phil and buy a Big Hunk or Butterfinger, but this was all a lead-up to another intention. We were hoping he would have a cigar box empty. He would usually have one or two behind the counter and never charged kids who bothered to talk to him. The colorful gilded cardboard cigar boxes were all about regal Cuban cigars and would often have elaborate prints of historic people or events or ships or mythological characters on their lids. On a really lucky day Phil might give you a cigar box of Spanish cedar. I owned only one.

This Saturday Allan's dad chauffeured the five of us kids to the Santa Clara. The matinees ran continuously from ten in the morning. You could start with either feature and stay for a repeat showing after the two were finished. That was my mistake.

Allan's dad dropped us off in front of the Santa Clara an hour before the first matinee began. At nine o'clock in the morning, the smells from the Genova Deli to the right, the movie house snack bar, center, and University Smoke Shop to the left were overwhelming at times. The salty smells of meats, cheeses, briny olives, and pungent garlic, were virtually unknown in our house. My dad was strictly a meat-and-potatoes kind of man so that's what we ate, and expected to smell. Those strong foreign aromas combined with the buttery smell of theater popcorn and rich, sweet varieties of pipe and cigar tobacco from Phil's, were good reasons to have someone else save your place in line, to my way of thinking. I could never understand how the old guy who owned the box-sized watch repair shop right next to the theater could work on the intricacies of a watch with the distractions of foods and people constantly attacking his senses, especially when mobs of kids were around every Saturday. When I would sometimes come home from the movies with a stomach ache after having eaten a ton of candy, I think those smells were at least a contributing factor to my discomfort. Yet all those smells and tastes were also a part of going to the matinee. I was spared some of them today when Michael lost at RoShamBo and held our spot in line. We had plenty of time and wasted it around town as usual, hitting up the bike shop, Santa Clara Sports Shop and Phil's. By movie time, I had designs on a new bike and new glove and proudly carried my newest H. Upmann *petit corona* Cuban cigar box with me.

Thanks to Michael, we got good seats three rows up from the front of the screen, and we were well stocked with candy, popcorn, and large fountain cokes. The Newsreel was kind of boring, except for the update about Elvis Presley's tour of duty in Germany, but everybody enjoyed the Donald Duck cartoon, even though it was about math. After several hours of movie thrills and kids screaming, laughing and sometimes heckling the movie, Art, Allan, Carl, Michael and I agreed. The original *Fly* was better than *The Return*. But all five of us liked *The Alligator People* best.

When we were ready to go home, Allan was supposed to call his dad at the tow shop to pick us up. Both his parents were working there this Saturday so it really didn't matter when we were done as far as they were concerned. I, on the other hand, had told my dad that we would be back after the matinee, sometime after one o'clock. Going to the movies had usually given me a way out of going grocery shopping with my parents on Saturday mornings. I had no reason to believe this Saturday was different, but it was.

After the first matinee we decided to stick around for the beginning of *The Return of the Fly* a second time. We watched the Newsreel again and were right at the beginning of the cartoon feature, *Donald Goes to Mathmagic Land*. At the very beginning, Donald enters a dark cave looking for something. Eerie music in the background was all you could hear until—

"Benny, Benny Collins, are you in here?" It wasn't the voice we expected. A creepy feeling came over me, especially when I looked to my right and in the darkness of the theater, striding down to the front row and guided by the narrow beam of the usher's flashlight, was my father! I was mortified. My stomach went sour. I felt like the fly. *"Cecile, help me. I'm here on the floor."* But I didn't want to be found. I signaled by reluctantly raising my hand as if I were in class admitting to some wrong in Mrs. Fay's room. The usher shot the flashlight's beam into my face briefly so my dad could grab the right kid, and my dad pulled me from the seat by my arm and told me I needed to get home now.

As I got up in the semi-dark theater, kids started screaming, laughing hysterically. Were they laughing at me or at the cartoon that was now in competition for everyone's attention? I was convinced it was me, and I slunk as low as I could as my dad escorted me up the dim theater aisle and out the door. I left Allan, Michael, Carl, and Art in the theater. I was embarrassed, angry, and fearful at the same time, so much so that I left my latest cigar box under my seat. All I thought about was what kids would say in class come September. I never made it to Briarwood in September to find out.

CHAPTER 9

---

all 1959
F   *Adults in charge of schools must sit around in big offices and figure out how to make kids' lives miserable, or they don't consider them at all.* I hadn't been a bad student these past two years. I had learned a lot. I had learned to get along with Mrs. Fay in second grade. I had definitely learned how to organize my schoolwork better than I had. My mother confided in me that after my incident with the penmanship project and the phone call she received that she spoke with vice principal Mr. Nutt (that really was his name) about Mrs. Fay. He assured my mom that Mrs. Fay had a short fuse and not to worry about me. Saying as much, both my mom and dad impressed on Lyle and me the notion that schools and teachers are always right so I wasn't to talk badly about my teachers.

Third grade with Mrs. Hageman was definitely an improvement. I did well on tests and usually did my homework. In other words, I kept under the radar. So it was quite surprising in the early part of July that my parents received a letter from the school district announcing I was to be transferred to a new school in the fall for fourth grade. Art and I had spent several months watching the construction of a new school across Lawrence, not knowing that I would be confined there.

Construction started with taking out another orchard. This time they bulldozed about a third of farmer Jim's cherry orchard which grew in view of our house to build the school. It only took two days to annihilate any traces of cherry trees. One Tuesday morning in February two huge yellow caterpillars began uprooting the still dormant bing trees. By the time we got home from school, row after row of cherry tree roots, trunks, and limbs were violently piled in dozens of stacks like kindling, ready for burning. By Wednesday evening, all that was left of these purple bing bearing trees were ashes, traces of smoke in the air, and open space, ready for leveling and construction.

I was sure orders for me to attend the new school were somehow personal. Darn city. But as it turned out a bunch of the kids plucked from my block were heading to Bennett school in September. Somebody drew a line on a map that ran across the street between the Jacksons' house and the Ruffinos' on our side of Cabrillo and the Snowdens' and Millers' on the other side. What was most baffling was that the new school wasn't even in Santa Clara. It was on the other side of Lawrence Station Road. If the Santa Clara and Sunnyvale police couldn't even agree about jurisdiction of an accident on city boundaries, how did I end up in a school half a mile away from the boundary? Surely, it had to be a mistake.

For some reason the Jefferson district, of which half of the Santa Clara elementary schools were part, also included kids and schools in some Sunnyvale neighborhoods. As the Jefferson district letter explained, to relieve overcrowding in both Santa Clara and Sunnyvale, the cities decided to build a single new school and shift school boundaries. Surrounded by a tomato field, remains of the cherry orchard and a prune orchard, Bennett school would transplant third and fourth graders from each city its first year. Some of the Briarwood kids that were supposed to go on to Jefferson as sixth-graders ended up rooted another year in elementary school.

You could see part of Bennett school take shape from our kitchen window as it was being built. The red brick and green mint stucco front of it set back a good hundred yards but faced Lawrence Station Road. It was a "tract school," a near duplicate in most respects to other Santa Clara schools like Briarwood, Bracher, Bowers, Miliken, and Pomeroy. Designers did to new schools what they did to new houses—built them all the same. Builders constructed two more "roads to nowhere" to get to Bennett. The first new road, off Lawrence, headed into Sunnyvale, just west of Cabrillo, sandwiched between Bennett's side lot and playing field on the left and the Kiely family's prune orchard to the right. The freshly paved road ended with the familiar white ranch end-of-the-road fence at farmer Jim's remaining cherry trees. The second new road, Halford, ran parallel to Lawrence in front of Bennett school and abruptly ended just beyond the classrooms, heading directly to the tomato fields in front of it, El Camino Real in the distance. I sensed the tomato fields weren't long for this world.

The only advantage I could see going to Bennett was that our house was at the corner of the new school bus stop, but even that seemed wrong. For one thing, I couldn't walk or ride my bike to school, no more tortillas. The people who planned these things didn't want kids crossing busy Lawrence Station Road by themselves. It didn't matter to them that Briarwood school, where all my friends were, was only two more blocks away than Bennett.

So in the fall, a busload of "bootlegged" kids took the ride to Bennett. The trip was scenic. I'll give them that. We could have been at school in five minutes, tops, but the bus went deep into a couple of Sunnyvale neighborhoods to harvest other unhappy kids and made the ride a thirty-minute trip. I admit, I did learn my way around Sunnyvale. It's funny how kids can live only a couple of blocks from one another and never even know anyone in another neighborhood because they end up in other schools. I now would know two school populations.

In my new fourth grade class, Lorraine Jackson, Jimmy Carpenter, Sheryl Snyder, and Catherine Epolite were the only kids I knew. On my block, families from the Ruffinos east continued at Briarwood school. No more Allan, Michael, Art, Carl, Carlotta, Sarah, Susan, or any of my other classmates. The wheels of progress had struck me personally. That hurt.

Miss Krammer, a young auburn haired, short, freckled teacher (every visible part of her body was covered in rich brown freckles), tried to put a good spin on everything. She always wore cotton dresses with bright flowery prints and painted her smile with blinding red lipstick. She sensed our difficulty being displaced. She told us on our first day of class that each of us was a "tabula something-or-other," a blank slate, starting over. Well, I didn't entirely agree. It's not that easy to forget. I still wasn't going to speak to Lorraine, and I'll never forget my first day in second grade when Hubie and I got into a fight. And I certainly didn't want to forget my old friends, especially Art, Allan, Carl, and Michael. You can't pile old memories like uprooted trees and then burn them, which is what they did when they cleared another orchard around us.

Out on the field I met Pauly Owens. He was a small, dark haired, freckly-faced guy, who was talented on the playing fields. He was Flash fast on the grass. He made some pretty impressive throws and catches with the football. It turns out he was even better at baseball. We hit it off immediately. For a while, he lived on the Sunnyvale side of Lawrence down by the old Lawrence Station, not too far from the tracks. His family moved a lot.

On the bus I met Billy Preacher. He was bigger and taller than most fourth-graders, and he'd sometimes tease other kids or give them a knuckle head rub, because he could. We both seemed to discover Melinda Johnson on the bus at the same time, but we both got over that, too. Billy lived in a tract home behind the Corn Palace farm. Like me, he could see no good reason to take the bus to school. After the first couple weeks, he simply didn't, and no one challenged him. He rode his beat up blue Schwinn everywhere. When I suggested to my mom that maybe I too could ride my bike to school, I was reminded of the old dictum, the people in charge of school (and everything else, for that matter) were always right. In other words, I would take the bus, as instructed. Eventually, Billy and I would have some good biking adventures outside of school.

The big redwood house was somewhat of an eyesore on Lawrence Station Road. It was a holdout from the orchard days of the neighborhood. As quite often happened in the days of builders buying out orchard owners for large chunks of land on which to build yet another tract of houses, an owner would make demands the builders would refuse to accept so they would simply build around them. Not all these homes were stylish. Pauly Owens' family rented such a house in October. It was surrounded by the homes of Lawrence Meadows. The house was identifiable because it was made of wide redwood clapboard, stained a dark-brown with both high and flat rooflines and irregular add-ons that made it twice the width of the neighboring homes. The main house, situated midway in the lot, was narrow but tall enough to be two-story and occupied the right side of the double lot. An enclosed pass thru hall, a flat roofed enclosed breezeway/bedroom, and a dilapidated garage with a gravel floor filled the left side. Most distinctive of all was that the house faced the wrong way! Its front faced the highway. The Lawrence Meadows tract houses on either side of it faced the newly created Del Monte Avenue behind it. The Owens' backyard, facing Del Monte, unenclosed, was a doublewide field of patchy grass. It made the yards surrounding it look puny. The "field" served Pauly, his six brothers and sisters, and neighborhood kids quite well for play once his family moved in. Prior to that it was just another vacant lot at the back of a quiet old farmhouse in disrepair.

It was a welcomed surprise to me to see Pauly's family move in just down the path from my house, just beyond my mother's walnut trees. Pauly was second oldest of seven kids. Nobody ever called him Paul. His oldest brother Renny was two years older than he. Pauly's parents had a child every year for eight years! Pauly's older brother Patrick had died before he was a year old. That meant all other brothers and sisters were one year apart. Pauly was nine when we met at Bennett school. In order were his brother Johnny, 8; his sister

Carrie, 7; his brother Jeremy, 6; his sister Jill, 5, and his youngest sister Mindy, 4.

The Owens were poor by Lawrence Meadows standards. The main house had a living room and dining area, two bedrooms, a cramped galley kitchen, and one small bathroom, for nine people. The three girls slept in the house proper in one wooden framed double bed. An always-leaky tin-roof covered the pass-thru that linked the back of the kitchen to the boys' room opposite the main house. The drafty pass-thru was skinny, but wide and long enough for the four old wooden dressers that were lined up in a row on the wall for the boys' clothes. An old washing machine was wedged in at the edge of the porch door in the pass-thru, not leaving much room to pass through to anywhere easily. Soiled stacks of jeans, shirts, shorts, and socks were always piled on its lid, and opened cardboard boxes full of unfolded clothing lined up along the near wall of the pass-thru. Two thin cotton ropes hung tautly over the boxes and were used for drying clothes when it rained instead of using the big lines that stood below the kitchen window in the driveway area. Even in good weather these two lines were seldom completely empty. There was always the smell of wet clothes in the air.

From the left end of the hall, you could go out to the true front of the house, which mostly consisted of a gravel driveway, junk, a pigeon coop, and a lot of tall weeds facing the highway. Go out the right door of the pass-thru, if you could maneuver through the dressers, boxes, hanging clothes, and clutter, and you were at the "field," their backyard. A storm door opposite the kitchen door on the other side of the pass-thru led to the boys' bedroom, a converted breezeway with a flat tar roof that always leaked. The room had a single double-hung curtainless window facing the driveway. Its dark walls and low ceiling were knotty pine siding, long ago painted the brown of the house's exterior. A threadbare brown carpet remnant covered most of the iron concrete floor. At the far end of the long room was a burnt-brown sheet metal gas room heater, with a dusty black chimney flue pipe that disappeared into a poorly cut hole in the ceiling. Attached to the center of the warped ceiling was a tarnished brass lamp fixture missing its glass shade, exposing two bare light bulbs. The room contained four brown metal-framed army surplus barrack beds equally spaced along the long wall, each with its own two drawer night stand to its right, none the same in style or material. Each boy had a dark-colored rumpled flannel blanket and a misshapen canvas feather pillow on his bed. There were no sheets on the lumpy three-inch thick pinstriped mattresses. Absent a closet, pegs on the opposite wall held jackets, jeans, and shirts. The air was sour and damp.

Pauly's dad was a construction worker. He was a heavyset man with burly arms and a swarthy complexion. Around the house he wore greyish ribbed tank-top t-shirts, and his curly chest hairs erupted to his thick neck and collided with the grey and white stubble of his muffin top chin. He had a constant open-mouth grin on his face, exposing tobacco-stained yellowing crooked teeth and a large gap between two of his upper teeth where he had lost a battle to decay. Although he was only in his thirties, his hair, always cut close, was nearly completely white. When he was home, he was mostly enwrapped in his dark green naugahyde recliner watching TV or snoozing in t-shirt, jeans, and soiled off-white socks.

From his point of comfort, he would also play with all his children. The youngest would climb all over him as they told him about their day or he of his. The older ones he would entertain with a silly story or parlor trick. He would prompt Mindy or Jill to get a sewing needle from their mother's tin. Then he would place the needle between the flesh of his lower and upper arm at the inside of the elbow as he raised his lower arm to a 45-degree angle so that each end of needle appeared to nearly pinch the skin. With needle in place, he would slowly close his arm in on itself—to the oohs and awes of the children—and the needle would disappear between the arm of flesh, appearing to pierce the skin as he tightened his arm, but, alas, upon opening his arm there was no harm done. He could entertain his own kids and their neighborhood friends for hours.

CHAPTER 10

---

*W*inter 1959

     Christmas had always been a big event at our house. It probably had to do with the fact that both my father and mother came from large families. I can remember in Utah how my dad's eight brothers and sisters would bring their families to my grandma's stone Victorian on South Second Avenue, every Christmas after church. There was always a bountiful family dinner with all the trimmings, lots of cousins running all over the house and clusters of relatives sitting, standing, eating, drinking, and visiting. It was the best of times and never about gifts.

Christmas in Santa Clara was new. After moving to Santa Clara, our Christmas was rather small, though we would usually have dinner with Clara and Mac or Aunt Betty and Uncle Cliff and their kids Steven and Renee in Hayward. Compared to the Collins gatherings, our seasonal get-togethers were puny. Mom and dad made up for that in other ways.

First, there were the gifts shipped to parts of Utah, Nevada, and to Los Angeles. It seemed like the entire Collins clan had moved to somewhere else by 1959. None of my dad's family lived within four hundred miles of us, and only two of my mom's sisters lived in the bay area. The gift exchange was kind of silly. My mom boxed up a set of sheets or bath towels from Penny's or Harts department store in Sunnyvale, weeks before Christmas, and my dad took a backseat full of packages to the post office on Franklin for delivery. Then the gifts from aunts and uncles started trickling in from the mailman to our house. My grandmother and my dad's sisters always sent their packages unboxed. They arrived slightly smashed in abused brown grocery sack paper covered with rows of U.S. postage stamps and patches of scotch tape. Names and addresses were always poorly scrawled in blue ink across the top, obviously written once the packages were wrapped. Surprise! The lumpy gift-wrapped packages were invariably sheets or towels. Often the green terrycloth of towels or the floral patterns of new sheets were peek-a-boo visible where the packaging was torn. It was an even exchange of gifts. Sometimes, my grandma folded two pocket-handkerchiefs inside, one for me, one for Lyle.

My parents were cheap most of the year, no name brand soft drinks for us, Cragmont or Shasta. We never really celebrated birthdays or other events in a big way. Going out to a fancy dinner for a special occasion meant going to Burger Pit or, if they really splurged, Mr. Steak on El Camino. A fancy breakfast was at Uncle John's Pancake House.

Christmas was the one time they spent without reservation. Every year, whether there was a family gathering or not, my mother decorated the house with various Santa replicas, green plastic boughs and wreaths, assorted cotton snowmen, silk gauze angels, papier-mâché bells and miniature gold painted styrofoam reindeer. Outdoor red, green, white, blue, and orange lights hung from the eaves of the roof, unless, as he did one year, Paul Ruffino sneaks around one night and steals most of the neighbors' lights. Mother didn't like what she called "tacky" outdoor decorations so we never had a plastic Santa and his reindeer on the roof climbing up the chimney.

We've had some extreme Christmas trees. This year my mom bought a fresh-cut seven-foot Scotch pine at the Stevens Creek Plaza Christmas tree lot next to Emporium and had it machine flocked with fake snow and glitter in a huge outdoor tent. At least it wasn't pink as it was the year before that or aluminum before that. (The aluminum tree lived on for years and years at my Aunt Betty's house.) The Scotch pine was prominently displayed in the living room window and lit with a turning translucent color-wheel that stood on the floor in the corner of the room and projected the whole tree and living room a different color—red, green, blue, yellow—as the ten-inch wheel spun slowly in front of a floodlight.

My mother and father made up for small Christmas gatherings with big Christmas gifts for Lyle and me. Christmas was now less about family and more about getting new things. We always got at least a couple of big-ticket items like bicycles or sports equipment, and always an array of clothes, from underwear to shirts to pants to jackets. I thought that was the way everyone celebrated Christmas now.

Christmas 1959 I woke up to a brand new red and white J.C. Higgins Flightliner. It's the very one I picked out at Sears on San Carlos a couple of months ago when my dad was getting his brakes redone in the auto area. We were wandering around the store with bags of popcorn we bought at the Sears rear diner, killing time. The Flightliner was with all the other bikes lined up on kickstands in the store, right next to the gas lawnmowers. I had made a big deal out of liking it, but my dad appeared more interested in a Craftsman mower than a bike. I also got a Spalding Collegiate basketball from Lyle. It would be another good excuse to allow us to put up a backboard and hoop above the garage door, though mother resisted us. I opened up a new pair of Union strap-on roller skates. I had worn out the straps on the old ones and taken the skates apart. By removing the heel and toe metal clips and separating the sliding front section from the back, with a little bit of hammering you could get two good sets of mounted wheels for making a skate cart. There were plenty of wooden lugs lying around across the highway in the prune orchard. One of those on end, nailed to a two-by-four with skate wheels, made a great scooter. My now new skates would have a second life when they got old.

Lyle got a Tudor electric football game. The little metal blue and silver players skittered along the sheet-metal gridiron, which vibrated when you turned it on. The football was a small white chunk of felt cut to resemble the shape of a football. The kicker was spring-loaded to "kick" the ball at a player when you released the trigger. We spent hours playing it in his room while listening to his Elvis Presley *White Christmas* album over and over. Mostly electric football was a game of chance. The players weren't too predictable once the power was on and would usually bunch up in one corner of the board or head to the wrong end zone. Lyle also got a new pair of Riddell football cleats and a pair of low-cut Converse All-Stars. He finally got to unwrap his MacGregor Willie Mays glove he had picked out at the Santa Clara Sport Shop downtown last month.

Before the day was over, Lyle had already soaked his new mitt in the garage sink, dried it out in the oven, battered it around with my dad's ball pein hammer, saturated it with Rawlings glove oil, and wrapped it shut over an old softball, secured by a worn leather belt tied around it. He wanted it broken in as soon as possible. I bought him Bas ket, a box basketball game that uses a ping-pong ball and finger flippers to shoot baskets at miniature hoops. We both got good at that after a couple of weeks. Oh yeah, we both got a bunch of new clothes.

Excited to show off my new bike, I road up and down Cabrillo two or three times, and then decided to go to Pauly's house. Their family had only lived there since October so I wasn't much familiar with their family celebrations. I took the gravel path to the front of the house. Most of the time a group of neighborhood kids were playing some kind of ball on the field in the backyard. I would show off my new bike at the right time. I put my bike under the kitchen window area, near the pass-thru door and the clothesline, but behind an old dead washer and trash can, where you wouldn't even see it unless you were looking for it. I figured it was safe there and not too close to the wire pigeon coop that sat next to the garage. Pauly's mom raised about a dozen pet pigeons so the garage and driveway area was usually a mess of gravel, weeds, pigeon feed and poop. The pigeons all looked the same to me, but anyone in Pauly's family could name each pigeon. They were part of the family and just as plentiful. Anyway, the pigeons weren't fluttering about today.

On an end table at the front window stood a rather pathetic-looking three-foot high Douglas Fir Christmas sapling. Excessive silver tensil and hand-made paper ornaments hung from its sparse and flimsy branches. A threaded string of popcorn draped unevenly from top to bottom. Upon my knocking at the front door, I was ushered in by freckle-faced, curly haired Carrie, on whom I had somewhat of a crush. Inside, the house was a whirlwind of activity.

Pauly was busy talking with Johnny, comparing their fishing poles. Jeremy was in the corner rolling a foot-long blue metal dump truck on the carpet and up the arms of an overstuffed chair. Mindy and Jill were busy "conversing" with their identical Nanette dolls. Pauly's dad sat in his recliner commanding Renny's full attention with an elaborate story about a guy on the job cutting his index finger off with a circular saw, and his mom was busy cooking in the cluttered kitchen, where Carrie had re-joined her. Lots of conversations and laughter.

"Hey, Pauly, I didn't mean to interrupt your opening presents. My mom made me wait until eleven before I came over, but I guess you guys get up later than we do Christmas morning," I said apologetically.

"Are you kidding? We've been up since six this morning. We go to church at 7:30 and have a big pancake breakfast when we get home. Nobody opens any presents until the last plate's washed," Pauly said as he handed me his new fishing pole to examine. The pole looked good to me, but I didn't know anything about fishing. I could see it still had a small red Payless $1.95 tag hanging on it.

"That's a Shakespeare reel. Isn't it cool?" he asked.

"Yeah, but where do you fish?"

"We mostly fish Stevens Creek or the dam. Sometimes my dad takes us to Uvas or Lexington. We have cousins in Gustine so sometimes we fish the Merced and the Delta Mendota."

Fishing was a whole new world to me. Back in Utah we lived in the city, but Lyle and I had once gone on a fishing trip to the canyon country with our Uncle Mike and Aunt Noan. They were avid fishermen. We stayed three days at a camp that had old cabins and not much else. To get a drink of water you had to go to the one spigot on the edge of camp. It was a hose faucet on a three-foot pole that rose from the ground. I don't recall catching any fish, but I remember reaching out to turn the faucet on and sticking my head under it for water when face-to-face I encountered the largest snake I'd ever seen, wrapped tightly around the faucet. Everyone in a mile radius knew I was in camp—or leaving. I screamed my head off. All I remembered about fishing itself was being told to have patience.

"We can ride up to Stevens Creek in a couple of months if you want and I'll show you how," Pauly added.

"That would be great," I said, but before I could continue, Pauly was showing me what each of his brothers and sisters gave him. Renny gave him hand-me-down baseball cleats, which Renny had carefully cleaned and shoe shined black. From Johnny, he got a quart Mason jar of marbles Johnny had collected or won over the year just for Pauly. They were mostly catseyes and pearls, but I saw a couple of steelies. Carrie had made Pauly a black and white keychain out of braided strips of plastic, no doubt made at the Parks and Rec program during the summer. He had homemade fudge from Mindy. As a matter of fact, all of his six brothers and sisters exchanged gifts that they had either made or renewed. I thought about how my mom gave me money to buy gifts for the family. I knew I was not going to show off my new Flightliner that was sitting beneath their kitchen window today.

Moments later, Pauly's aunt and uncle arrived with their five kids and a couple of second-cousins. The families had already seen each other earlier this morning at church. They carried plates of Christmas cookies, divinity, chocolate walnut fudge, a pumpkin pie, an eight-inch fruitcake, and a chocolate Yule log, and then they worked to find room for them on the edges of the already overburdened table in the dining area. After an exchange of hugs and kisses by all the relations, Pauly's mom paused the action to introduce me to everyone as if I were member of the family. Kids bunched off into all corners of the house. Pauly's aunt and the older girls immediately assembled in the narrow kitchen for tasks Mrs. Owens delegated in preparation for even more food. Mr. Owens narrated a new tale from his recliner to a fresh audience of men and boys. Pauly later told me his relatives had been here just a month from Oklahoma and living with Pauly's older cousin in a two-room basement apartment in Sunnyvale. The Owens' crowded house got louder and tighter to move around in, but nobody seemed to mind. As soon as Pauly unleashed his jar of marbles onto the well-worn family marble race roller apparatus he had dug out of the hall closet, the steady hum and clack of glass marbles rolling down wooden rails played background static to the ten conversations and Bing Crosby crooning from the radio at the same time. The scene reminded me of a past Collins gathering.

A little later, the boys went out back and played some football with other kids from the neighborhood on the field. The Owens' field had already become the gathering place for most of the kids living near Del Monte Avenue. It was home turf to a lot of us. That day I ended up telling Pauly only about my new basketball, and only when he asked me about my Christmas. He'd find out about my new bike soon enough. Pauly told me that his mother had invited me to Christmas dinner if I could stay. They were having roast pigeon.

The most memorable Washington's Birthday I ever had I was February 1960. First of all, it was a day off from school, but there was some extra excitement in the air. Looking up at the night sky for several nights, you could see metronomic searchlights' crisscrossing beams circling the night and drawing you to the event, and it was just down the road from our house. Lawrence Square Shopping Center was finally opening. It was a three-day weekend celebration, complete with discounts, food, and prizes. My mom kept reminding us that the new Safeway opening meant not having to wait to grocery shop on the weekends when my dad was able to drive her to the big Safeway out on Winchester or to Littleman's Market.

Lawrence Square was a mile from our house on the corner of Lawrence and El Camino Real. Its new Safeway was one of the largest in the Bay Area. My mom was always clipping coupons from the *Mercury News* for sale items at Safeway. Finally, she had a Safeway she could get to on foot, but the funny thing was Saturday shopping trips continued. The ride was shorter but the shopping took longer. I was dragged along virtually every Saturday morning while she shopped, up and down every aisle. Sometimes, I would walk the shopping center with my dad while my mother loaded up the grocery cart. He would chat with store clerks and other husbands waiting for their wives, with me in tow. Once a month we would get haircuts at Haircuts, a shop just two doors down from the Safeway. It didn't have the comfort of our old barbershop on the Alameda where everybody knew everybody there, but that was closing because El Camino Real was being widened. I had never heard of Drug King, some kind of chain store, but it turned out to be much more than a drug store. It was in direct competition with Bob's Glendale Pharmacy on the Bell Plaza.

We knew Bob personally, but we ended up shopping mostly at Drug King unless my mom or dad needed medical advice. Then they turned to Bob. Drug King had just about everything. More than one Christmas I found just the right gift for my dad, like a set of Old Spice or Aqua Velva shaving lotions or a Timex watchband, and things were cheaper there than at Bob's. My friends and I spent many an afternoon at Woolworth's fountain when we were rich in coins, eating a rotisserie hot dog or a Velveeta grilled cheese sandwich or slurping a thick chocolate shake or a fountain Coke, but there was virtually no pet shop as there was in Valley Fair, where they devoted a quarter of the basement floor to birds, fish, hamsters, and turtles.

Baldwin Toys *looked* promising. It was jammed with stuff for kids, from a box of Pick-Up Stix to a Duncan yo-yo to a Slinky to an Etch-a-Sketch to a View Master to the out-of-my-price range toys like an Ant Farm or Erector Set. They even had Jerry Mahoney dummies. The more expensive the toy the higher it was on a shelf. What never made sense to my friends or me was why the shriveled old couple that owned the place ever bought a toy store. Kids were the enemy. Whenever we ventured in they would "man the battle stations." Mrs. Baldwin would stand ready at the cash register, where she could also watch the ceiling convex mirrors from the best angles, and Mr. Baldwin would follow us at a short distance, holding his arms behind his back, crooking his head in our direction, looking out at us from above his drooping glasses, and watching our every move. You dared not touch anything. The only thing I ever bought there were a few TopFlite Man in the Moon and Jolly Roger kites, and then only because Woolworth's was out of stock. Even those they kept behind the counter in an out-of-the-reach cardboard box. You would point to the one you wanted from the assembled samples pinned high on the wall, name your color, and Mr. Baldwin or the Mrs. would get your pick out for you and get easily irritated if you rejected the wrong one they would invariably put on the counter. Paper ones were 15 cents, plastic ones 30 cents. At Woolworth's you could pick through them on your own, and they were a nickel cheaper—when they had them.

I never got a pair of shoes from the Gallenkamp shoe store, too expensive. The anchor store at Lawrence Square was J.M. McDonald Co. Department Store. It was busy from day one. That's probably because there were not a lot of other department stores around. McDonald was where I got my first pair of genuine Levi's jeans and not until I had saved up my allowance money. My mom refused to buy them for me. She would say, "I'm not spending money on those until you can learn to stop wearing out the knees of your jeans. That's too much money to put into pants I'm only going to have to patch a month after you've had them." No matter how I pleaded to have the real thing, she refused, so I a saved up $4.50 and bought my own. By that time the store had been there a while.

Stores opened at eleven on Saturday morning of the Grand Opening. The gala event had been announced in both the *Mercury* and the *Santa Clara Journal*. But it was the grand opening of McDonald Department Store I was anxious to see. For me, it was all about the raffles. McDonald was primarily a clothing store, but it had a kitchenware area, a small appliance section, and even a baby furniture area. One of its best features turned out to be free professional gift-wrapping, especially when a kid was in need of such for a birthday or Christmas gift.

The morning of the center's Grand Opening I was anxious to get some of the goodies promised. I just knew I was going to win one of the door prizes. Safeway was decorated with red and blue crepe paper twisted around the windows and bunches of colorful balloons blowing above the automatic doors. At each entrance, a greeter gave out red and white paper cups of Carnation vanilla ice cream with little wooden spoons. Drug King, with its orange and blue color scheme, also adorned with balloons, set up tables on either side of the door, and teenage girls gave out little sample bottles of shaving products or containers of cosmetics, not much for kids, though I did get a travel-size tube of Brylcreem that I didn't really need for my crew cut. Mr. and Mrs. Baldwin were ready for business, no frills, no smiles, just the two of them, arms akimbo, waiting at their door. Woolworth's passed out midget bags of popcorn they popped in a glass machine in front of the store and helium balloons to the little kids and merchandise coupons to the adults. I got a free red Duncan top at Gallenkamp Shoes, and we looked around the store.

J.M. McDonald set up a long table at the front door for the raffles. To my disappointment, only adults could sign up for the drawings. So my mom and dad each filled out a red ticket and put them in the wire hamster-like cage on the table while I looked over the prizes all displayed on a shelf behind the tabletop. There was a door-prize drawing of the tickets Saturday, Sunday, and Monday, at 2 p.m. The store gave out each of the displayed prizes each day: an aluminum electric cooker-griddle-skillet-roaster, a portable stereo hi-fi console with two detachable speakers, a five-speed blender with a chrome-plated base, a lunchbox leather-bound transistor radio, three wrist watches, and numerous small items like fingernail file kits and cufflinks and earrings and pins. Of course, I wanted us to win either the hi-fi or transistor radio. Store workers were serving slices of cherry pie on paper plates near the giftwrap area so we mulled around eating our pie for a while. A framed poster on a metal stand in the area proclaimed the first 228 customers through the door Monday morning would each receive a whole baked cherry pie to take home in honor of George Washington's 228th birthday.

After walking the entire store, we went back to Safeway to grocery shop, calculating a two o'clock return for the first drawing. We walked away from J.M. McDonald that day with a shiny black lunchbox transistor radio just like Lyle's brown one. Pauly and I went back Monday and each won a whole cherry pie.

CHAPTER 11

*S*pring 1960

There must have been two hundred boys, baseball mitts in hands, out on the fields surrounding the brand new Briarwood Little League Park. It was ready to go, but no kids were allowed on it. We were herded off to the grasslands of Killarney Park and Briarwood school. It was stadium and park dedication day, but the boys were all there for the little league tryouts.

Vice President Nixon showed up to throw out the first pitch at brand new Candlestick Park last week, but we settled for Mayor Rebeiro and a gaggle of city officials and local reporters, tie-less with rolled up long-sleeve white shirts and dark slacks, who droned endlessly, thanking various parent groups and coaches and a tall suit-clad Killarney Farms representative. They officially changed the name of Killarney Park to Machado Park, named after the farmer whose crops once stood where we were. Still no kids were allowed on the new diamond, and in front of the small crowd of adults that sat on the newly constructed concrete bleachers behind the backstop, the city mayor threw a first pitch from the mound to the new little league president at home plate. Then it was over for the adults.

All the while, a mob of kids was gathered around the outside of the three-foot high home run cyclone fencing, waiting patiently for tryouts to begin and the mob to become teams. When the dedicating was done, we were divided by age groups. Signed in, and in smaller groups we shagged fly balls, traded off taking infield, and even got to hit at pitches thrown by coaches. Other coaches, many wearing their team's ball caps, the Texaco Chiefs, Gallenkamp Shoes, New York Sausage, and Grandview Hardware, observed us, making notes about us on their clipboards. Only the eleven and twelve year olds actually tried out on the new diamond.

It was turning out to be a pretty good day. Little League had arrived at Briarwood. I got to see many of my old friends from Briarwood school. Coaches Wright and Tanaka chose Michael and me. We would be on the same farm team. Our first practice would be Monday after school back at the big field.

I had seen Carlotta on the chin-up bars in the distance on the jungle gym at the playground when we were shagging fly balls during tryouts. She had been there all morning, watching. I was guessing she would have liked to have been out there with us. She was better than half the guys trying out.

"Michael, I'm going to go see Carlotta at the school. Wanna come?"

"No. I gotta get home. I told my dad I'd report straight home after tryouts. We're going to my cousins' house for a barbecue. I'll see you tomorrow." Michael, the obedient son, rode off on his bike. Michael was one of the guys at Briarwood who didn't take too well to Carlotta.

I cut across the big field where we'd tried out and headed toward the school playground. Most the guys were already gone from the teams they were assigned to except for a half dozen of the older kids going to be on the majors this season. They were on the newly dedicated field along with a couple of the coaches. Next year Michael and I will be eligible for the majors, too, and we will get to officially play on the new diamond if we make a team.

I waved at Carlotta as I closed the distance to her. She was sitting on the taller of the two chin-up bars, her hands holding her upright, but she released one arm to wave back.

"Hey, Carlotta. Long time no see. I saw you out here earlier. Did you go to the Little League field dedication ceremony?"

"No. Not too interesting to me. My Uncle Steve was out there. He's going to help coach the Chiefs."

"I thought you liked baseball," I said as a question.

"I do. That's just the problem. I can't play because I'm a girl. That's not fair. My uncle told me I could sell candy in the snack shack. Big deal," she said, and then she let go her hands from the chin-up bar, slipped backwards, turned a full summersault in the air, and landed squarely with her feet on the ground. It looked like an Olympic gymnastic dismount.

"How'd you do that?" I asked, both my arms pointing toward the chin-up bar.

"I learned that when I was seven. That's what happens when you live with a schoolyard behind your house. I thought you moved away or something."

"I got transferred to Bennett. Don't you remember?"

"Oh, yeah. Hey, did you make a team?" she asked.

"Yeah, Michael and I are both going to be on the Pirates farm team. The rules say you can't be on the majors until you are eleven or twelve. Some of the guys our age are good enough to play majors now. It's not fair." The words shot from my mouth before I realized how stupid I must have sounded to Carlotta.

"Uncle Steve and I got into a big argument. He said baseball's a boys' sport. Where are the girls' sports? That's what I want to know," Carlotta said, looking to the ground for an answer.

"You're right, you know. But lots of things are changing around here. Maybe that will too," I said, trying to cheer her up, even though I didn't really believe myself. "Say, can you teach me how to do that flip off the chin-up bars?"

We spent a good hour together, catching up on old times, my watching her go through the steps on the chin-up bar over and over, sitting on the bar with her, sitting on the bar by myself. Still, I didn't have the nerve to do a flip.

Easter Sunday, singer Eddie Cochran was killed in a car accident on a road in England. I don't know much about the roads in England, but I know Highway 17 to Santa Cruz is a driver's nightmare. My dad says that anyone who drives the center lane of that road's an idiot. Yellow lines are all that stand between you and a head-on. There are always news stories about head-on crashes and rollovers, especially along Big Moody Curve. The few times my dad has taken us to Santa Cruz, I have paid little attention to the dangers of the road. The trip through the redwoods is a fast-moving adventure of turns, drops, and climbs. I focus on the landmarks that signal how far we are from our usual destination, Santa Cruz. The two giant cat statues just outside of the town of Los Gatos, Lexington Dam, the painted plywood CHP patrol car at the summit just beyond Cloud Nine restaurant, and Denny's tall spinning yellow and red sign just before the Tree Circus in Scotts Valley mark all but the final stretch to Santa Cruz and points north and south along Highway 1. Denny's restaurant also signals Santa's Village, an amusement park on the other side of the highway. It is only a blur when you're heading southbound, but I always stretch my neck to get a glimpse of the fake snow-covered red and white North Pole cottages or the octopus-like snowball ride other kids are riding. We will probably never go there, no matter how often I ask.

"How many times have you been to Disneyland? Santa's Village is nothing compared to that," my dad says every time we pass it. He says the same thing about the Tree Circus. But I would prefer to make my own comparisons by going to them at least once.

Lyle's football buddies were going to Santa Cruz this spring break. It was already a tradition at Buchser, and even though most of the students going were seniors, the football players booked enough rooms at the Peter Pan Motel in Santa Cruz for the week that a handful of juniors were invited along, probably to keep the cost down. Spring break at Santa Cruz was about sun, surf, girls, and I'm pretty sure, beer. Lyle was a star player of sorts so he had a lot of buddies who wanted him to go. It took some persuading for the guys to say Ron Maloney could tag along, too. Lyle spent a good month getting the courage to ask dad if he could go. When he finally did, all hell broke loose in our house.

"I don't care whether you think it's fair or not. You're not going and that's final," my dad said for the tenth time in a week. So Lyle pulled a "Lyle" and shut himself off from the rest of us. He'd come home late from school—but before my dad got home—eat supper, and promptly retreat to his room and his music. In other words, Lyle was his old self, not very happy, not very social, and not about to give up a fight. The one concession my dad made was telling Lyle he could go next year.

Ron Maloney couldn't go either, but at the time Maloney told Lyle he wouldn't go out of loyalty to his friend. So Lyle and Maloney did the next best thing. They went anyway.

With their friends already in Santa Cruz by the beginning of the week and no wheels of their own, Lyle and Maloney decided to hitchhike. Just in front of The Cats Roadhouse outside Los Gatos, Lyle and Maloney got the ride of their lives.

After nearly a twenty-minute wait, a black beat up Olds 88 station wagon pulled over in a cloud of dust next to Lyle and Maloney. A wiry-haired young woman dressed in beads and a peasant blouse stuck her head out the passenger-side window of the front seat. The back seat was already taken by two teen girls dressed for the beach.

"Hop in the back. You'll have to sit on the deck. We've got a full house already," the young woman said and then directed the two hikers to unlatch the backend and jump in.

Lyle and Maloney slid into the back with their rolled up beach towels where there was really nothing to grab onto. They sat with their legs bent at forty-fives on the ribbed plastic floor of the deck. Backs against opposite side windows, they faced each other, and slid down on their butts as the Olds spun on the gravel where they had been and headed south on 17. When they finally got their balance, they raised their heads and got a slightly obstructed look at their driver in front of the girls in the back seat. From behind, he looked not unlike his front passenger. His long wiry black hair was down to his shoulders, but they could see traces of a scraggly dark beard on his chin. He was wearing some kind of paisley tunic. His black Ray Ban sunglasses tinted dark green hid his eyes from the rearview mirror reflection. He was Jesus in Ray Bans. The passenger cranked up the radio volume of the already-loud guitar sounds of Dick Dale's "Let's Go Trippin'" playing on the car speakers, pulsating out of large woofers in the wagon side panels behind both Lyle's and Maloney's lower backs.

Lyle regretted this hitchhiking idea too late. The Olds picked up speed as the volume on the radio increased. By the time they crossed Lexington Dam, the Olds was moving in and out of the curves of the two lanes of southbound traffic to get another car length ahead. The wheels were screech'n on the sharp turns. It was only a matter of time before the giant Olds crossed the double yellow lines. And the cars heading north were tearing downhill in their own race home.

Sure enough, the Olds clipped an oncoming red Ford Falcon as the two vehicles entered the extreme of a curb. But the Ray Ban man accelerated after separation, a serious bash in the Olds' left front fender. No telling whether or not the Falcon recovered. By this time, the backseat teens were crying to get out. Lyle and Maloney were sliding around on the deck, trying to wedge themselves by stretching out between the sides of the car that was just a bit too wide for a solid body hold. Between slides on the deck, Maloney tried to hide his eyes in his towel. The driver revved the engine whenever he could and the Olds sped up the hill, through the hairpin turns, and between slower cars. His female passenger held on tightly and said nothing.

"Stop. Stop. Oh, please stop and let us out," cried one of the teens in front of Lyle and Maloney.

"I can't stop now, man. I'll get arrested. There's no place to pull over anyhow. We've got to get out of here."

At that moment, Ray Ban, again in the center lane and passing another car on his right, over-corrected as he turned right out of another turn, and narrowly missed another oncoming car but sideswiped the car to his right, metal raking metal, against Maloney's backside. Again Ray Ban accelerated away, out of the turn.

"We're all gonna die!" moaned one of the teens between her sobs.

"Man, this guy's high on something," Lyle said to a spaced-out Maloney and the teary-eyed teens.

"Hey, hey! Hey, hey!" Lyle yelled until he finally got the attention of the wiry-haired passenger. By this time they were near the summit and then it would be all downhill—and even faster. "Tell your friend I know a backroad he can take. He can get away," Lyle yelled.

"Did you hear that, babe? The guy says there's a back way."

"I don't know anything about no back road," Ray Ban said, still swerving between lanes and cars. They zoomed right by the plywood CHP car at the summit. Where were the real cops?

"Hey, tell him to look for the Denny's at the bottom of the hill," Lyle yelled. It was a last chance. Hunting for Denny's seemed to give Ray Ban a different focus, and he throttled back a little as they headed down into the valley.

At Scotts Valley, Ray Ban turned off as everyone directed. "There it is. There's Denny's!" In the Denny's lot the four weary hitchhikers jumped out of the Olds and slammed the doors shut. Lyle walked up to the open window of the driver-from-hell, looked directly at the dark green lenses, and gave the bearded lunatic wrong directions to Boulder Creek. As the Olds peeled away, Lyle ran into Denny's to tell someone to call the cops.

Lyle and Maloney just sat on the curb outside Denny's for a while, gathering their emotions. The teen girls were long gone. Two minutes later, two CHP cars raced up Glenwood Drive in hot pursuit of Ray Ban and his girlfriend. Lyle and Maloney did the unthinkable and took a cab back to Santa Clara. They were at Cabrillo and Machado by noon and walked their separate ways home. Neither one had remembered to grab his beach towel from the Olds. Lyle was so wound up when he got home, he had to tell someone and invited me into his room to hear the story of his resurrection.

The news this week was full of stories about the Nazi "big fish" being caught in Argentina. Pauly showed me how to hook a big fish over the weekend. Pauly's Uncle Cecil had just finished a construction job with Pauly's dad near De La Cruz, next to the Corning Fiberglass Plant. His Uncle Cecil used to live in Gustine, a small farming town, not far from Merced, in the San Joaquin Valley, and had promised to take Pauly and Johnny to Gustine to go striper fishing in the Delta Mendota canal this week. I was invited.

My parents weren't really keen on the idea of my going all the way out to Gustine, especially since it meant a drive over Pacheco Pass. I had heard tons of stories from my dad, the trucker, about horrible big-rig accidents he had witnessed or heard about on that windy, winding two-lane mountain pass, and he'd say it didn't matter what time of year it was that road was deadly. There was talk of a new wider highway being constructed in a few years and even a dam in the valley to meet the demands of progress.

Pauly's uncle came to our house Friday evening to talk to my dad about my going along, and the two of them spent a good hour discussing all the construction going on around the area and all the people they knew in common. The fact that Mr. Owens knew my dad's best friend Elmer clinched the deal. We would be back late Saturday night.

I was thinking the most difficult part of the trip was going to be getting up at five in the morning for the nearly four-hour drive, but Pauly, Johnny, and I slept most of the way in Mr. Owens's '55 Dodge station wagon. I knew from vacations to LA that Monterey Highway seemed to go on forever before you would get out of the valley—orchard after orchard, field after field, and a local fruit stand about every two hundred yards. Of course, coming back, it would seem even longer. We stopped at an old bait shop along the highway, just before we reached Gilroy, and Mr. Owens bought a big plastic bag of frozen anchovies and smaller bag of oysters and put them in the green metal Coleman ice chest. We took a break at Casa de Fruta, one of the last stands before Pacheco Pass, and ate tuna sandwiches Pauly's mom had packed for us. We sat at the picnic tables that were set up off the roadway among the fruit trees and watched the traffic zoom by as we ate.

Back on the road, the Dodge climbed unevenly against winds to the top of the gusty and winding pass and we looked down at the huge expanse of gilded rolling hills and dry valley below where the San Luis Creek ran. There was a horse ranch at the very bottom.

By the time we reached the Delta Mendota in the valley floor near the town of Gustine it was almost ten. I had only seen the canal as a blur along the highway before now. The concrete canal cut sharply through the yellow grasslands around it. We headed a quarter mile down the graveled service road along the canal's berm and parked where the canal made a slight bend.

"PELIGRO. DANGER. PELIGRO. DANGER," read the signs stenciled red on the top edges of the concrete walls. Apparently, a lot of people drown trying to swim in the twenty-four foot wide river of water or fall into the deceivingly calm but swift-moving current of the canal. Not all of those who attempt swimming speak English.

Pauly and Johnny got right to work and had their poles in the water within minutes while I merely watched. Mr. Owens unfolded his patio chair and opened a beer. Then it was my turn to fish. Pauly showed me how to bait my hook by threading the sliced off chunk of half-frozen anchovy on one of the two hooks. I readied the second hook. The anchovies were salty and sticky, but I liked using them over worms I had to deal with on my trip with Uncle Mike and Aunt Noan years ago.

Within ten minutes, Johnny had hooked a striper. I instantly understood the challenge. The fish would swim with the current and make catching it a duel. Johnny's rod arched like a rainbow and line kept ratcheting out. He'd crank in and an occasional glimpse of silver reflected in the water just below the surface. But the fish would pull down, the line would buzz, and the striper would be out of sight again. This went on for several long minutes before his cranks would outnumber the fish's pulls. Eventually, the sleek silver scaled striper surfaced, and Pauly stepped down the concrete side to net the fish. I could see how easy it would be to fall into the canal.

Just as we were about to measure and further admire Johnny's fish, my line hit. I was pulled toward the water a step before I regained my balance. I had learned the routine from Johnny, but it wasn't as easy as he made it out to be. By the time I got my fish in, I was physically drained, though too excited to think about it. Pauly netted my first striper. After he assured me the fish would not bite, I grabbed the gyrating creature from the net once it was above land to remove the hook, not realizing at the top of its rough, scaly surface were two razor-sharp dorsal fins along its back. They cut my palm like pickle fork's tines, ripping across my flesh, and I dropped my first fish to the ground. Instinctively, it flipped back into the water, quickly breaking loose from the hook, and that was the one that got away.

We each caught three fish within the couple of hours we were there. Johnny caught a twenty-four-incher. The other stripers were sixteen or better. I learned to grab my fish with a rag. I replaced the duct-tape on my bandaged palm several times that day. Mr. Owens never did fish, but he seemed to enjoy watching us and drinking his

Falstaffs. Before we left, we each cleaned our stripers, not too bad of a job, but scraping the translucent scales off their backs made quite a mess in the dirt.

"Okay, are you boys ready to do some real fishing now?" Mr. Owens asked, as he was folding up his chair and getting ready to leave.

"I thought that's what we were doing," I remarked, happy with my day's return.

"It's time to catfish the farm canals. We've got to get at least a few to take home," said Pauly as he and Johnny were already loading up the gear into the back of the wagon. "That's why we bought the oysters," he said. I had completely forgotten about them.

Mr. Owens knew where he was going. We turned off the highway, down a long dirt road until we reached a long metal gate on some farmer's property. We stopped and Johnny jumped out and opened the steel gate. We drove through and Johnny shut us in, hopped back into the station wagon, and we made our way down another dirt road along a field of greens. At the junction of three fields was a six-foot wide canal flowing murky water onward used to irrigate the fields.

This time we baited our hooks with oysters. The spit-laced blobs, long ago thawed, slid through my fingers as I wove the flesh into a pair of hooks. Even after rinsing my hands with water from the jug, my hands smelled of salt and metal. We fished a solid hour without a bite, and then it happened (and thankfully not to me). Pauly jerked at a bite and got the pull of his life. You would have thought a full-grown man was at the hook end. I was sure Pauly's Shakespeare reel was going to snap in two. He struggled at least fifteen minutes with that catfish but eventually got the best of it. It was close to three feet long and with its huge head, expansive mouth, and tentacle whiskers, way too ugly and nasty for me. I was told that the fins of a striper were nothing compared to the deadly spikes of a catfish. Even

Johnny knew better than to grab at this fish barehanded. Out the corner of my eye, I saw Mr. Owens heading for the car.

Once Pauly and Johnny landed the fish, it was obviously unfazed being out of water and even more lively on shore, thrashing wildly. What I saw next made me want to turn away in disgust but I watched.

Pauly's uncle threw down a three-foot long two-by-six board at Pauly's feet near the fish.

"Put the fish on the board so I have a solid surface," instructed Uncle Cecil. Pauly did as told, and cocking his arm above his head, for a forceful wallop, Mr. Owens began striking the catfish on the flat of its head with a hammer. After a couple of blows, the catfish slowed down its thrashing. Its spread eyes seemed to glaze over, but it wasn't over. Mr. Owens pulled a massive nail from his shirt pocket and proceeded to pound the nail a good three inches into the center of the catfish's head to secure it to the board. Blood shot about as he completed the catfish crucifixion.

"You've got to do this, or they'll just suffer," he explained as he took one last blow. The whiskered barbels rattled to a halt. "I'd say this sucker weighs over twenty pounds. Way to go, Pauly. That will be enough to feed the whole tribe. Now we've got to skin it. It's much easier to do when they're just killed."

From his rear pocket, he pulled out a large pair of needle-nose pliers and a pocketknife. Now standing on his knees and straddling the fish and board, he made a surgical cut behind the gills of the fish, all the way around, carefully separating the skin from the meat. Then he put the pliers to work. The fish moved even as Uncle Cecil began peeling at the grey-brown skin, prying it off the fleshy pink meat that remained, pulling it toward the back of the board. I had seen enough.

That one catfish seemed to satisfy everyone's fishing appetite for the day, and it was a story to be told many times. I was glad our fishing day was done. On the way home Pauly, Johnny, and

Uncle Cecil talked on and on about the triumphs of the day and the upcoming fish fry. Pauly wanted to take me trout fishing next. I feigned sleep in the corner of the backseat to end the discussion. At least Mr. Owens hadn't insisted that we eat the catfish right there and then.

CHAPTER 12

S ummer 1960

The Summer Olympics would play on television for the first time ever this August. My father made sure we would be back in time from Big Basin State Park this year to see the games. As we would typically do, the family would meet up with Aunt Betty's family and stake out a campsite for the week. My uncle Cliff and my dad would take us there on a Sunday, set up camp with a huge Coleman tent, and then leave my mother and aunt and the four kids there for the week while they worked. They would return Friday night. We wore Big Basin ragged, running along the trails, hiking up and down the creeks, climbing every fallen redwood trunk within reach, visiting the nature lodge and the stuffed wildlife museum dozens of times, and buying ice cream sandwiches and sticky candy at the camp store. For a nickel, you could buy a bag of oats and feed the deer that milled about in the long flattened grass area in front of the store. Lyle and my cousin Steve would often ditch me so I would play with my younger cousin René. She was a good sport about it. But by the end of the week, she pretty much was sick of the boys and spent most her time with the moms.

When I was eight, I tagged along with Lyle and Steve on a trail to the site of Maddock's cabin. John Maddock was some historic settler of the area. At least that's what the trail sign said. It was a three-mile hike. Before too long, Lyle and Steve had decided to give me the slip. I never saw them backtrack so I figured they must have continued to the cabin destination.

I hiked and hiked. I yelled for them but got no response. Maybe they were waiting for me at the cabin. Finally, I reached a large brown park sign that read, "Maddock Cabin Site," followed by a bunch of historical information about the cabin. I figured the cabin itself must be just around the bend. I kept hiking. I hiked another twenty minutes, at least. The trail kept getting smaller and the terrain was steep. Somebody had played a trick on me. I was nearly convinced there was no cabin. As I climbed the next ridge, I came to a chilling stop. At my feet was a coiled rattlesnake, rattling away, glaring at me, preparing to strike. I turned on a dime and ran and ran and ran. I ran the full three miles plus of the trail. Then I ran another half mile to our camp. There were Lyle and Steve, sitting at the picnic table, with big grins on their faces, slopping up chunks of watermelon from paper plates. I was exhausted. I collapsed on the bench, and then threw up, inches from the watermelon eaters whose melon had suddenly lost its flavor.

My mom told me I could bring Pauly along camping this summer. Lyle was not going with us this year and Steve would probably stay home, too. Camping at Big Basin would not be the same without them. For all Pauly's fishing adventures, he had never really camped, unless you count sleeping in a car near a riverbank. We had made it through school, and in two months we would be off to Big Basin. We needed practice.

With my mother's permission, we created a tent out of three old army blankets and a couple of white flannel sheets strung across our backyard clothesline. We attached everything together using wooden clothespins. It was a fine tent, and almost as comfy as the underground fort Pauly and I had built last spring on the far side of Pauly's house, on the path alongside Lawrence Station Road. Of course, there was no way my mom or Pauly's would have let us spend the night in any underground fort. Besides, it was a secret fort, anyway. We had managed to dig a sizable four-foot deep hole between a couple of walnut trees, only twenty feet from the zooming cars along Lawrence Station. The Corn Palace was visible on the other side of the road. We retrieved a couple of faded, discarded plywood painted billboard signs from the side of Pauly's garage that had once also been used as the rooftops of the wire pigeon cages, and we made a roof for our fort, which was wide enough and long enough for us to stretch out in. We propped it with 2x4s, especially since we covered the fort with dirt to keep it hidden from view. A couple of old burgundy Persian rugs with exotic gold-thread prints served as our floor. We kept votive candles in empty tuna cans for light and rigged a section of broken metal irrigation pipe in the corner for ventilation. The vent seemed to let in more dust and dirt than good air. We even brought down some comic books and magazines, but we never spent much actual time in the fort. We would occasionally disappear from sight when other kids were on the path, hoping they would wonder where we suddenly went. Once we tried smoking a couple of Chesterfields Pauly took from his dad's bedroom, but we didn't see the point in it once we started hacking the trapped smoke. Another time we shared a can of Hamm's beer we stole from the refrigerator. We were almost caught when Pauly had to sneak back to the kitchen to find the "church key" so we could open the can. I once suggested we could bring a couple of girls down there but then thought about how that might spoil the good thing we had already. It was just building the fort and knowing only we knew about it that made it fun.

For our camping out in the backyard I retrieved two of our family sleeping bags from the garage rafters. They were Coleman bags my dad bought at Sears right after our new house camping adventure when we arrived in Santa Clara before our beds. Flannel-lined with a duck hunting scene pattern and stuffed with cotton, they were bulky, and, surprisingly, not that warm. Nevertheless, they would work for our night in the backyard. We each had a flashlight and candy provisions so we were set. Lyle came out to investigate our getup and told us about a news report of a madman on the loose from Agnews State Hospital, only about eight miles away, north off Lawrence Station Road. Very funny. Just about the time we were falling asleep—my dad had checked on us at least twice—we heard a rustling along the back fence where the pyracanthas grew. We figured it had to be a cat, or at least we hoped it was. The pyracantha branches were prickly and dangerous for a person stupid enough to get near them. Although the blackbirds loved the red berries, they wouldn't be in them at night. Then we saw the flickering light.

Through the flannel sheet that served as our tent siding, we could make out what appeared to be a candle, and then as the light got stronger and closer, we could make out the figure of a man carrying what looked like a rifle in his arm and heading our direction. The light behind him silhouetted his body as he moved back and forth at the side of the tent.

Pauly and I were frozen in our sleeping bags. Suddenly it came to me, and I thought of the story Lyle had told us earlier of the escaped madman. It had to be Lyle. With my flashlight in my hand, I hit the switch and charged out of the front of the tent, roaring at the unknown. There stood Lyle, a broom in his arm, and his friend Maloney holding a candle behind him. They ran into the dark.

"You kids keep it down. People are trying to get some sleep around here," my dad yelled from the bathroom window he had cranked open in the dark of the house. He was unaware of the prank.

"Tell Lyle to get out of here," I yelled. By then, Lyle and Maloney had disappeared, running to the far side of the backyard and over the side fence to the gravel path. I could hear Maloney whispering in pain to Lyle something about his arm being burnt as they scurried away trying to get traction in the loose gravel.

When Pauly and I awoke in the morning, the sun heating us out of the tent, we heard my dad and our neighbor George Schlegel talking in the front yard.

"It happened sometime past eight last night. The hubcaps were on the Ranchero when I went out front for a smoke. Did you hear a ruckus in the *nacht* about eleven?" George asked my dad.

"Yeah, but it was just Benny and the Owens kid Pauly sleeping outside."

"That explains it. I don't trust those Owens boys. Those kids are dirty and poor. They are always scrounging for pop bottles and the like. You know they are Oakies. Don't you? I'm going to call the authorities. We'll find *mein* hubcaps fast," George said with surety. Pauly just stood there listening with me, his head studying the ground.

"Now wait a minute, George. I don't think those kids had anything to do with your missing hubcaps. Those are some of the nicest kids around here. Just because they are poor, doesn't mean they are dishonest. Don't jump to conclusions," my dad said. I suddenly felt a new respect for my dad. I knew Lyle would never steal from George, but I wasn't quite so sure about his friend Maloney.

By this time next year, there would be a new first family in the White House, either the Nixons or the Kennedys. The big white house of our block belonged to the Ruffino family. Before they owned their house a year, they had put a two-bedroom second story on it. It is the only two-story on the block. Mrs. Ruffino's family was from Armenia; at least that is what my mother told me when I asked her about the funny-sounding language she was always speaking to someone on the phone. Though I never addressed her myself by her first name, all the neighbors called her Neneh. Talking on the phone was one of three activities that I ever saw or heard her do.

Her primary activity was housecleaning. Her curly black hair mostly hidden behind a factory girl scarf, a flowered apron around her torso, tight-fitting dark slacks, and black flat shoes made up her standard wardrobe around home.

The Ruffinos had the cleanest house on the block and a sharp contrast to the Jacksons' house to their left. Mrs. Ruffino made it clear to her kids they were not to play with the Jackson kids. The one and only time I went inside the Ruffino house was because

Teddy wanted to show off his new Flying Tiger model plane in his bedroom. That plan was cut short as soon as both of us walked through the garage back door into the family room, even though we had both removed our shoes.

"What do you think you're doing, young man? Neneh asked Teddy as she turned toward us and momentarily from the black and white image on the TV screen. Seeing her profile silhouetted as she exercised, I suddenly realized Mrs. Ruffino had a big nose.

She was in the middle of her second favorite activity, working out with Jack LaLanne. It seemed like any morning I was near the Ruffino house, at some point I could hear the television fitness guru, counting off a face or thigh exercise or providing some healthy wisdom to the "friends at home." This time I saw Neneh in action. She didn't miss a beat as she sat on her white vinyl kitchen chair, which she had positioned squarely in front of the TV, air bicycling with Jack LaLanne, pedaling her legs at the ceiling, in her fashionably black pedal-pushers and pink exercise sweatshirt.

"I just want to show Benny my new model. We won't mess up anything."

"Benny can wait in the kitchen while you bring it out," she ordered. I could see her thinking. In the kitchen I would be standing on linoleum, not carpet, while I waited.

Almost every other time I saw Neneh she had broom and dustpan in hand, in the garage or heading into the garage from the family room door. When Teddy and his brother and I would play out front, Neneh was mostly in the house but always within earshot. We would hear her, on the phone. She would go on and on in Armenian with every Armenian she knew, unless she was talking to Mr. Ruffino.

"Paolo, I miss you, darling. How is work today, sweetie? The kids have made such a mess of the house. How's your turkey sandwich, dear? Did I put too much mayonnaise on it, babe? Are you going to be home by four, love?"

It was enough to make any boy sick. Though I do not think she knew any of the neighborhood boys by name, she seemed glad to have Teddy and Donny play at home where she could keep an eye on them. It was too late to control Paul.

Mr. Ruffino was a short chubby guy who was very important. To hear him tell it, he ran the Ford plant. I don't know if he attached bumpers to cars on the assembly line or directed everyone else on the line, but he was a Ford man through and through. Every year, when the new models were first out, he would drive up in a new Ford Fairlane, with all the latest features. After 1959 it was always a Galaxie 500/XL. In the daytime, the new car would sit in the driveway instead of the garage, for weeks, for all the neighbors to see. We kids figured Ford gave him a new car every year, but our parents straightened us out about that. Mr. Ruffino loved to have the newest, biggest and best.

One Saturday afternoon, while a bunch of us were playing whiffle ball in the street, or trying to—Cabrillo kept getting busier and busier—we heard a police siren come from the direction of the Ruffino' garage. It was loud! It was kind of scary. The siren barely rose in its howl before it cut off short. Then, when everyone resumed play, it whined again. This happened three or four times before we all decided it was time to investigate.

Four of us were standing outside the Ruffinos' closed garage door. Their new green Starliner Galaxie 500 was parked in the driveway so we knew they were home. Someone yelled out for Paul, but no answer. Just as we were about to give it up, the siren went off again. Its shrilling shattered our ears and came from just the other side of the garage door. Muffled laughs on the other side became clear as Paul slowly lifted the door from the inside so we could see the action. On Mr. Ruffino's workbench sat the real thing, a red cop's siren, the domed red light attached to wires and a car battery.

"Wow, that's neat," the four us exclaimed, practically in unison.

Just as we were about to take a closer look and get the details, Mr. Ruffino's attention turned from us to the street. A Santa Clara police black and white was slowing up at the curb.

Mr. Ruffino deftly picked up the siren from the workbench, turned his back to the street, slipped off his sandals at the back door, and quickly went into the house in his white sock feet. Paul, Teddy, and Donny hushed us and told us not to say anything if asked. But we didn't have to. The police officer promptly got out of his car, headed toward us, nodded, and then turned to go to the front door. Apparently, he had seen Mr. Ruffino's quick exit.

The boys went into the house through the garage back door; the neighborhood kids, myself included, headed down the street. We learned later that Mr. Ruffino relinquished the siren to the officer and was ticketed.

Another Saturday afternoon Mr. Ruffino came home with a nine-inch red Cox prop rod gas motored tether race car. It had a propeller on its rear end. These hobby cars were usually raced out in hobby lots and controlled by a steel wire attached to a pole. The "driver" would prime the gas engine, spin the propeller until ignition and then let the car swing, racing around a fixed pole.

Mr. Ruffino had a better idea. He went out to the middle of the street in front of his garage and drilled a hole in the asphalt where he placed a large hex bolt. He attached the car wire to the bolt, started the engine, and let it rip. The loud, high-pitched engine sounding like a mutant mosquito propelled the little car around again and again and again until it ran out of gas, which was the usual way of stopping these tethered cars. Repeat performances went on for an hour. Any oncoming real car was flagged to stop and witness the event. Somebody, either an angry delayed motorist or a safety-conscious neighbor, reported Mr. Ruffino. Again the police cited him. The hex bolt was removed

.

Never to be outdone by another neighbor, Mr. Ruffino always bought the so-called "Neighborhood Hero" 4th of July fireworks package, the largest and most expensive available, full of bottle rockets, flairs, fountains, Roman candles, side-winders, ash cans, and sparklers, but he had bigger fireworks than that, which we never saw until they lit up or exploded the skies. They surely didn't come from the Lawrence Station fireworks stands. His source must have been the same guy who got him the siren. He would also put on a sound show for everyone before, during, and after the Fourth, with M-80s, cherry bombs, and firecrackers. One of his favorite stunts was to light multiple packages of firecrackers that he hung with wooden clothespins to the backyard wire clothesline. A ten-foot string would go off for minutes and smoke up the entire yard. I can't remember the number of times the cops were at their door because of firecracker and cherry bomb explosions in the Ruffino vicinity. There were no cats around their house. Come 4th of July night, his firework show would rival the Washington Park city display, yet it was a single hot sparkler I accidentally threw into our "empty lot" across the street that created the biggest inferno on our block.

When Paul entered junior high, he officially took up his father's magnetism for trouble with the police.

Paul seemed to tolerate me after he had been at Jefferson a year. Maybe that's because I wasn't a threat to him, and his brothers Teddy and Donny seemed to like me. Paul's "big man" days didn't go over too well at Jefferson. It started in sixth grade when he showed up in P.E. with his "modified" P.E. uniform. That didn't sit well with Coach Jones. Coach Jones had had stomach surgery that summer and was still recovering. He couldn't eat solid foods so he ate what he could, constantly. That was usually a small plastic bowl of some yellow phlegm resembling pudding or applesauce. He had a reputation of being a butt to begin with; now he was a butt with a spoon always in his mouth.

On the second week of school, all boys in his sixth grade P.E. class were to have their uniforms by then, which they could buy at the student store. They consisted of a white Jefferson Physical Ed labeled t-shirt and a pair of cobalt blue shorts that had a Jefferson Jaguar logo on one corner. Tennis shoes and white socks were the student's choice. When the bell rang, all fifty sixth-graders in Coach Jones' first period class were lined up ready for calisthenics on their assigned numbers, which were stenciled in yellow on the asphalt in front of the locker room. Coach Jones selected two students to lead the group, beginning with repetitions of jumping jacks, while he ate his applesauce and ran through a roll card an office runner would soon pick up. When he got to Paul's name, he stopped the action.

"Ruffino, what the hell is this?" he asked Paul, pointing to his gym shorts. Paul had pegged his shorts like many people pegged their jeans. They fit skin-tight to his thighs. Not waiting for a response, Coach Jones handed off his applesauce and roll card to a bewildered kid near him, took his pencil from his ear, grabbed Paul's shorts with them still on, first the left and then the right sewn seam, and ripped each pegged seam apart with the pencil's point. The pencil broke along the way but that didn't slow him down. The threads, torn and shredded, hung on the shorts. The broken off half of pencil lay on the ground. Paul stood there mortified. After a pregnant pause, kids started laughing. Coach Jones had made his point, *almost*.

"For that crap, Ruffino, be at detention after school for the next three days. Anybody thinks that's funny will serve detention with him." It got quiet quickly.

For the most part, Paul learned to stay clear of Coach Jones from that point on, except one grey morning in November. As the calisthenics were about to take place and just before the bell rang to start, kids were horsing around as they usually did, which often meant finding loose gravel bits on the weathered asphalt to pick up and flick at another kid's bare legs. The tiny gravel rocks would sting, but usually that meant no harm done. As Coach Jones turned the corner, someone threw a gravel pebble and, deliberately or not, hit him high on his bald forehead. Not only did it hurt, it bled. Coach Jones was furious. He pulled a white handkerchief from his black trouser pocket, dampened it with the tip of his tongue and held it to his wounded head. He demanded to know who threw the stone. No one responded, but they all knew who did it.

Calculating the stone's trajectory, Coach Jones announced that the twenty students to his far right were all guilty, and he stretched his free arm out to make a line in the air to indicate which kids he meant like he often did to designate teams. Somehow Paul had avoided even being identified. After class was over but before showers, the befuddled students all obediently lined up at the coaches' office for two swats with the big wooden waffle paddle. Kids dressing at their lockers below the coach's office could see the action above through the large plate glass window as the accused bent over and grabbed their ankles for their respective swats. Nobody squealed on Paul.

Paul Ruffino was becoming legendary. In seventh grade, the police showed up on campus. It seems a lowly sixth-grader, who was unfortunate enough to be assigned a locker near Paul's in the hallway, left a family volume of the Encyclopedia Britannica atop his locker. Apparently, the kid was not supposed to have brought the book to school in the first place. After realizing he had left it at his locker only moments ago, he returned to find it gone. The next day he retrieved a note someone had slipped into his locker vent. It read:

If you want your encyclopedia back,
be at 3443 Cabrillo Ave.

at 3:30 tomorrow, and bring $10.

The poor kid was caught between a rock and a hard spot. With the volume missing, the family encyclopedia set was ruined. He faced his dad and got a ten-dollar bill for the next day. The transaction took place in Paul's garage, and the book was given back. As usual, Paul threatened the victim if he said anything to anyone: "You know what happens to squealers?" But it was too late. The next day Paul was removed from school by a Santa Clara police officer and charged with extortion. It seems the kid's father had kept the note and notified the school. Paul was suspended from Jefferson.

One evening last August Paul's neighbors saw him taking BB shots at their front window from his own upstairs bathroom window, which was slightly opened. He denied doing it when they marched across the street to confront him and his parents, and when the Santa Clara police arrived, his mom and dad supported Paul's denial, until they found the rifle on the toilet tank upstairs.

Just last month, the fire department and an ambulance showed up at the Ruffinos. Apparently, Paul had syphoned gasoline from the lawn mower in the garage and filled a mason jar to concoct some kind of Molotov cocktail. It exploded in the garage and severely burnt one of his hands. I haven't heard about his high school adventures yet.

I spent a lot of summer days at Bennett School in the parks and rec program after fourth grade. Although we didn't have a building for organized recreation like they did at Machado or Merry Gomez parks, Bennett school was close by, and the city emptied one wing of three classrooms for park activities on one side of the school. In one room we learned arts and crafts and wove bolo ties from thin bright colored plastic strips or made potholders from yarn crisscrossed back and forth on crudely made weaving looms of wooden blocks and nails. In another room we played table games like carrom board pool or checkers, or Ping-Pong on the one well-worn, slightly warped plywood green table provided. It sat on two wide sawhorses the school carpenter built. The third room was used to store sports equipment and whatever else needed a place to hide. Kids spent most of the time outside sitting at the picnic tables on tasks or playing foursquare, tetherball or basketball on the asphalt. Sometimes the teen leaders would organize flag football or softball teams and we'd use the school field. Of course, everything done by parks and rec was co-ed.

I was content going to play that summer at Bennett school now that I had finished fourth grade there and had a bunch of new friends from the west side of Lawrence Station Road. Living in Santa Clara for two years, I hadn't met any of the kids on that side of the road until the school boundaries changed. This summer, Jefferson district was hosting a big July holiday carnival at Jefferson School. Jefferson was about the oldest school in Santa Clara that was not part of the original downtown area. I don't know when they tore the old classroom buildings down and built new outdoor wings, but only the auditorium and bell tower of the Spanish-style stucco white and red tiled structure remained, and they were marked condemned and closed for renovation at the time of the carnival.

Each Park and Rec group in the area had a specific quota of tickets to sell, baked goods to collect, and an event to man. Our group of kids was about twenty in number. Selling tickets meant hitting up your parents and relatives, going door-to-door in the neighborhoods, and digging up a couple of your own quarters. Admission tickets were good for entrance, five game tickets, and on-going raffles of baked goods or sometimes a store-provided gift like two passes to the Skate Palace down the street. It was not unheard of for a kid to win a fruit pie or chocolate cake at a carnival that his mother had baked the day before the carnival. The truth is that most adults who bought a ticket had no intention of going to the carnival. Some would give you a quarter and not even take a ticket in exchange. Ninety percent of the participants were kids. The adults that did show were usually there to watch their toddlers or help run an event. The teen parks leaders ran the show, but, mostly, it was a mass of kids having fun.

In our group, everybody was asked to sell ten tickets. That was easy enough for Pauly and me. We figured out quickly that the big new apartment complex across the street from the front of the school would be the perfect target. The backside of these two-story apartments now lined Lawrence, buried sight of Bennett school, and all but blocked our kitchen view of El Camino. Only the black walnut trees lining the road remained. Views of fields and orchard from our kitchen window were nearly gone in less than the three years I had lived in Santa Clara. Except for the Kiely prune orchard, directly to our right, you wouldn't know the place. That Saturday, Pauly and I sold thirty-three tickets altogether. Most of the occupants were adults with no kids of their own and were readily willing to give us a quarter or two.

A second task everyone had was to bring a baked cake or pie or a dozen cookies or cupcakes to Bennett before Friday afternoon on the day before the carnival. The idea was that you would help your mother bake the goodies, but I don't know of any boy who did. I guess some of the girls did. Thursday night my mother went the extra mile and baked two dozen oatmeal raisin cookies, one dozen with walnuts we had harvested ourselves and one dozen with just raisins. I took them, arranged in a cardboard lid, covered with wax paper, to Bennett the next day. Pauly's mom baked a cherry pie made from bings she had picked from the orchard along Reed Road.

To show our team spirit, we decided to all go to the carnival in team t-shirts. Each kid had someone's mom Ritz dye a t-shirt dark brown. My mom dyed t-shirts in her canning tub for me and five of my friends. The shirts hung out on the backyard clothes line for the day. At the school the next day we ironed on yellow felt lettering to the backs that spelled out BENNETT. Our group was in charge of the fishing booth.

The fishing booth was a game of chance, a chance where everybody won something. A long wire about five feet high was stretched across two corner walls of a classroom. Bed sheets were attached to the wire to make a closed curtain area. The curtain was supposedly the ocean so we decorated it with colored paper cutouts of fish and waves and seahorses and whatever else we thought belonged in the ocean, which we had made and outlined with crayons the week before in our arts and crafts classes. Kids from our group sat at two long tables directly in front of the curtain. When a kid exchanged a ticket, he or she was given an eight-foot bamboo pole with a short kite string attached to its end. In place of a hook was a wooden clothespin. The fisher would flip the fishing pole line over the curtain at the open area between the two tables. Once the line went over, another kid from our group would attach a prize to the clothespin from behind the curtain and then tug on the line for the angler to slowly pull in the catch. Most of the prizes were Woolworth's toys like plastic jewelry, rubber amphibians, or sets of jacks or small bags of catseyes. I worked behind the curtain for an hour. It was fun hearing the littlest kids giggle with delight when they got their prize.

Pauly and I spent all our money on games and candy after that. It was a hot afternoon, but we talked the Bowers Park people into letting us take a couple of turns sitting in their dunk tank where kids we knew paid to cool us off. At the end of the day, we walked Lawrence to our houses. Our bodies were streaked with brown where the t-shirt dye came off on our bodies from our being dunked. I managed to bring home a somewhat droopy Boston cream pie I won at the cakewalk.

• • • •

WHEN I WAS SIX, LIKE most kids, I would take on the trappings of Superman or Davy Crockett or the Lone Ranger (who I thought was the long ranger until I got a few years older). I broke my leg when my neighbor Joyce got her older sister Charlotte to give us turns riding double on the back of her sister's bike. Unfortunately, Charlotte crashed into a curb during my turn, and my leg got mangled in the spokes. Despite the fact my leg was a bloody mess when the accident happened, I was told by Dr. Fishler it was a clean break, and I was to wear a cast for several weeks. We still have a family photo of me sitting on the front porch, proudly displaying my cast, wearing a bath towel cape, a straw cowboy hat and holstered pearl-handle guns. I would initially tell my school friends that I broke my leg jumping off the roof of a house being newly constructed down the street. It was a much more daring and noble way to break a leg than crashing on a bike someone else—a girl—was steering. My friends believed me since a few of us had indeed jumped off that roof into a six-foot pile of sand below it that sat at the site for several weeks. Of course, the truth got out before long (there were witnesses), but years later after we had moved to Santa Clara I began to tell my broken leg story from memory as if I really did break it jumping from a rooftop in an effort to take flight. Later, I would project the abilities of athletes like Mickey Mantle and Whitey Ford and singers like Ricky Nelson and Elvis Presley to myself, but reality always brought me back to earth. Earth was calling Ron Maloney, but he never got the call. I'm not sure who he really is. Maybe that's why Ron Maloney turned out to be such an Eddie Haskell.

"Good morning, Mrs. C. What a delightful dress you're wearing. Is Benjamin home?" Maloney was a phony. He spent most of his time trying to impress people and being cool. He was always telling Lyle how he was gonna "make the scene," whatever that meant. Whenever I saw him in Lyle's room he was usually primping in the mirror, pampering his sandy flattop with the palms of his hands or preening his teeth and gums with a tongue massage. But his thick black horn-rimmed glasses gave him a Buddy Holly kind of goofiness. He was tall and skinny and anything but cool.

Outside Lyle's bedroom door, I overheard him last fall tell Lyle that he was sure he would be cut from the football team by the time the season started. His confession of doubt was rare to my ears. He wanted so much to be on the football team, and he was one of Lyle's few friends who lived nearby (they met on the daily bus rides they took together across town to school) so I guess Lyle took pity on him, and came up with a plan. Lyle taught Maloney how to long hike, a football skill Lyle excelled at, among many others. The two of them would spend hours in the backyard hiking for imaginary punts. Maloney made the thirties team his junior year, hiking for punts, even lettered. It was the only playing time he got, but it was enough. He joined the Letterman's Club and wore his black letterman sweater whenever possible after that, strutting around like he was the star quarterback. I guess he had finally made the scene.

For some reason I was his favorite target for ridicule, true to Eddie Haskell form. He'd see me and all civility was gone.

"Hey, runt. What's the little momma's boy doing in big Lyle's room?"

I would occasionally banter with him, but most of the time I took Lyle's advice and simply ignored Maloney. He had long ago earned my disrespect.

One afternoon in late August just after the Big Basin trip, Art and I were sitting on the front lawn, watching cars go by on Lawrence Station Road. A strange sight emerged from Briarwood Drive, heading up Cabrillo on the sidewalk toward us. Three guys lugging some kind of huge cage were approaching. As they neared and the cage wobbled in their grasp, I recognized Lyle, Maloney, and Gaylord Talbert. Gaylord lived at the far end of Briarwood and Warburton, one house before the block's end and behind Lawrence Square. He was another buddy of Lyle's, but he was never around when my father was at home. One day Lyle told me why.

"Well, if it isn't Happy Jesus!" my father said to Gaylord one Saturday afternoon when Gaylord and Lyle cut through the garage. My dad was surgically repairing another pen machine he had to bring home. It most probably had been jammed with a metal slug by someone trying to con a free 25-cent ball-point pen. The greeting my dad gave Gaylord that day fell flat, and Gaylord never spoke to my father again. My dad often joked with our friends, but they didn't always appreciate it. Gaylord was very sensitive about his name, and my dad had hit a nerve.

As the three of them got closer to our house with the gigantic cage, they stopped at least three times to regroup on the sidewalk before getting the cage to the middle of our driveway. It was apparent this was no ordinary cage. It had some local history to it, as well. I recognized it as Eddie the mynah bird's cage from Mr. Johnson's garage. Mr. Johnson was part owner of Me-n-Ed's pizza parlor on El Camino, across from the PW Shopping Center. His bird Eddie was a celebrity, both at the pizza parlor, where he would sit on a perch near the counter and entertain for hours with rambling phrases he had learned to speak—-talking to customers or no one in particular, and on local radio and TV ads, where he'd sing a catchy little tune:

"We always go to Me-n-Ed's for pizza, for pizza."

Lyle is always telling someone about the grand opening at Me-n-Ed's when he and his buddies got in line more than once for a free pizza that day.

Mr. Johnson lived next door to Gaylord Talbert, and I had been to his house once when Lyle had to pick up a wheat dough relief map of America he and Gaylord had built on a half sheet of plywood painted dark blue. Their joint school project pin-covered map identified American Indian tribes and eventually hung out in our garage for years after that. Gaylord and a couple other guys were in Mr. Johnson's garage when we pulled up in Lyle's Ford so he let me go over with him to see the famous mynah bird in action.

Eddie's cage was originally in Andy's Pet Shop on the Alameda near Race Street, which was a local attraction for neighborhood kids. Andy's sold exotic animals from monkeys to birds to tropical fish, turtles, lizards, and snakes. Once they had a kangaroo in the window. We would spend hours in there, checking out the animals and scheming about how to talk our parents into letting us get a monkey or hamster or parakeet or maybe just a goldfish. I once got a red ear slider turtle and a plastic lagoon, but the turtle died about a month later. A gigantic neon sign in the shape of a brightly colored scarlet parrot perched above the pet shop sign and entrance. You could give people directions by it. "Look for the big red, blue and yellow parrot."

Andy had given the cage to Mr. Johnson for his famous bird. It was eight foot long and four foot high and deep but also sat on foot-high legs made of 3/4-inch pipe. Somebody spent a long time making it. It was solid steel framed with square mesh wire on all sides but the back. The frame and cage wire were painted jungle green. The two-foot cage door latched and locked on the right side. But the most impressive feature of the cage was the elaborate back plywood wall. It had been hand-painted with a jungle scene of ferns and vines and limbs in various greens, yellows, browns, and blues that included a Capuchin monkey hanging by its tail from a tree branch on one side and a colorful tree-sitting macaw, very similar to the one atop Andy's shop, perched on the opposite side. Three half-inch dowels were mounted at different levels across the cage for Eddie to move around.

After catching their breaths from the long trek, Lyle, Maloney and Gaylord set the cage inside the garage to admire it and show it off to Art and me.

"Look what Mr. Johnson gave me—for free! He got Eddie a brand new indoor cage and said I could have this one if I hauled it away," Lyle exclaimed to me.

"That's pretty cool," I responded and by then had already got down on my knees and was poking my head through the cage door.

"I think the cage would make the perfect place for your brother to spend a few hours," said Maloney to Lyle, and then he looked around for Gaylord's and Art's approval of his humor. I backed away from the cage door and stood up before Maloney decided to get any funnier. It had been awhile since I had had to deal with Maloney and his meanness, and I liked it that way.

"What are you going to do with that? Mom isn't going to like some old thing in the garage. I'll bet she makes you take it back," I said to Lyle.

"Nah. She already said I could get a couple of parakeets this spring. Now I already have the cage."

Well, my mother wasn't too happy about the cage. It's not exactly what she had in mind when he asked her about parakeets, but the cage, which we always referred to as "the monkey cage" from then on, ended up on the far side of the house in the backyard along the fence, out of sight. In the spring Lyle bought five parakeets from Charles.

My mother explained to me that Charles was a kid in a man's body. He lived on the corner of Briarwood Drive and newly named St. Lawrence Drive with his parents. Everyone in the neighborhood knew Charles but no one knew much about him, except that he was different. He was probably in his early twenties, but he was mentally about six. He never went to school, at least as far as the kids in the neighborhood knew. But he was a friendly, grinning neighborhood fixture on his oversized bike. He was at least six-four. He was huge in every sense of the word. He wore farmer's denim overalls everyday and the same long-sleeve red and black plaid flannel shirt every day. He would pedal along on his spray-painted black Schwinn, with its gooseneck handlebars, big black basket, and an excessive number of red reflectors, up and down the neighborhood streets routinely in the late afternoons. He'd greet everyone with "Hi, I'm Charles. Good evening" but never really talked to anyone. He always had a wad of Bazooka gum in his mouth and he loved to show off his bubble blowing skills, which often resulted in disaster when the wind blew back at his face as he rode along, but he'd just keep on grinning. He looked somewhat like Curley on *Three Stooges*. Unfair rumors had it he slept locked up in the backyard in a cage with his birds. His parents kept to themselves and were rarely seen. Everyone knew he raised birds in his backyard because you could hear them chirping, singing and squawking whenever you walked by along Willow, I mean St. Lawrence.

One Saturday morning Lyle came home with a rattling grocery sack and a brand new indoor birdcage he had bought at Woolworth's at Valley Fair. He had completely abandoned idea of using the monkey cage in the backyard. In the sack were five "dwarf" parakeets, each no more than 3/4 of an inch tall and almost identical with lime green, lemon yellow, and olive black feathers. Their fingertip snowy white faces were speckled with tiny black spots.

In the family room he set up the cage with a clear plastic feeder and water cup and released the tiny birds to their new home. Five birds were not what my mother had agreed to, but Lyle argued that because they were "dwarf" birds, the five were no more than two regular birds. When he told her he had bought the birds, not at Woolworth's but from Charles, she was bothered again.

"How do you know where those birds come from? They might carry some disease. I've never heard of 'dwarf' parakeets. Wash your hands thoroughly when you finish with them and don't touch them." She left the room somewhat upset but shortly returned with pages from yesterday's newspaper so Lyle could line the cage bottom tray for his new pets. They were cute. They grew very little in the short time we had them and never seemed to really fly, but they jumped around a lot. By late summer they had all died. Lyle was pretty upset when the last bird died. "No more birds," my mother declared and Lyle spent more time in his room again.

Saturday afternoon my mom and dad had to go to city hall for another meeting about plans for widening Lawrence Station Road. Lyle was forced to keep an eye on me for the afternoon and stay around the house. I made myself busy with my latest Revell plastic model. I was never any good at putting them together, but I liked the idea of model cars, and they sure looked good on the box cover. I was too messy with glue and paint. I would always smear the glue somewhere on the car it wasn't supposed to be, like on the clear plastic windshield. Cousin Steve's models inspired me. He had all sorts of cool detailed model hotrods and planes. And I vaguely remember the piles of Fort Apache miniature soldiers, horses, and Indian warriors Lyle had painstakingly painted one by one and played with for hours in Salt Lake City on the living room floor when we were both smaller. My mother quietly gave away the entire Fort Apache Stockade, along with his Lincoln Logs, to our cousin Harvey before our move to California. Her "spring cleaning" of *his* things only fed his anger about being uprooted from Utah and his past.

I didn't have the patience it took to do the classy work Lyle or Steve did. Today was no exception. I was working on a '57 "Fireball" Roberts Ford, with every intention of making it the coolest car ever. I had succeeded gluing it together without too many mistakes, and I actually had no leftover pieces, which was rare for me. I decided to paint it two-tone, red and creme, but I got some red on the top and then on the plastic seats that should have been creme, and changed my plans. I opened a fresh little bottle of green paint. Pretty soon I had a real mess and a brown unevenly painted blob that looked like something you'd leave behind in the toilet. Meanwhile, I could hear

Maloney next door in Lyle's room, between 45s playing, giving him a hard time about having to babysit me. Just what I needed. Maloney hadn't been around as much this school year, but I could hear he was already zeroing in on his favorite target, me.

I cleaned up my mess and quietly headed for the backyard with my latest model disaster. I had an idea. I used to play with toy cars and trucks in the dirt along the flower border that lined the back of the house so I decided to revive my old habits and make this disaster a real disaster. I got a book of matches from the kitchen junk drawer and a gallon-can of paint thinner from my dad's workbench. I hooked up my old garage-stored 18-inch metal fire truck to the garden hose. The once bright red fire truck had been a Christmas gift from my Uncle Jack the first year we moved here. By hooking up a real hose to it, you could shoot water from a straw-sized black fire hose on the truck and control the flow with a valve on the truck's side panel.

Uh-oh. My Ford overturned in the flowerbed. From out of nowhere, it was doused with paint thinner, and then poof! The model became a genuine "firebird." It blew into a flaming torch when I threw the match at it. Just as I was about to send in the fire brigade—turn on the fire hose and use it on a *real* fire—here come Lyle and Maloney, witnesses to the entire event.

"What the hell are you doing? Trying to burn the house down?" Lyle yelled and then rushed over and kicked dirt onto the still-blazing plastic blob before I could even turn on my fire hose. I was mad, but a little worried I had been caught playing with fire.

"Go to your room. This isn't over. Wait 'til dad hears about this." Lyle was in charge, but Maloney had to put in his two cents.

"Yeah, wait 'til dad hears about this," he mimicked. "The little shit needs to be properly punished," he said, but I didn't stick around to find out what he had in mind. I was off to my room.

Maybe five minutes went by as I lay on my bed, my pillow covering my face. Lyle opened my door and demanded my attention.

"Hey, get up. First you're going to clean up that mess. Then you're going to do some time," Lyle said to me, his shadow Maloney smiling, looking over Lyle's shoulder with a kind of eagerness.

They followed me in and out of the backyard and garage and to the trash can. I couldn't imagine what they had planned for me and why they had me clean up the evidence.

"Alright, now head for the backyard again." I led the way until we reached the scene of the fire, but Lyle told me to keep going to the far side of the yard. We stood in front of the monkey cage and finally Lyle spoke. "I've got a proposition for you. I won't tell on you if you shut up and take your punishment like a man." Maloney stood at his side holding his laughter back with his fist against his mouth.

"What's that?" I asked. Suddenly, Maloney moved in front of Lyle, rapidly twirling the loop of a gym lock around his index finger, but it flew off his finger and hit the fence with a bang. He quickly retrieved it and Lyle gave him the stink eye and then spelled out his conditions to me.

I spent the next two hours in my underwear locked inside the monkey cage.

Crouched in the cage in only my briefs, I sat there thinking there were worse things. At least my mom and dad wouldn't find out about the fire. Lyle calculated he would get away with this sick idea of humor, though I knew whose idea it really was.

Sunday, my dad found what was left of my "Fireball" Roberts Ford in the trash can and Lyle and I had some explaining to do. After some yelling from my father, I was off the hook and sent to my room. I guess they figured what Lyle and Maloney had done to me was punishment enough. My dad yelled at Lyle much louder and longer before sending him to his room. I half expected Lyle would get a whipping, something he hadn't gotten in years. Years ago Lyle had even taught me the art of avoiding really getting hurt by the "belt." All you really had to do was cry and my dad would be satisfied and stop striking you. I couldn't imagine Lyle crying at seventeen. Things were changing. Lyle was put on restriction and Maloney didn't visit our house anymore.

Maloney gave up football his senior year but became a shining star on the gridiron in a new role. Dressed in his snow white wool uniform, single-point jacket and flared slacks, replete with an eighteen-inch-high matching bearskin hat, tassel-bouncing epaulettes, embroidered red and black BHS sash, silver whistle, white cotton gloves, and a forty-five inch red corded drum major's chrome mace, Maloney marched the entire forty-five piece mighty Bruin Band, 8 to 5 step, to the fifty-yard line for an always spriteful musical showcase every halftime. In high-lift mark time, his white patent leather shoes mirrored the night lights of Townsend Field, and the band played on to his commands. Ronald Maloney had finally made the scene.

all 1960

F*I was right.* Apparently the boundary makers for the school district realized their mistake and put the missing third of Cabrillo Avenue back on the Briarwood map. The lives of more than fifty kids who were bussed into Sunnyvale and removed from their neighborhood were back where they belonged. I got the feeling people in charge of all the changes going on in Santa Clara and Sunnyvale were making new rules as they went along.

My parents got official notification from the city in August that the future of Lawrence Station Road was in for some changes, just like everything else around here. To accommodate all the cars, the city was discussing how to widen the roadway and perhaps to turn it into an expressway. Just what that would mean for the neighborhood was a big topic among adults. My mom and dad began to talk about moving since we were so close to the pavement already. I didn't think much about it.

My first day back at Briarwood school was rewarding. Like Miss Krammer, Miss Childrey, our new fifth grade teacher, was young. She was our Miss Landers of *Leave It to Beaver*. If the TV people had needed someone to replace Miss Landers, they could have easily done so without the viewing audience knowing, and our Miss Childrey was her identical in more ways than one. She had us (at least the boys) mesmerized from the first day. The first thing she did was to tell us to pick our own seats. That was a new and promising experience.

"Welcome to the fifth grade. My name is Miss Childrey, and I am going to be your guide on an adventure into learning about the world. Just last week, I returned to Santa Clara from Paris, France, one of thirty stops I made last year, and I would like to share parts of my world with you. But first, I'd like to make you official co-pilots on this journey, so as I come around the room, tell me your name and I'll give you your wings."

And she did. Up until September, Miss Childrey had been a United Airlines stewardess. The three-inch plastic chrome wings she gave to each one of us to pin on our shirts, read: UNITED, Future-Pilot. The rest of the first day was a blur, but we did whatever she asked.

My mom was the only one who watched the presidential debates at our house Friday nights. Buchser football season had begun. Lyle became quite the star of the thirties football team that fall. He played offensive center and defensive linebacker. My dad rarely got off work early enough to see Lyle play—something Lyle constantly complained to me about—but I saw every home game at Townsend Field, even one at Buck Shaw Stadium. By the end of the season, Lyle had made First Team All-League as both center and linebacker.

Before the season was over, Lyle was seriously shopping for his first car. He had spent the past two summers working at the Ravizza's apricot orchard out on Homestead Road in Sunnyvale. Lifting boxes and trays of cots from shed to drying areas had earned him muscle and money. He had saved almost $200 toward a car by the time school started, and he scoured the *Mercury News* classified section for a month, looking for just the right car. He found it—a Chevy Bel Air. Lyle became much more talkative around the house. Wednesday and Thursday evening he even waited for dad to get home before he ate in the evenings so that he could sit at the dinner table with him to talk about cars, the Chevy in particular. Being a trucker, my dad knew a lot about cars and what to look for in a used one. Each discussion Lyle tried to have with dad ended pretty much the same: "Something practical and reliable is what you need." The last thing to impress my dad about a car was how cool it looked. In a small victory for Lyle, dad agreed to at least look at the Bel Air. If dad was in the right mood after work, the plan was to go see the car Saturday afternoon. Lyle called the owner Saturday morning while dad was out collecting pen machine quarters.

"Lyle, come out to the driveway. There's something I want you to see," said dad in the hallway outside Lyle's bedroom door. Lyle was startled by the knock and request. Dad was home early. This couldn't be good.

In the driveway sat a two-tone Raven black and Sungate Ivory topped '52 Customline Fordor Sedan V-8 Ford, complete with fender skirts, sun visor and Coronado deck on the trunk for the spare. Lyle was blindsided. It wasn't what he had in mind, but he had no say.

"It looks like an old lady's car," Lyle grumbled at my dad, then turned around in the driveway and marched into the house. Dad and I could hear the bedroom door slam from the driveway. Dad muttered something about an ungrateful son-of-a bitch. Then headed in after him. I knew better than to stick around. Anger spreads too easily so I grabbed my glove, got on my bike, and headed for Briarwood field.

Later that afternoon when I got home the Ford was in the garage. The ivory sun visor was on the garage floor and dad and Lyle were working on detaching the black fender skirts. There was no removing the trunk deck.

Lyle once shared with me one of the advantages of having your own car as a teenager is being able to take others along for the ride. He discovered quickly one of the disadvantages is not always having a say about who you take. Mother didn't drive so Lyle the chauffeur quickly learned the art of being invisible at the right time. Nevertheless, he spent more time in shopping center parking lots, listening to the radio, waiting for mother. Of course she would always give him gas money for her trips. Easy money he would tell me.

It was a good three weeks before Lyle ever took me anywhere he wasn't told to, but that changed one memorable Thursday night.

Friday nights, after school games, are cruising nights, especially in downtown San Jose. It is the place to be seen if you have a hot set of wheels. Lyle wasn't about to take his Ford there, but he and his Buchser buddies knew the Santa Clara main drags quite well. They made a loop out of El Camino Real, Scott, Winchester, Stevens Creek and Lawrence Station roads.

Anyway, over the past two years I have secretly acquired and put to memory most of Lyle's favorite hangouts and ignored the boring details about girls they scope out as he and his friends talk about them in Lyle's room or out on the driveway as they get ready to leave or come back to our house. I know where the hangouts are even if I haven't been in them all. I have it my goal to go to them all if I ever make it to high school, which seems like a long four years away. Along El Camino their favorite stops are Pippino's, Vesuvio's, Bob's, Si's, and Me 'n Ed's. On Stevens Creek they hang out at Vesuvio's No. 2 and Futurama Bowl.

I guess school boundaries define who most of your friends are and where you hang out. Construction on a new high school on Monroe is supposed to begin this year. If I end up going to the new Wilcox High School and not Buchser, I guess my hangouts will be different from Lyle's, but I don't like to think about that.

Like any respectable teenage brother, Lyle is not about to take me with him on a Friday or Saturday night. Thursday evening Lyle had the driving urge and finally took me in his new car along some of the Friday night route. We headed east on El Camino from Lawrence (which still confuses me since I have it in my head that San Jose is south of Santa Clara, but I guess the world isn't laid out in straight lines). Lyle pointed out hangouts I already knew from eavesdropping on him and his friends, but I liked hearing about them firsthand, for a change. But mostly he played music on the car's AM radio. The radio was one of the few features of his Ford that Lyle truly liked. By the time we reached Keily Boulevard just beyond Vesuvio's, traffic was crawling.

"I thought cruisin' nights were only Fridays and Saturdays."

"Does it look like people are cruising to you?" Lyle remarked, obviously irritated at the slowdown that on a Friday night probably wouldn't have bothered him in the least. I was taking it all in and enjoying my first official ride along in Lyle's new car.

♬ ♬ ♬ "My challenge was answered in less than a heart-beat; The handsome young stranger lay dead on the floor. . . ." ♬ ♬ ♬

Lyle turned up the radio as we made our way through our version of the town of "El Paso" by Marty Robbins. I didn't see the need to hurry anyhow.

We virtually crawled past Mariani's restaurant. Traffic was almost to a dead stop by the time we approached the Si's Burgers neon sign to our left. Something big was going on. Lyle turned off the music. People on sidewalks and driveways were hoofing it to the curb's edge on both sides of the four lane road like spectators seeking the best spot for the action at a parade. To our left, four identically dressed Si's car hop girls in their royal blue side caps, white cotton blouses, short blue skirts, and powder white saddle shoes had abandoned their posts and were lined up at the curb, a squad of cheerleaders looking at the aftermath of a crucial third-and-one play on the road just ahead of us. Traffic was a snail's pace in both directions.

All traffic in our direction was funneling to the center lane, the right lane dead stopped. Some people in that lane were leaving their cars. We could hear the frightening whine of sirens from both directions threatening to deafen all of us. The stench of sulfur from road flares filled the air and we rolled up our windows. Fragmented voices broke through our windows but their words were unrecognizable. Rotating red beams of light began to bounce off storefronts on either side of the road as emergency vehicles closed in on the spot. The Western Motel neon sign looked like cactus afire. Stuart's Furniture store plate glass windows caught the approaching red lights and threw red spears back at the crowd, strobing everything they hit. One guy struck a second or third road flare a few feet from us and dropped the long red stick on the ground. Lyle swore at the added obstacle. A man hurried by my window from behind, carrying a dark wool blanket cradled in his arms. Two men were kneeled down just ahead in the lane to our right tending to a person lying on the illuminated asphalt. Headlights from all the cars maneuvering around and stopped at the scene lit up the road like a stadium. Cars inching into his lane of traffic took Lyle's full attention and we were smack in the middle of the action. It was a test of his new driving skills.

Neither of us spoke. Just as we were about to roll pass the scene, the guy with the blanket removed it from his arms and handed it off to one of the kneeling men. I looked down and saw a glimpse of the lifeless gray face of a boy lying on his back just as the blanket draped his body permanently from everyone, and we pulled away from the scene. We were the last car through before emergency forces arrived. The ambulance passed us and slid to a stop. I looked through the rear window just as an ambulance attendant dressed fully in white pulled the wagon rear door open wide. Then I lost sight of the action. The cruise was over. We headed for home. I had seen more than I had bargained for that night.

The next morning Lyle and I read the story in the *Mercury* about the eight-teen-year old Santa Clara High student killed trying to jaywalk El Camino last night. The sight of his face is imprinted in my mind.

Lyle never did like the Ford Customline, but he kept it through his last year of high school. He was a hit with some of his football buddies from our side of town and charged them a quarter a week to get a ride home in his "old lady's car." Easy money he would tell me.

A month after he moved out of the house, he traded the Ford for a Chevy.

Saturday afternoon I was out with my dad in our 1956 Pontiac Star Chief, collecting quarters from ballpoint pen vending machines he had in stores in downtown San Jose. The bright yellow and blue machines were often just inside a store or shop along with gum ball, jawbreaker, and peanut vending machines or next to the check cashing booth in a grocery store. We were near the end of his rounds in the Thrifty's Drug on Santa Clara Street when I saw the mask I would wear this Halloween. No Bugs Bunny, no skeleton or ghost, no hobo for me this year. I was going as the absolute biggest devil ever devised. The mask itself was three-quarters of my height and twice my width. It was a plastic molded devil's head in relief. The eyeholes for the mask were cleverly hidden in the mouth of the devil. It stood at least thirty inches above my chin when on my face. An elastic adjustable band secured the mask to my head, and, just in case of a head wind, there was an extra strap in the lower corner to hold on to the mask. The unpainted backside of the mask looked like the inside of the Disney Matterhorn, unfinished. The face was artfully spray-painted red, purple and black. Two wicked-looking black and red horns, also part of the shell, rose another eight inches from the top on both sides. I had to have it.

My mom keeps family photos in an old metal projection tin. Whenever Halloween comes around, I dig out some of the old pictures of a family Halloween party we hosted in the basement of our little white house in Salt Lake. It was a huge costume party, much like the family Christmas gatherings we used to have. We had a "Best Costume" contest, bobbed for apples, feasted on potluck dishes and stuffed ourselves with hand-cranked vanilla ice cream and pumpkin pie. I went as a skeleton, but so did my cousin Russell. My eighty-year old grandmother was dressed as a gypsy.

My older cousin Jimmy took Lyle, me, our cousin Harvey, and Jimmy's two boys, Paul and Jay, to a farm outside of the city to get some Halloween decorations the day before the party. He had a 1948 Kenwood green Plymouth Special Deluxe he rigged with a trailer hitch. We loaded his six-foot hauling trailer with a couple of haystacks, some corn stalks, gourds, and pumpkins from a farm in a town called Sandy. Jimmy, Harvey, and Lyle sat in the car on the way home. Paul, Jay, and I pleaded with Jimmy to let us ride in the trailer. We sat sandwiched between the farm-grown items on the way home.

"Now don't be fooling around back there. We've got to keep the trailer balanced," he told us so the trailer would ride right. When we entered the city, we had to cut across town. Lots of the roads were steep. We came to the top of a hill on a busy boulevard and waited for the light to change. Suddenly, there was a big snap. The trailer had detached from the car. With the hitch dragging and sparking against the asphalt, the trailer began rolling backward, throwing the Halloween freight and us toward the upcoming traffic. Three feet, six feet—the trailer was picking up momentum, skidding and screeching as the rear end scraped the asphalt of the road, and we were screaming for Jimmy, arms covering our heads as we crouched wedged between hay bails, cornstalks, and pumpkins, waiting for a sure crash. In a flash, Jimmy was out the driver's side of the Plymouth, chasing us down the street. With Superman's strength, he caught the trailer hitch with his bare arms and with all his might, pulled the trailer, farm's harvest, and kids to the side of the road. Lyle and Harvey stood at the curb, dumbfounded. We were three scared but thankful kids. We rode the rest of the way home in the backseat of the '48. Now that was a Halloween scare.

Back to Saturday, my dad had finished putting his collection of quarters from the Thrifty's store into one of several deep canvas bags he used to keep his store accounts straight. He drew it closed by the string and tied it off. We would count quarters at home. As was his routine, he would spend another fifteen minutes or so talking with the manager and settling up the store's share of profits based on the machine's mechanical counter of actual ballpoint pens dispensed. I knew better than to interrupt him when he was at his best, chatting up business.

When he was finished, I described the devil's mask to him with eagerness enough to get him to go to the costume displays. That was half the battle.

"Don't you think it's kind of big?" he asked me, as he handled the mask.

"Yeah, but that's the point. I want to standout."

"You might get *worn out* before the night's over wearing this," he warned.

"I won't. I won't," I insisted. And so he relented, not something he did all that often. The fact that he had a bag full of quarters in one hand probably made him feel more generous, and I was certainly grateful.

The final stop for the day was always a place where he could make a last vending machine transaction and have a cup of coffee. Today, it was special, the Carnation Creamery on the Alameda. I would be rewarded for tagging along with him with a chocolate shake. As we sat at the counter, enjoying our beverages, my dad reminded me about all the great creameries in San Jose and Santa Clara that were disappearing. Living far from old Santa Clara, I missed out on a lot of things downtown like soda fountains, parades, and celebrations, and I knew nothing about Santa Clara University. The suburbs were about newness. I was beginning to understand why Lyle was damaged by our move out of the city where he grew up with places like the Seventh Avenue Drug and Fountain.

Halloween night this year was cold and windy. Halloween now was about candy. Pauly, Art, and I had strategically worked out the most efficient route for getting the most candy in the least amount of time. We devised a plan to cover half of Briarwood tract, all of Lawrence Meadows, and half of Killarney Farms before our night would be complete. Our parents had no idea we could cover such a range. With Pauly's face hidden behind a caricature gangster mask that looked a lot lot my uncle Mike, and my own face consumed by my towering devil's head, we left the house with great intentions. By the time we reached the short distance of Cabrillo and Briarwood Drive, I could see, or more accurately put, couldn't see, the devil's mask was a mistake. It would slide down my chin every five seconds so I couldn't see out the eyeholes. It caught the wind, even when I was just walking. When I tried to pick up the pace, the mask would blow hard against my head and came off completely at least twice, and all this before we had even reached Art's house. Art was done up as an unshaven hobo, complete with cold cream and coffee grinds to make his beard. His hobo bindlestiff would come in handy for carrying extra candy. We each had a medium brown grocery sack for our booty. We did not want to walk up to people's houses with big bags. That would look like we were greedy, but Art sneaked three white pillow cases out of the linen closet for candy we would keep out of sight.

It was time for the devil's mask to go. Arturo's mom found us a suitable grocery sack and we cut out slots for eyes and a mouth. I was a. . . . I am not sure what I was supposed to be, but the bag on my head was much better than the devil on my face.

My mother had given me a two-hour limit to trick-or-treat, but since I didn't have a watch, or any sense of time once we got going, we trick-or-treated until we were ready to drop. Proud of my night's success, I came home with a grocery sack and pillowcase of candy to some bad news waiting at the front door.

It seems my cousin René and her two girlfriends had been holdup while trick-or-treating in their Hayward neighborhood. A group of teenage boys ripped their bags of candy from their hands in the dark of night.

"Benny, you know what I think you should do?" my mother asked, obviously unhappy with how much candy I had in the first place. Of course, I knew what she had in mind, but I played along, hoping I was wrong.

I had to wait almost an entire week to give half my candy to René since we weren't going to Hayward until the following Sunday. My mother watched me from the kitchen as I counted out my candy with exacting precision by separating each piece of candy into one of three stacks, based on sizes and desirability, spreading my hoard wide on the living room shag carpet. Like a guide to my conscience, my mother was there to see that I didn't leave René with only candy from one of the three stacks. At least I didn't get into trouble for staying out so late. My mother put René's half in a bag in the cabinet above the Frigidaire. It was a temptation the entire week. The devil surely had had a hand in this Halloween.

John F. Kennedy was elected the 35th President of the United States this week, and Sarah Sanderson and I were named Briarwood cafeteria workers from our class. Miss Childrey had a merit system for people who wished to work in the cafeteria for a two-week period during the school year. You earned points by completing your homework, scoring high on tests and quizzes and behaving in class. You had to be in at least fifth grade to work in the cafeteria itself. In fourth grade, you could sell 5 cent milk at the milk lines, but you couldn't fold out the cafeteria tables, serve food, or wash the big green plastic trays and silverware unless you were at least a fifth-grader. By sixth grade, you were supposed to be attending Jefferson School, but some sixth graders remained at Briarwood due to overcrowding. Those kids didn't want to work in the cafeteria of an elementary school.

In this round for our class for cafeteria workers, "Too-tall" Sarah Sanderson and I made the grade. We had become pretty good friends over the four years and had had all our Briarwood classes together since second grade. Of course, I was bussed away for fourth grade, but I adjusted to being with my old classmates the first day back. The cafeteria at Briarwood was a great place to eat, but only on certain days of the week. Hardly anybody ate there every school day. Fish Fridays and meatloaf days were two of the least popular, but come hotdog day or pizza day or sloppy joe day, count me in. Working in the cafeteria got you a free 35-cent lunch every day you worked.

I suppose the hotdogs were not anything special, but the secret sauce of mayonnaise and mustard made them different, and the fries were baked. The school smelled particularly aromatic on pizza day. That's because the pizza was also baked on thick sweet bread with fresh sweet tomato paste, layered with cheeses. A lucky day was when you could get a second helping. Working in the cafeteria assured that. Nobody but my mom could match the sloppy joes at school, made entirely from scratch. My mother was friends with Mrs. Florence, the head cook, and she gave my mom the recipe. Sloppy joes were a favorite in our house. Oh, yeah, baked spaghetti days were also good at school.

Cafeteria workers got to eat first and last. You would eat just before the mad rush for food after the bell, and after cleanup, you might get an extra slice of pizza or an extra dessert. Best of all, the other kids thought they had an in with you, especially if you were behind the serving counter. "I want the corner piece of pizza, not the middle. "Give me an extra sloppy joe scoop." I always obliged, but the cafeteria ladies did most of the serving.

Sarah and I made a good team at the dishwashing area. We wore industrial strength vanilla colored rubber gloves. Kids left their mint green cafeteria trays at the open window area when they finished. With a wide spatula, Alex, a fifth-grader from another class, would shake and scrape the remains on the plastic trays into the trash can. Sarah was usually the rinser. The metal hose that contained the sprayer was on a tall, looped mechanism. Her height made it easier for her than others of us, although one day the sprayer snaked from her hand and she ended up with a misted face. We all had a good laugh.

My job was to take trays from Sarah, put them on edge in racks, and place the rinsed silverware in a small plastic bucket, which were all in a rolling metal framework that I slid into the big box metal washer. Loud rumbles and whiffs of steam would generate from inside the washer in action. When the machine was done with one load, a shrill buzzer would sound and the big stainless steel lids would lift automatically as clouds of fog dissipated into the air. I would push another tray of dirty dishes into the washing contraption while the clean tray rolled out the other end. Another kid would collect the hot clean plates and stack them for tomorrow. It was a bit wet and steamy back there, but our heavy brown plastic aprons and gloves kept us fairly dry. It was kind of fun, and we became good friends with the cafeteria ladies and other kids working.

Right before Thanksgiving my mother began retrieving Christmas decorations from the garage attic. Lyle and I were crossing our fingers, hoping that this year's Christmas tree wouldn't be as bad as the tree of '58. What could be worse than a pink flocked tree with blue ornaments inside a pink house? She had reminded my dad several times in the last few weeks that she intended to go to the annual Harvest Bizarre at the San Jose Civic Auditorium this year for some fresh holiday ideas. That meant he had to commit to taking her there and hanging out while she shopped. I thought it was kind of funny until I was informed that morning I would be going with them. It was bad enough when I had to go to the grocery store on Saturday mornings, but this was beyond reason. The last thing I wanted to do on a Sunday was look at arts and crafts holiday junk made by ladies in sewing circles. But there was no arguing the point.

Before my mother got into the car, my dad turned around to me in the back seat and said, "Just be quiet about this, and we'll figure something out." I had no idea what that meant, but I played along.

Traffic was thick on San Carlos when we got downtown. We circled the Civic twice looking for parking. The third time around my dad told my mother we would meet her inside after we found a spot to park, but it was a long time before we would make it inside the auditorium. We didn't even try.

It was a men's day out, or so my dad told me as I got into the front seat alongside him.

"Where are we going?" I asked and knew I would be glad with any answer that didn't have to do with holiday bizarres.

"You'll see. I think we need a bit of fresh air." My mind was spinning. It was not like my dad to do anything that wasn't somehow related to work or hauling my mother around shopping.

My dad was old as long as I can remember. I can't remember the last time we threw catch or did something for fun. Even when we went to Big Basin in the summers, he spent most of his time there putting the camp together—staking up the tent, building a fire, breaking up block ice for the ice chest or pumping the white gas Coleman stove so my mother could percolate the coffee. When he sat down, it was to smoke another Camel, drink another cup of coffee, and discuss what else needed doing with the adults. He was always working.

We headed out of downtown on San Carlos. At Bird we made our way to Santa Clara Street. We headed toward the Alameda, a part of town I was a bit more familiar with. My dad parked the Pontiac just beyond the A&W on the Alameda at Stockton.

"Let's go to Schurra's. They've got the best licorice buttons in town, not to mention they make their own chocolates." I was always up for candy of most any kind. My dad, on the other hand, pretty much focused on licorice, lemon drops, and root beer barrels. He always had a ragged paper white bag of one of those candies in his glove compartment.

The giant Muffler Man watched over us as we walked across the Alameda. At the corner of Sunol, I could see two large women in white kitchen aprons and black hairnets inside the chocolate shop behind the corner plate glass windows. One was working over cream fillings with wide scrapers on a huge marble slab. The second woman quickly rolled the fillings into snakes and put them into a rolling mold, which cut them into perfect rounds she would hand dip into melted chocolate and place in rows on metal trays. She was mechanically fast.

I took a deep breath of sweet buttery air as we entered the store and a little bell above the door jingled at our entrance. A man dressed in all white and wearing a white paper cap came from a back area to the glass counter opposite where the candy ladies were working when we walked in. The glass case revealed two paper-laced shelves of every assortment of chocolates imaginable. On the top of the glass case was a foot-tall milk chocolate figure of Santa Claus and another of a chocolate angel sitting next to large glass canisters that held colorful candy balls, stick candy, gumdrops, suckers, and licorice. Tin candy molds of creatures and objects hung on nails on the wall behind the counter. A March-Of-Dimes collection can stood next to the tarnished NCR register on the lower counter.

Without even asking me what I wanted, my dad ordered two caramel dark chocolates for our immediate consumption, a small box to go, and a half-pound bag of licorice buttons. Whenever there was a box of chocolates at our house, everyone went straight for the chocolate caramels. My dad knew us well. There were more times than I can count when someone took a nibble of a chocolate creme and then put it back in its brown ribbed sleeve after finding no caramel inside, and it wasn't always me who did it.

With long metal tongs the counterman put ten matching chocolates into empty brown paper cups in a perfect-fit box, placed two cupped chocolates on the counter, and then with a silver metal scoop measured out a half pound of black licorice buttons from the big jar onto a scale on his first scoop and shoveled them into a small white paper sack.

My dad and the owner talked about how business was doing and what trucking outfit delivered their goods and whom they knew in common. I immediately devoured my caramel. The sweet smell of chocolate, cream, and sugar was a treat in itself, and I watched the two women behind us work the chocolate while my dad chatted, but I was ready to leave by the time he paid the candy man. Had we stayed any longer, my stomach would have lost my urge for anything sweet for awhile.

"Now your mother doesn't need to know anything about this. Remember, we're still looking for parking." My dad ate his chocolate caramel on his way out the door, pulled another out of the box for each of us, handed me the package of remaining caramels and told me to save some for Lyle. He shoved the white bag of black licorice buttons into his jacket pocket and we headed up the Alameda, eating our second piece of chocolate. The caramels were the best I had ever had. I knew where to find the licorice buttons later.

On the opposite corner of Sunol stood Scotchman's Chris-Craft boat shop. We walked through the parking lot in front of the warehouse and cupped our faces at the French window panes to admire the several wooden boats on display in the sunlit showroom shut up tight for Sunday. I asked my dad which one he'd pick from the four gleaming lacquered mahogany boats we could see in the boat warehouse, but he didn't want to play the game and told me boats like that were for rich people and we moved along the street beyond Cummings Tires shop, as we both finished off our second caramels. On the roof of an old pale yellow and brown stucco craftsman house at the corner of Morrison, atop short metal scaffolding, a tall yellow sign trimmed in brown lettering and the silhouette of ballroom dancers announced Arthur Murray's Dance. Many Tuesday evenings my parents watched *Arthur Murray Party* on TV. Once in a while the show would have some good guests on like Buddy Holly or The Platters, but mostly Arthur and Kathryn Murray waltzed around on our Zenith TV screen when we could have been watching *The Rifleman*. At least it's on only a half hour now.

"You know, when I was young I was quite the dancer. I could really jitterbug and foxtrot. My sister Grace and I even won a couple of trophies. We would dance to all the big bands that came to town, Tommy Dorsey, Glen Miller, Artie Shaw, even Ozzie Nelson." My dad seemed lost in the past as we walked along. I had heard his dancing stories many times. I even once asked Aunt Grace what happened to the trophies. She laughed. "We never won any trophies." But I didn't want spoil the moment so I didn't say anything to my dad today.

As we neared Race Street we came to San Jose Roller Land. I had been rollerskating there a couple of times with Allan and Art. Everything about the place was old. It was an old red brick building with old wooden floors and old skates. My friends and I preferred the new Skateland out on Reed Road in Sunnyvale. My dad and I watched a handful of skaters go round from the limited window area out front.

"You know, this place wasn't always a skating rink. It used to be called Auditorium Skate Rink because before that it was one of San Jose's biggest gathering places. It was used for political conventions, town meetings, dances, theater, boxing matches, even basketball games. That changed pretty much after they built the Civic Auditorium in the thirties. I once took your mother here to a big band dance right after the war." My dad was talking to me, but he was in the good old days again. I guess this day will be a good old day for me someday.

As we made our way to the corner, I imagined how fun it must be to shoot a bow and arrow inside the Archery Shop, a red painted building on our left, but I knew my dad would have none of that. When we reached Race Street, my dad suggested a coke for me so we sat at the half-round counter at Tiny's Drive-in. He drank two mugs of coffee, smoked some Camels, and talked the leg off the waitress about what used to be along the Alameda. Spinning on my stool and enjoying my coke with a bird's eye view of the Alameda from Tiny's curved plate glass windows, I tried to make out all of the animals on Andy's Pet Shop mural across the street down to our left. I had once eaten at Ed's Chuck Wagon that stood on the next corner beyond Andy's. The imposing Falstaff beer tower stood in the distance at the brewery, rising above all the buildings in the area.

When we finally got back downtown in the Pontiac the traffic was as thick as ever. My mother was standing under the arched porch of the Civic Center, a loop-handled shopping bag in one hand, another bag on the ground next to her as she waited for us. She seemed to have a chokehold on a three-foot tall cotton gauze stuffed snowman under her left arm. As my dad spotted her with her holiday finds, he told me to lie.

"Just tell your mother we've been circling around every few minutes for an hour, that we parked across town for a while and lost track of time. That should work." The story about losing track of time sounded a lot like what I would often hear him say to my mother in the late evenings when he finally made it home from work and she was re-heating dinner for him, or when he didn't make it to a football game or a school program in time.

CHAPTER 14

S pring 1961

The world eventually found out the truth about the United States botched invasion of Cuba, but all the kids in our neighborhood knew George Schlegel's secret by the next day. Mr. Schlegel was a complicated man. He was a master carpenter who immigrated to America sometime after World War II. His thick German accent was right out of the *Stalag 17* movie. He and his wife Emma had no children, and he did nothing to encourage neighborhood kids to like him. His house, his yard, his 1960 Belmont blue Ford Falcon Ranchero, and even his carpenter-equipped garage were always picture perfect. He had a "keep-off-the-lawn" sign near his front porch. That made him a magnet to some kids who would often disrupt his yard just to be mean by running across his lawn on their bikes or tossing their litter on it. Older kids, like Maloney, referred to him as "The Fuhrer" behind his back. Mr. Schlegel was sure everybody was against him and promoted that treatment by speaking only in grumbles to neighbors or to no one at all, except to my dad. My dad could befriend anyone. My dad loved to talk to adults. I can't say that he was that way with Lyle and me. My dad defended Mr. Schlegel for his abruptness with people when I persisted asking why he was so mean.

"George has had a tough life. He lost his entire family in the war and barely escaped Germany alive. He had to start over. He's done pretty good for himself, remarried, started a business here, and even bought a house. Maybe he is afraid of losing it all again," my dad suggested to me when I asked him why Mr. Schlegel never talked to anyone. I often imagined he had something to hide from his war days, but I never said that to anyone. I still didn't get why he didn't like the Owens. He didn't even know them.

Miss Childrey gave us a writing assignment in English class: Write about a memorable event in your neighborhood. I wrote about Mr. Schlegel's secret.

After four years of construction and traffic in the neighborhood, Cabrillo Avenue was scheduled to be resurfaced, which meant a lot of loose gravel and a slurry coating of tar. It was messy, stinky, and the work upset the normal flow of traffic and parking on the street. Tow-away signs hung from white wooden street sawhorses along our block, warning people not to park on Cabrillo for the next two days. People who lived on our street usually parked in their two-car garages or in their driveways anyway. But someone down the street—Mr. Snowden, I think—came up with the idea of simply parking in the vacant lot across from our house and avoiding having to drive on Cabrillo at all while the paving took place. With a little caution, a driver could simply pull out from the vacant lot onto Lawrence Station Road directly. By five o'clock Wednesday night, Mr. Snowden's idea had caught on with neighbors. Before the night was up, at least a dozen sedans, station wagons, and pickup trucks were parked in the lot, even Mr. Ruffino's latest Galaxy 500. Thursday morning everyone went off to work and the scraping and graveling began. Thursday evening and the lot was full again. Friday was tarring day. By the time most people got home from work, the pavers were just finishing up, and so many people left their cars in the lot for one more night. They could easily retrieve them Saturday morning.

Tom Watts was the *Mercury News* newspaper boy in our neighborhood. His newspaper delivery pickup spot was just across Lawrence on the corner of Halford and Lawrence, about fifty yards south of Cabrillo. By 5:30 every morning, Tom would be sitting on the curb, folding newspapers for delivery. He had a birds-eye view of the daily action along Lawrence. This Saturday he saw something out of the ordinary. About six o'clock, Mr. Schlegel came out of his garage with a stack of cardboard signs. He crossed the street to the vacant lot and quickly placed 12-inch square signs on the windshields of all the parked cars and then hurried into his garage and pulled down the door.

Cabrillo was waking up by eight Saturday morning.

"Why do you suppose all those signs are on the cars across the street?" my mother standing at the kitchen sink asked my father who was sitting at the kitchen table reading the paper and working on a cup of coffee. He hadn't noticed a thing. He got up to look out the kitchen window at about the same time a car heading south on Lawrence pulled over to look at the cars across the street. My dad watched as the driver got out to check out the cars.

"I don't know, but somebody's headed over there. Maybe the city posted warnings on the cars. No, I think those are "For Sale" signs." About this time, Mr. Snowden showed up across the street to get his car. He didn't look too happy when he saw a stranger giving his car the once over. By now, I was out of bed and at the window asking questions. The three of us watched the silent comedy in action from our front row window. Mr. Snowden was obviously upset—at everyone. He pulled the sign from his own windshield and then began ripping them away one by one from the windshields of the other seven or eight cars. Each sign had a price and phony phone number written on it in thick black felt pen. It seemed almost instantly that the other men on our block were in the lot to get their cars and to get to the bottom of this.

My dad told me to stay in the yard. He headed over to get into the fray. Mr. Schlegel was already there. A couple of men thought the entire incident was funny, and I could make out their laughter. Most of them were angry. I could hear Mr. Schlegel blaming those "dammed kids again." He even said something about the Owens. A disappointed potential customer returned to his car and headed down Lawrence. Eventually everyone dispersed and the neighbors put their cars back to the safety of their garages and driveways. The mystery remained among all the adults, but by Monday all the kids at Briarwood and Jefferson schools knew what the old German guy on Cabrillo had done for April Fools Day.

As Miss Childrey read the handwritten version of my story to the class, my face was ten shades of red. When she finished it, everyone applauded and she went on about how we all have hidden talents if we just give ourselves a chance to find them. From that point on I took a different view of writing. I would sometimes write stories without being assigned. I even worked on my penmanship. Mrs. Fay would be proud.

When something goofy or interesting happened at school, some of my classmates would tease me and ask, "Are you going to write about that, Benny?"

"I might," I would reply.

It was one of those "zip-a-dee-doo-dah" days, or so I thought, as I biked up to my driveway after school the Wednesday after Mothers Day. We had had both my aunts Clara and Betty and their families to the house for Mothers Day dinner. As usual, Steve and Lyle quickly disappeared from the company into Lyle's room. The renderings of Chuck Berry and Little Richard reverberated from the other side of the door. I knew I would not be welcome. It was a teenage thing, my mother told me.

I hadn't seen Aunt Clara and Uncle Mac for a long time, but I knew Aunt Clara had been sick and in the hospital. It had to do with her heart. She looked fully recovered to me. The only difference I noticed was that she had changed her smoking habits. It was the subject of adult ribbing she took for much of the day. Oh, she still smoked, but now she was "fashionable," as she put it. She now inhaled her Salems from a six-inch long black plastic holder, to which she attached each cigarette she smoked. Apparently, her doctors had told her that she had to stop smoking. Sitting at the kitchen table, cross-legged in black slacks and a black and white polka-dot blouse (the blouse was a Mothers Day gift from her daughter Marlene), she amused everyone with her Hollywood red-lipped smile and humorous anecdotes, punctuated by long gusts of hazy grey smoke she blew out her nose. She reminded me of a much kinder Cruella de Vil in Disney's *One Hundred and One Dalmatians*.

"Well, when he told me I have to give up smoking completely, I told him I'd compromise. These new filters are made from something called asbestos fibers and are guaranteed to reduce the tar and nicotine intake in any cigarette."

We rarely saw Aunt Clara's children, Mark and Marlene. They were much older than the rest of our cousins and lived somewhere north of San Francisco, but today Marlene and her husband Ange brought their seven-year-old daughter Kimberly to the Sunday dinner.

Kimberly was my proof polio was real, not just something we saw on TV news. Kimberly was a brown-eyed curly-haired Shirley Temple look-alike. She was always smiling and loved by everyone. She had had a tough past three years. In and out of hospitals, at one point she had nearly died. My aunts and uncles were always talking about the Shriners Hospital for Children and how they had saved her life. It seemed she was always preparing for another surgery when she was not actually in the hospital.

Today Kimberly, with great effort, proudly walked on her own wearing matching steel metal hinged-braces attached to her thick brown leather shoes. Each cumbersome brace, paralleling both sides of leg and hinged at the knee, stayed fixed with dark leather straps and metal buckles. The braces disappeared up her thighs beyond her white cotton dress and petticoat. It was a struggle for her, but she never stopped smiling as she tirelessly moved one leg stiffly ahead of the other, the metal hinges slightly clicking with each motion. Word had it that she would be able to toss off one of those braces someday—if the next surgery went as planned. My mother told me once that Kimberly had been lucky to not end up in an iron lung or totally paralyzed. She didn't seem very lucky to me.

Mothers Day dinner went off without a hitch. Afterward, we all—minus Lyle and Steve—sat around the living room and talked and talked. Cousin René played a couple tunes on my dad's Thomas organ for the adults but made a quick exit when she heard the opening theme song to *Disneyland* on the TV coming from the family room where Kimberly and I had retreated.

So it's Wednesday afternoon, and I am feeling pretty good about myself. I had gotten an *A* on a book report I had written about John Steinbeck's *The Moon is Down*, and, as always, I got some flattering compliments from Miss Childrey, which she had written in the margins. As I enter the family room from the garage, I see my mother sitting at the kitchen table facing the wall, her head bent into the palms of her hands. She looks up and over, her eyes red from crying.

"Clara died of a heart attack, early this morning."

To this point in my life, I had avoided the specter of death, except of course for the lifeless face of the boy I had seen on El Camino Real last fall. I had somehow channeled that picture in my mind as make-believe. Aunt Clara was forty-six years old when she died. Her death affected everyone I called family. Many feelings came to surface, and I am still trying to forgive my parents.

Aunt Clara's funeral was held in what must have been the oldest building in San Francisco since the 1906 earthquake. Of course to me most of San Francisco seemed that way, coming from reborn Santa Clara. I never went to San Francisco unless our family had out-of-state company, like my aunts and uncles from Utah, and then we would only go to the tourist spots, like Fisherman's Wharf or Coit Tower or Golden Gate Park or the zoo, certainly not a place like Gray's Mortuary. I was not prepared for this event.

The four of us drove to the mortuary in our white '61 Tempest station wagon. Lyle and I sat in the back seat and didn't say much to each other during the ride. My mother and father talked in muffles the entire trip. My mother made one thing clear first thing this morning. She wanted us to be at the service early. We were.

We walked into the ancient mortuary chapel, greeted by two aging, well-manicured men in dark suits with pink carnations in their lapels. My focus was immediately drawn to the burgundy-curtained wall at the far end of the chapel, beyond the Sunday-dressed people who had begun to shuffle into the building, beyond the overwhelming musk of flower sprays and wreaths, beyond the padded upholstered wooden benches on either side of the floral carpeted aisle, to the opened, satin-lined polished walnut coffin, front and center.

Even from forty feet away, I could make out features of Aunt Clara's face, illuminated by unnatural red light from eerie tall lamps on either side of the coffin. That was close enough for me.

"Come on. Family sits up front," my dad said to Lyle and me. There was no turning back, no time to think at all. My mother disappeared into a group of women, all hugging and talking in whispers. Steve intercepted Lyle before my dad noticed, and the two of them were gone. Then we were there.

Inches from Aunt Clara, we looked down at her face. My dad's attention was taken by one of Uncle Mac's brothers who approached him. The moment was now mine alone. There she was dressed just as she had been Sunday for Mothers Day in her black and white polka-dot blouse. Her red-lipped smile was vaguely there, if you used your imagination. Her makeup seemed thick and caked with rouge and powder. Her curly black hair was too perfectly set, and of course her eyes were closed. This was death, and I didn't like it.

Just then my dad whispered we were to sit just there, and he pointed to the front row maybe three feet away. He sat me down, leaned down at me and spoke.

"Stay here. I'll be back."

It wasn't fair. For a slow-moving hour I sat by myself having a stare-down with death, three feet away. Sitting on the bench, I was in a direct line to Aunt Clara's face where she rested in her coffin. Occasionally, one of the mourners who came up to view Aunt Clara nodded to me or spoke my name, but I remained alone until the service began.

President Kennedy had just recently announced on television the rest of America was going to the moon so we felt the need to get on board.

"Now class, I need everyone on best behavior today when you board the city's brand new bookmobile. Remember, it is a library, not a playground on wheels. Your parents' hard earned taxes paid $36,000 so you young people can have the world of knowledge outside your door. Isn't that remarkable?" enthused Miss Childrey to a class of excited fifth-graders. We had all heard about the bookmobile over the past two years. Now it was finally here, and it inspired our imaginations.

To wet our appetites, Miss Childrey told us all about the launch of this year's city library reading program: Rocket Ship to the Moon. Today when the gleaming yellow bookmobile rolled into the circular drive of Briarwood school, most of us entered the big new bus with big new plans to reach the mesosphere. Before today, the only library I knew outside of school was the city library on Main Street in downtown Santa Clara. I had been in there a couple of times in the summers, but my excuse for not reading much during the out-of-school months was that the library was too far away to go to regularly, even though I could find my way to War Memorial pool constantly, and the library was on the way to the pools.

It was hard to believe that somebody could turn a bus into an entire library, but practically every inch of the bus held something to read on the floor-to-ceiling narrow wood shelves that surrounded the walls. Along the bottom row on both sides of the marbled green linoleum floor was a step/bench where you could perch yourself going through books, except that we had only fifteen minutes to make our selections that first day, since only half the class could enter the bookmobile at a time. Even then, it was tight quarters for kids all vying for books in the same sections.

Climbing high into space in the summer reading program meant reading an astronomical number of books. Half the fun was just scrambling through the tall tilted stacks and claiming a pile of books to check out on the dogtag library cards we were issued. Today even the boys checked out the maximum five books allowed until the bookmobile returned in two weeks. I found plenty to read with the likes of *Old Yeller, Davy Crockett,* and *Mike Fink*, but as always, despite my spring enthusiasm, I lacked the time and patience to read everything I checked out so anxiously and so did my friends. Allan, Art, Michael, Carl and I had good intentions. It's just that it seemed more natural to create our own adventures outside than read about them. On the other hand, Lyle was a reading fanatic who locked himself in his bedroom for hours reading, traces of dull lamp light escaping to the hall carpet from beneath his closed door into the late night hours. Following a gentle but routine knock on Lyle's door at least once every weeknight, my father would remind Lyle of his duty growing up: "You need to get to sleep. Tomorrow's a school night, you know." He would later use that same line on both of us as we started to watch more nighttime TV.

By the end of August, my personalized tinfoil cutout rocket wasn't very high in the black cardboard outer space displayed on the bookmobile easel. By the looks of the display, the girls in my class were much more determined reading astronauts. But in defense of guys, Allan was a comic book addict, and Michael read every sports magazine and baseball book he could get his hands on and could spout almost any baseball statistic of the last twenty years.

During the summers the bookmobile would continue its stops at the school but also roll into the neighborhood. Cabrillo Avenue was a regular stop every other week, and that summer and the next my friends and I would start off for the moon and get the bookmobile ladies excited helping us find just the right books, but by fall our visits to the bookmobile were rare like the fruit left on the trees.

The guys learned in part from our bookmobile experience that we could accelerate in the world of counting books we read much better if we shared what we read and our book reports in our classes with each other. We learned to avoid suspicion; no reports on comics or watered-down classics. Out of necessity, we learned the art of "re-composition" also. By the time we reached the sixth grade we had mastered the "art" of book reports. We had found the back issues of "Boy's Life" and "Junior Scholastic" in the school's library periodical section. They were rich with adventure stories that didn't demand the time of *Kon Tiki* or *Robinson Crusoe*. We figured out pretty fast that no teacher could possibly know the difference between a short story and a novel all the time. Just as long as we turned in a report on a story every two weeks, Mrs. Musson seemed satisfied, and if we didn't get the details correct, no one was the wiser. There was a time or two when I even reported on a story found only in my own imagination. I think maybe Mrs. Musson knew all along what was going on, but she had us reading and writing, so all was well.

Summer 1961

Last week it was a record 107 degrees in Santa Clara. Billy and I postponed our trip to the dam for a couple of weeks. I met Billy at 8 o'clock in front of the Corn Palace. Between us, we had enough money for a couple of sodas, some fries, and some candy we would buy later. That would suffice us for the day. Our destination was an nine-mile bike ride to Stevens Creek Dam. I told my mom I was hanging out with Billy today at Bennett school so that she would not get suspicious. We would go up El Camino but take the back way up Lilly St. by the Francia's farm, head into Sunnyvale, and then cut across Henderson behind farmer Jim's cherry orchard, and out to El Camino. I wasn't allowed to go far into Sunnyvale or El Camino on my bike, so of course I had many times. Last year I had gone all the way to Helen Honeyback's house. She lived behind the Sunken Gardens Golf Course.

Helen was one of three girls I liked in fourth grade. The girls heavily outnumbered the boys there for some reason. To add to my popularity, I was from Santa Clara and most of the kids at Bennett were from Sunnyvale. I had the advantage of not arriving with any baggage, except of course Lorraine and the others bussed to Bennett with me from Briarwood. Helen was a fair-haired blonde. Helen was also a bussing victim and had been taken away from Fair Oaks school in Sunnyvale to attend fourth grade at Bennett. Without a doubt, she was one of the smartest girls in school, one of her appealing qualities, so it didn't hurt to be close to her when there was schoolwork to be done. Our relationship usually involved spending recess and lunch together. We shared lots of lunch goodies (There was no cafeteria at Bennett) and occasionally we held hands as we walked around. I decided to take things to the next step by actually accepting an invitation to her house one Saturday morning.

Helen lived two miles up El Camino on Ham Avenue, another short road to nowhere. I had ridden up Lawrence to El Camino that day. When I passed the tomato fields along El Camino, I sped up to quickly get beyond the palm tree-lined road to farmer Jim's house and his cherry orchard. Stories about farmer Jim put fear into all the boys in the area. I could see his two brown dogs, running about near the big house in the distance. We would hear their barking all day long when we were in class at Bennett but rarely see them.

The turn to Helen's house was just before Wolf Road. There were only three or four houses along her street. Construction people were already leveling out land for a tract of houses just before Ham. Newly scraped courts were being laid out behind Helen's clapboard house, directly in front of rows of pines lining a park or something, and tractor dirt roads ran in several directions. When I arrived, I was surprised to see her house was much older than ours and on a big wooded lot without fencing. Mrs. Honeyback met me at the front door. Violin music sounded from the far end of the house. She greeted me by name though I had never met her, and that felt reassuring.

"Helen has five more minutes of practice but come into the living room. She'll be in soon," she said in a soft, inviting voice. As I timidly sat down on a silk white sofa with my bare legs and cutoffs, I expected *Neneh Ruffino* would be in any second to chase me out. Delicate glass objects and dark walnut furniture surrounded me.

It turns out Helen's mother was a classical music teacher. I was not too familiar with orchestral music. I was more into rock and roll, the sounds that drummed from Lyle's bedroom constantly. I'm glad her mom didn't stick around and quiz me on it.

It wasn't long before Helen made her appearance. She looked dressed for Sunday School. She took my hand and led me out back beyond a large patio to an enormous yard of scattered fruit trees and sycamores. I was immediately drawn to the dense pine treetops beyond the property that rose just behind a cyclone metal fence along the back edge of the construction area, at least a hundred yards from the back of Helen's house.

"What's behind all those pine trees?" I asked.

"That's just the Sunken Gardens Golf Course. It was built when I was in first grade," she said without any interest. I insisted we cut through the trees and to the cyclone fence for a close-up look. She wasn't happy about it, especially with her nice clothes on, but she went along. The trees were rooted below, a thirty-foot drop into the course. Helen told me the canyon was once a rock quarry but three years ago a company bought it and converted it into a golf course. Peeking between fence and tree branches, I could see large areas of manicured green lawn below surrounded by pines and palm trees, and on the outer edges of the lawn were huge telephone poles holding up black netting. Fouled-off golf balls sprinkled the edges of the green fairway like an invasion of pesky mushrooms. The severely steep paved road at the far end must have been the entrance. I could see myself biking down to the bottom of it.

"How do you get in there from here?" I asked, expecting Helen to reveal to me her own shortcut, some hole in the fence or a back path. But she came up with nothing. She told me that she had only been there once, in a car, and had never even gotten out of the car. Where's the adventure in that? Her parents had bought this house when she was a baby when the quarry was still there and cherry trees filled most of the space behind it. Her parents had owned some of the property where the cul de sacs were being constructed and they planned to sell their house. They were moving next year to a new house they were having built in Los Gatos.

Helen's mom served us fresh lemonade and petifores on the patio once we returned. It was very civilized, but I kept thinking about biking down into the golf course. I wrapped a couple of frosted French cakes into a paper napkin and slipped them into my pocket when Helen wasn't looking to have for my ride home. We talked about school and our classmates. Helen told me about her music and a recital she was preparing for and even showed me her violin. It was a nice day, but within an hour we had run out of things to talk about. I'm not even sure she owned a bike.

Billy and I knew we were close to the Wolf Road turnoff today when we spotted the tall white and blue Golfland sign along El Camino. Helen Honeyback's house was gone and so was Ham Avenue now. In its place were partially completed apartments and Poplar Avenue. I told Billy about the Sunken Gardens Golf Course, and he looked at me like that was old news. Anyway, we decided to take a spin into the course and check it out. The ride down was great but not so much getting back to the top. Three times down and up was enough. While we caught our breath, we discussed Helen, and Billy pointed out that she was GUD, geographically undesirable, now that she had moved to Los Gatos. We had a good laugh. We thought about checking out Golfland but decided we had better get going. It was still two miles, just to Stevens Creek Road.

Wolf Road was busy, and there were fewer orchards and more houses out that way from the last time I was in that area with my parents. Many of the remaining cherry orchards were tagged with huge plywood painted billboards advertising a new tract coming soon. When we finally reached Stevens Creek Road, we had to make a decision. If we backtracked along Stevens Creek about a quarter mile, we could stop at A&W, or, if we forged ahead, we could stop at the Stevens Creek Store and get a Nehi. In fact, their bottling factory was near the store. We chose to go ahead.

Reaching the little white store at the top of the hill was probably the most difficult part of the ride. After the Nehi plant, Stevens Creek Road headed straight down to a canyon past Blackberry Farm, a private picnic area, where they had a swimming pool, volleyball courts, a playing field and barbecue setups. Stevens Creek ran through it. I had been there once a couple of years back when Willig Freight lines hosted a summer barbecue for employees' families. There was a golf course called Deep Cliff buried in there also. Most of all, it was a good place to collect pollywogs in the creek and swim in the pool until your eyes clouded from too much chlorine.

Once you biked to the bottom of the canyon on Stevens Creek Road, you had to ride up the hill. That was the tough part. Of course, both our bikes were one-speeds. The reward for the climb was the little stucco store at the top. Planted in front of the store was a yellow and red refrigerated three-foot tall cooler full of ice-cold Nehi bottled sodas. I loved the blue cream; Billy had a Nehi orange. Before we left, we got a couple of candy bars and some Bazooka gum.

It was a hot day and the Kaiser concrete trucks were busy in the hills, hauling chunks of the mountainside, churning up dust along Stevens Creek Canyon Road, but we were within a couple of miles of our destination, the dam. The rest of the way was along an up-and-down, winding and narrow road. We were too near our goal to let it bother us. When we reached the top of the canyon, we had reached the dam.

By now it was almost noon, and the parking lot was full of cars and bicycles. Along the concrete top edge of the dam were dozens of mostly teenage bathers. It was a colorful sight of beach towels, bathing suits, and flesh. Most of the bathers were laid out near the dam's top where the concrete angled toward the water's surface some twenty feet below. Their legs rested on the sloping concrete as if it were a reclining chaise lounge for their bodies.

The swimming action took place at the near edge where dirt and weeds met the water's edge, below the exposed concrete dam wall. Our destination was the spillway at the far edge of the dam where water met a long concrete ten-foot wide slide and then disappeared from sight, heading forty yards down to the creek below. The crowd was far younger at the spillway, and predominantly boys, almost all shirtless and in blue jean-cutoffs.

Spillway sliding was a hit and miss proposition. When the reservoir waters were high, nature took over and water flowed torrentially down the spillway. Sometimes it would flow so hard a person would have to be a fool to slide down—too dangerous, and at times there was an undertow where the creek began. Other times, when the dam was low, the spillway was just a concrete shoot. Still kids would show up with flattened cardboard boxes retrieved from behind grocery stores and "dry slide" the spillway. While it was fun, it was also treacherous on the body. The slightest contact with the cement path down was ten times worse than landing on the asphalt when your rollerskates hit the road, because here you just kept scraping against concrete, rocks, glass shards, and any other standing debris, all the way to the bottom. Ideally, we looked for controlled runoffs down the spillway, wet enough to keep you sliding lightly over the crap on the spillway floor.

"You can't have everything," my mom used to say. Today, the spillway was dripping with slushy, mucky water. After the recent heatwave we had, we were lucky there was running water at all. There were probably about ten boys who were actually sliding the spillway. They were the muddy and scraped-up ones. Another group of boys cheered them down. Billy was going down, no question about it. Like the other daredevils, he kept his Keds on. That was the only smart thing he did. By the time he reached the bottom, he was covered in mud, skin-scraped all over, and even had a huge tear in the butt of his cutoffs. Any thought I had had about going down vanished when Billy climbed back up. Billy laughed it off and gave me a bad time for not sliding, and we spent the rest of the afternoon roughhousing in the swim area and checking out the girls, especially the few teenage girls wearing bikinis. At the end of the day, his body scuffs were varying degrees of grapefruit pink and most hidden by his t-shirt, except for the terrible scrape on his knee. Billy's knee scrape—it looked like a moist pink slice of spam—had clotted enough beneath the glob of gum he stuck on it after his spill to stop bleeding by the time we left. We swam, sunburned, and headed for home, but not before we stopped at A&W for fries and frosted mugs of root beer. At least we knew how to stay away from the poison oak.

I was determined that the summer was not going to be a total washout. Being cut from the little league majors because I had to go on vacation early in the season was not the way I wanted my life to be, but I played on the Pirates farm team again when we returned from Los Angeles in the middle of the season. Most of my friends, now eleven or twelve, played in the majors. I argued and pleaded with my parents, but my dad insisted that he could not alter his vacation time at work and that I would like it in L.A. Seeing as how we had gone to L.A. for vacation almost every other year since I was five, it wasn't like I did not know what to expect—another visit with relatives. Besides, they didn't make Lyle go. Why couldn't he just watch me in Santa Clara?

There were only two decent reasons to go to L.A. One was going to Disneyland with my cousins. My second cousin Carol was some kind of secretary for Walt Disney so whenever my other seven, eight, or nine cousins and I were dropped off for the day, we got the royal treatment. We'd walk in with a stack of E-tickets. E-tickets commanded respect. You could go on any ride, from Peter Pan to the Matterhorn, with an E-ticket, and the best part is no parents to boss you around. My older cousins Diane and Steve were in charge, and they would just tell us to meet them at the Main Street Rail Station at a certain time at the end of the day. To our parents the best part was probably the fact it was free, though I do think they slipped Diane and Steve a couple of dollars for watching us. Sometimes we would be so tired by the time the day was done, usually evening near closing time, we would waste an E-ticket on the horse-drawn trolley or the motor bus, just to avoid walking Main Street one more time.

The only time our parents went with us to the park was the first day Disneyland opened when I was five. It was also the last time Lyle had to go on vacation with us to L.A. I don't remember much about the day except that there were lots of people; it was hot, and Fantasyland was closed in the afternoon. All I saw and heard of inside of the castle were flashing red lights and sirens. I know the adults enjoyed celebrity hunting that day. "Oh, there goes Keenen Wynn and his kids," my dad said, near the Swiss Family Robinson tree house.

Out on Tom Sawyer's Island, TV crews were filming Bob Cummings and some other personalities. I was hoping to see Fess Parker, a.k.a. Davy Crockett, close up but didn't. I did get my mom to buy me a coonskin cap in Frontierland, but we didn't see anyone too important unless you count the stars in the Main Street parade who were too far from us to really see. We only guessed when a celebrity was around us in the park by the huge crowd moving through the park like a tidal surge in the sea of people. I do remember my mom and my aunts taking us to the bridge at the entrance to Fantasyland at a predetermined time. Although the castle itself was all cordoned off for the emergency, Disney ushers directed maybe two hundred of us kids under the castle arches and near the bridge, and then they had us run back toward them while they snapped some photographs with the castle as a backdrop.

The second thing I liked about going to L.A. was staying at my Uncle Blaine's house. He was a high school basketball coach who had once been a college star. He and my Aunt MaryJo lived in Whittier on Bluford Avenue with their four kids. They had a swimming pool. I spent hours in it, even late at night. Floating on an inner tube, the pool light shimmering in the water, was my kind of vacation. When the Zazadell cousins showed up, four boys, all near me in age, it was a splash party. My cousins Joyce, Nancy, and Diane traded off playing lifeguard. Steve, like Lyle, avoided family when he could. While my parents visited other relatives in the L.A. area, I tried to stay at Uncle Blaine's.

• • • •

BEING ELEVEN, I WAS a little bigger and stronger than most of the guys playing on the little league farm teams, and most of our games were at elementary school fields like Bracher, Bowers, and Bennett, instead of at the Briarwood Stadium, so I didn't see many of my friends in the afternoons or Saturdays after we got back from L.A. My dad said I would get over it, but I don't think so. Anyway, I still loved playing, and I was one of the best hitters in the league. Of course, the pitching was much slower, and I could often place a hit where I wanted it. I wanted to be sure coaches noticed me for next summer. Pauly's younger brother Johnny, who was too young to play majors, was on my team, and we became good friends. Just like being tossed out of Briarwood to attend Bennett, I felt like I was being ricocheted from my friends by some pinball force out of my control. My dad promised me no vacation next summer until after little league was over.

Last July, Allan and I took intermediate swimming at the War Memorial Pool. We weren't going to be on any swim team so we couldn't see the point of taking advanced lessons this summer when we could just go swimming for fifteen cents any day during free-swim time at the pool. Coach Haines, who supervised the summer swim programs, had already handpicked the real swimmers.

It took about thirty-five minutes to bike to the pool from Allan's house, but we seldom went straight to the pool or straight home. We would always window shop when we got downtown at Santa Clara Sports Shop on Franklin to admire the stuffed polar bear in the front window. We never got tired looking at it. Sometimes we'd stop at the bike shop and check out the ten-speeds or stop and say hello to Phil at the smoke shop.

By that time, scheduled swim classes would be nearly finished, and kids would be sure to be lined up outside the pool dressing room so we would ride around the library park and over to the pool.

Today we locked up our bikes with the rows and rows of other kids' bikes at the steel racks, waited our turn in line, paid our 15 cents, and got a wire basket to put our street clothes into once we had changed into our trunks.

Each basket had a large safety pin clipped onto it that was imprinted with a number that matched one also on the basket. You would pass off your basket of clothes to a teenage attendant who stood behind a Dutch door leading to an enclosed storage room and clip the safety pin to your trunks. It would be your claim-check at the end of the day. Ready for the chlorinated blue depths of the pools, you first had to rinse in the chilling and sobering water tunnel of overhead sprinklers and dip through the chemically treated icy-wet foot canal that stood between you and the pools.

The wading, racing, and diving pools were jammed with kids. Two or three lanes of the racing pool were roped off for coach Haines' swimmers. My goal this summer was to dive from the high dive my first day back at War Memorial. I was more than adequate on the low dive, and my Uncle Blaine's pool had a similar springboard, though much lower, where I got lots of practice, but I had only *jumped* off the twelve-foot high dive at War Memorial. I failed to dive from it last summer and lived with that all year. Even with his lousy eyesight, Allan had done it several times. I just never had the courage to run, spring, and dive, head first, from the high dive.

As he had been on my fight day the first day of second grade, Allan was still my biggest promoter.

"There's really nothing to it," he said. Then he took his turn. Climbing up the twelve-foot ladder, pacing off his distance, he ran to the edge, sprung in the air, and made a perfectly arced dive. I watched from the pavement at least twice before I made a practice *jump* and quickly cleared the pool.

The moment of truth had arrived. After waiting behind another six kids in yet another line, I made my way up the ladder, my heart pounding in my ears. I told myself it was exactly like the low dive. Allan was standing on the concrete walk below yelling inaudible words of encouragement to me. A teenage lifeguard sat in her tall chair, behind sunglasses and a zinc-covered nose, facing my direction at the far corner of the pool. It was now *or later*.

I did everything perfectly as I knifed head first into the pool, except stop before my head hit the cement bottom. My arms had failed to stop me. I was jolted to unreality and was up and out of the water in a blink, or so it seemed. Allan was right there to congratulate me, but I was only thinking how my head hurt.

"I gotta go inside. I hit my head," I told him. I held my open palm on the crown of my head and hurried back to the dressing room. I easily blended in with the crowd and noise, undetected by anyone in charge. Sitting on the pine bench in the changing room for a couple of minutes, I figured I was okay. When I pulled my hand down from my head, I could see my palm was covered in a red Kool-Aid of blood and water. I had cracked my skull, and it hurt.

Allan examined my head and assured me it was just a scrape. At my request, he pulled some toilet paper from a restroom stall for me. I licked a piece of tissue and stuck it to my cut like I had seen Lyle do when he sliced himself shaving and it seemed to work. Neither one of us wanted to involve the pool people. We turned in our safety pins, put on our cutoffs, t-shirts and tennis shoes, and made our way to our bikes. Our wet trunks and towels rolled and secured to our fender racks, we headed for home. My quarter-sized bandage dried in the wind. By the time we got to Franklin Street, we were both ready for an icy A&W root beer in a chilled glass mug. And I pressed the icy mug against my head wound more than once.

I wore my Pirates cap around the house. After about three days, my headache subsided and my abrasion scabbed over, but I never told my parents about the event, fearing they would not let me back in the pool. I have no plans to attempt the high dive again.

· · · ·

THE MOST POPULAR ADULTS in our neighborhood lived on Del Monte Avenue, known to every kid within six blocks. They had no kids of their own. Their garage was loaded with all the games that our parents wouldn't buy, a pool table, a mechanical bowling alley, a collapsible ping pong table, and a genuine Vegas slot machine. Jake and Cindy Molina lured kids up their driveway to their open garage with their Wurlitzer jukebox blaring most Friday nights during the summer. They were our idea of what adulthood should be.

They both worked at Ampex, a company that designs audio and video recording devices. They also knew all the parents in the neighborhood, who thought they were saints for putting up with us kids. Friday right after dinner would usually start off with ping pong challenges. Jake Peavy and Renny Owens were the aces, but we all had a good time, often playing teams. The Molinas provided free popcorn they popped in a full sized glass popper, the kind you'd see at the fair. Sometimes, even some of the neighborhood teenagers showed up. Before I met the Molinas, they knew me, or at least my name. It seems Lyle had a secret he kept well hidden. He had become a pinball wizard of sorts, all because of Jake and Cindy's *Circus Queen* pinball machine. Later, I would find out that everyone at Moonlite Bowl knew him for his flipper skills. So he wasn't studying late at school *every* afternoon, and that explains why so many rolls of quarters would end up missing at home. Of course, my dad too often accused me of pilfering his pen collection money while Lyle was shut up in his room "reading."

Jake and Cindy rented some of their stuff out to church and school groups for bizarres and festivals. In a side storage shed they had a couple of coin-operated kiddie rides, like the blonde mechanical horse you'd see in front of Safeway. They even had a ride with three goofy looking turtles for very little kids that went around like a merry-go-round. They taught us how to dance, and we had big bowling tournaments on the arcade alley. All they wanted was a little bit of company or maybe some kids of their own.

Art, Pauly and I got free tickets to Roller Derby for a Saturday afternoon meet at Sunnyvale High School, where they would set up an entire raised rink on the football field. Cindy knew San Francisco Bay Bomber Joanie Weston personally and Weston was always giving Cindy tickets. Usually they were for the Cow Palace or someplace we couldn't get to. I did not know anybody whose parents would take a bunch of kids to roller derby, but Sunnyvale High was within biking distance.

All you needed was a note signed by a parent and you could pick prunes as a kid. Billy and I got our mothers to sign. But I argued with my mom before she'd put her name on something that would mean her own reputation.

"Picking fruit is hard work," she explained, and she would know, having grown up in the San Joaquin Valley. As a teen, besides working at her father's used furniture store and gas station, her jobs had been primarily in the fields.

"It's not just the picking, it's staying with it. You can't just quit when you get tired. It's hour after hour," she would tell me. Her concern was that I wouldn't last. But we were paid by the box, not by the hour. Besides, Lyle had gotten a job this summer at the cafeteria in the Libby's Cannery in Sunnyvale, and the two years before that he had a job as a shed boy, hauling drying trays of cots and fruit boxes. I needed an income of my own. I wanted a ten-speed some day just like my cousin Steve's.

One advantage of working in widow Kiely's prune orchard was its proximity to our house. It was just across the highway, not even sixty yards from my bedroom window. On hot summer nights, the window cranked open for a breeze, the sweet aroma of plums would overpower other senses, even the sounds of cars whining along Lawrence Station Road. The Kiely house was a gingerbread white Victorian that set just off Lawrence Station Road. It was surrounded by box hedges and red and yellow rose bushes, neatly manicured. In all the years we lived on Cabrillo, I never once saw widow Kiely come out of the house. Apparently, Mr. Kiely, one of a long line of Kielys in the area, had died before we moved there in 1957, and widow Kiely managed the farm from within her house, but my mother claimed Mrs. Kiely worked in her rose garden every morning before I was ever out of bed. Once in a great while, a family of relatives would visit Mrs. Kiely, and Art and I from my front yard would watch some of the kids playing around behind an old rusted corrugated shed, actually pushing and riding the dry yard carts back and forth on the rails at the backside of the orchard, having fun that we envied from a distance.

For three summers I had watched people work the prunes across the street. It looked easier than picking cots or cherries. For one thing, prunes were already on the ground when you simply put them into the galvanized buckets and then to large wooden lugs, lugs we would sometimes swipe to use for skate carts we would construct. Surely, gathering up the ripe purple plums couldn't be that difficult, I thought. But I didn't take into account that all of the work was in the dirt. At the crack of dawn, the farm boss, a no-nonsense leathery-skinned Filipino man, would go to rows of fertile trees to be picked and, with a long pole, artfully startle the waxy purple plums down from sagging branches to join other fallen fruit that gravity had already deposed. A dense round rug of dull purple would make a skirt below each partially-defrocked tree and the tedious job of picking would begin.

Billy and I reported for picking at seven a.m. so already things were kind of dim to two sleepyheads, but we could already feel the bright sun's heat about to beat down on us. The boss accepted our signed notes, explained the procedure to us and about ten other people, most of them adult seasoned workers, assigned each of us a row of trees to work, and gave us each two buckets and a stub of chalk to mark our lugs once they were filled with prunes. Two buckets would fill a lug. All we had to do was fill empty wooden lugs set by the trees to be picked and mark them as our own. We got thirty cents for every lug we filled. We were looking forward to making some easy money.

It was hard, dirty, sticky work. It was all done in the dirt, and it didn't take very long to realize it would take a long time to fill just one tall bucket, let alone one of those big lugs. And every time you cleared an area, you had to drag the getting-heavier bucket or lug along behind you over the dirt. Within an hour, my back and knees were killing me. Dirt clods were everywhere I stepped or knelt. My hands and pants and t-shirt were wet with mushy fruit from the ripe plums in no time and soon became caked with dirt transformed to sticky paste. Billy and I were both a sweaty mess almost instantly, and the flies, especially the annoying fruit flies, seemed more interested in buzzing our heads and ears than in the plums. It was also lonely work. There was no time to chat. You had your own trees to work by yourself. Despite that, Billy distracted me when he could.

"Benny. Come here," Billy called out to me from his knees under a tree the next row over.

"What? I've gotta keep working. What d'ya want?"

"Look." I looked down at his lug. He was already on his second lug, and he certainly didn't appear to be working any harder than I had been.

"How did you pick those so fast?" I asked, waiting for his advice.

"I lined the bottom with dirt clods just before I poured my first bucket." He could have been picking more prunes in the time it probably took to disguise his box.

"That's dumb, man. You're gonna get fired. Your number 'll be on the lugs."

"By the time the old guy sorts the lugs, I'll be paid and long gone," Billy assured me. What Billy hadn't taken in to account was that the boss wasn't born yesterday. When our first lugs were hoisted on the truck later in the morning, he inspected each lug before he logged it on his clipboard.

Billy was gone long before lunch. I, on the other hand, was struggling to fill my fourth lug of the morning. I looked up and like a godsend, there was my mother. She asked me if I was tired, but she already knew the answer to that. She tossed me my baseball cap, grabbed my other bucket, got down on her knees, and helped me earn my last thirty cents picking prunes. At least I made it until noon. My high-top Converse All-Stars never did come clean.

• • • •

MRS. MOLLOY HOSTED play times, homework times, and parties at her house. I don't think there was a dad around. The last full-blown birthday party I went to was at Susan's when she turned eleven, the summer of 1961. Three weeks prior to the actual party, Mrs. Molloy even hosted a smaller party of eight kids, myself included, to make cutout invitations to Susan's birthday party. It seemed as if our entire fifth grade class attended the big party that Saturday. We had the best of everything. A neighborhood teenage magician in a black suit did multiple card tricks with dovetail shuffles and performed a shell game with plastic walnuts. There were party favors (jacks, marbles, Play-Doh, Silly Putty, Slinkys, and balsa wood gliders), games, and lots of candy and food. We played Pin the Tail on the Donkey, Pass the Parcel, and Telephone, and broke a giant piñata loaded with hard candy that Art's mom had gotten from Mexico. When it came time to blow out the candles, we all helped. We had enough chunks of German chocolate cake and scoops of vanilla ice cream to make you sick. The cake was made especially for Susan at Wilson's Jewel Bakery downtown. The ice cream was hand-packed in a big cardboard tub from Mission Creamery.

Susan had recorded a thank you speech for us on her new portable tape recorder, which was enclosed in what looked like a lady's cosmetic case, with tab buttons and two little plastic reels. She proudly sat at the table, removed one curled hand from her cornflower blue cardigan pocket, and with her rickety index finger, hit the play button. In Susan's deep but crackly voice the recorder played:

"I w-a-n-t to t-h-a-n-k ev-er-y-bo-dy for com-ing to m-y par-ty and be-ing my fri-end." It was a kids' party truly beyond the call of duty for a parent. It was also Susan's last.

In the fall, Susan didn't show up for sixth grade. Her trike was nowhere to be seen, and nobody dared ask. When Art and I would pass by her house sometimes on the way to school, the house was always dark and closed up. We didn't talk about it. Sometime in November, I saw Mrs. Molloy walking home alone from Safeway, her grocery cart in tow.

F*all 1961*

What's with school boards? In July my parents got another official letter. This time we suspected it was coming because Miss Childrey had prepared us. She went on for at least the last month of school how we were a special class, very talented and mature. But we knew better. Her reasons had to do with the fact that again schools were running out of room in Santa Clara. We were more than ready for middle school at Jefferson, but Jefferson was probably not going to be ready for us. For all Miss Childrey had done for us this year, she couldn't bring smiles to our faces this time.

Our class and Mrs. Dunnett's fifth-grade class were not going to be attending Jefferson in the fall for sixth grade, but we would not stay another year at Briarwood like others had before us. We would be at Monticello elementary, another new school that stood on the backside of Jefferson's playing field. By last spring, we had already imagined ourselves at Jefferson middle school in September as sixth-graders. Now we would have to wait at least another half year while a new wing was being built at Jefferson. Except for P.E. and our elective classes, when we would trek the distance to Jefferson as entire classes, we would be two hundred yards away, separated from the rest of the middle schoolers. It had many of the markings of my fourth grade bussing experience at Bennett. Again, I was lucky enough to be chosen. Again, I would be at a separate school. Again, there was no cafeteria. Again, I would not see a lot of my friends, those who had not been in Miss Childrey's or Mrs. Dunnett's class in fifth grade. That included Carl. We were herded from the rest of Monticello elementary and fenced off from Jefferson middle school. We were given new labels. We were the A-1 and A-2 sections. We could call ourselves Jefferson students, but we were segregated.

Even at eleven years old, everyone knew what the labels meant. We were supposedly the smart kids. I didn't like being separated like that. It was an excuse to keep us away from friends of our choosing. We didn't get to share any of our classes with them, eat lunch with them, or even talk to them. It was prison. Like inmates, we had a special bond. After all, we did everything together. We had a single wing of three classrooms at the elementary school. The sixty of us would be shuffled up for math and science class in the third classroom and sent off in groups for P.E., shop, sewing, music, or art.

Mrs. Musson, our homeroom teacher, was nice enough, but even she knew it was hard on us being separated from our other friends. When we talked about current events that fall during social studies class, several of us asked Mrs. Musson if our being separated from our friends at Jefferson, fence and all, wasn't a lot like the Berlin Wall going up last month in East Germany. Mrs. Musson spent the first three months of the year with her own kind of propaganda, selling us on how we were to be the first class in the new Jefferson wing, where everything would be brand new. Newness had gotten old a long time ago.

The only co-ed elective we had was music, twice a week at Jefferson. Our music teacher, Mr. Holcomb, was an extraordinary man. He was dedicated to the performing arts, and he brought out the music in all of us. From "My Knapsack on My Back" to "Yellow Bird," our music class was loud if not harmonic. For the most part, the boys drowned out the girls as we sang traditional folksongs every other day. Even those most averse to singing joined in when Mr. Holcomb took the stage, his rich tenor voice, enthusiastically inviting you to find joy in singing.

Mr. Holcomb was a big man, six foot-three, pale skin, and jet-black hair. He was dramatic in every sense of the word. He was always performing in some municipal production. This year it was "Madame Butterfly." He was playing the role of an American Naval officer, B.F. Pinkerton. We learned all about the tragic operatic story and listened to opera on 78s he brought to class. You could hear a pin drop when Mr. Holcomb narrated the story and carefully placed the phono arm at just the right spot on the record for the opera to unfold. He sang along when his character performed. We were in awe.

Another day he displayed stage props in class, several elaborate Japanese kimonos, a large Japanese silk screen, and even a stage hara-kiri dagger with a carved bone sheath and handle. We learned about geishas and teas and etiquette, and Mr. Holcomb was himself dressed in a dark blue kimono and wore full stage makeup. The red lipstick was a bit too much for most of us, especially the boys, but he made an impression on us.

Mr. Holcomb would also bring professionals to class. He introduced us to Albert Muller, a famous fourth-generation violinmaker from San Francisco who had learned his trade from his German-born grandfather.

Atop three large tables set up in the music room were violin-making tools—a multitude of knives, scrapers, and planes—woods, models, violins and their parts in stages of the process, even genuine horse hair used for the bows. He told us it took him up to 150 days to complete one instrument. He talked to us about famous violins and violinists. He even brought a Stradivari model pattern from the 1700s he used for some of his violins. To assist him with all his master craftsmanship was none other than Reginald Pudlow. Reginald had earned our respect as a musician well before sixth grade. He, his twin sisters, and his mom had played as a string quartet at several Briarwood open house events. Reginald was already first violinist in the Jefferson orchestra. At the end of Mr. Muller's presentation, Reginald played a Vitali sonata on one of Mr. Muller's violins to a standing ovation from our class. Reggie was a celebrity at Jefferson.

• • • •

RITA MITCHELL'S SMILE was contagious, and she was definitely one happy camper when we sang. I cannot remember a time she did not put a bright light on even in the darkest of times. Early in our Briarwood days she would be the first to console you if you had a bad day with the likes of Mrs. Fay or did poorly on a test or report card. No one could bellow out "This Land is Your Land" like Rita. Like Sarah Sanderson, Rita was on the tall side, though most of the girls in our class now were taller than the boys. Long ago, Sarah had lost the name "too tall."

Rita took the fact that we were all in this Monticello thing together and helped to make us a community outside of school. She decided what we needed was our own version of Record Hop, not televised, of course, but a rock-and-roll dance party, something like the Wutzit Club out on Newhall that we only had heard about from our teenage brothers and sisters. So one Saturday evening in late September at her house in the garage, we had our first of many boy-girl dance parties. A couple more girls than guys, there were about two dozen of us—all from Mrs. Musson's or Mrs. Snyder's class (the other exiled sixth grade bunch), and we had known each other since most of grade school. Several mothers prepared some pretty good food for us, and we learned about hors d' oeuvres. The party was also dressy. Guys wore penny loafers, slacks, short sleeve dress shirts and thin neckties. Lyle taught me to tie a Windsor knot. Unlike school and a few church dances I had attended, where people mulled around and lots of guys never danced, nobody was afraid here. From the Marcels' "Blue Moon" to Dion's "Runaround Sue," we would find joy in music. "Limbo Rock" was a highlight of the night. Someone even brought an official limbo kit. Rita's party was such a success that we had one sometimes twice a month in someone else's garage. None of the guys ever hosted. There was always a portable record player set up on a card table or garage workbench, and we'd all bring a few 45s to play. I bought my first Ricky Nelson record at Bob's Pharmacy just for the dances. It was the beginning of romance for some of us. For others, it was a place to hang out with people you had known for a long time.

"Carlotta O'Reilly," Mrs. Musson called out, taking attendance the first day of sixth grade. "It's Lottie," Carlotta responded, and Michael and I looked at each other with a "what's with that?" kind of expression. But, like her name, Carlotta had changed. I guess I understood that. I often told people my name was Ben, not Benny. She was no longer the Tomboy we used to know. She wore her dresses comfortably and let her brown hair flow freely. All the guys thought she was hot. It was the other *girls* who were now competitive with her, and not on the school playing field.

So we did become a clique of sorts. Except for baseball, I hung around with only my A-1 friends. Some time after spring break, we all moved to the new wing of Jefferson, but by then it was too late for us to become truly part of Jefferson, and everyone sensed it. I never saw Carl anymore. Even Pauly and I only talked at school in passing. A-1 kids still had all our classes together, ate together, and hung out as if we were still at Monticello. We were the outsiders. Our former friends had established their patterns, and so had we.

My mother and father argued about Lyle moving out, all the way home from Hayward that Sunday night. I was in the backseat, not very successfully trying to stay awake.

"But, Pa. I'm old enough to take care of myself now. You don't need me at the Ponderosa every day. I'll just be 'cross town, and it's a lot closer to school," argued Little Joe to convince his dad.

Wait. They are arguing about Lyle moving to San Jose State campus. How did Little Joe get into the conversation? I must have drifted off.

We were returning from a full day at Aunt Betty and Uncle Cliff's. Sunday was loaded with new things. In the morning, Steve and I walked around the corner to Pepper Gomez's house. That was a treat. All this time, Pepper Gomez, a world-wrestling champion, the "man with the cast iron stomach," had been living just six houses from my cousin's. Steve didn't even know it until last week when he happened to see Pepper working out on a punching bag in his garage.

Pepper turned out to be a really nice guy. He even pulled a half nelson on Steve's head when we got there—not a serious one, of course. His garage was a fully equipped weight room, barbells, a lifting bench, several jump ropes, and genuine Everlast speed and punching bags. He even had a life-size color poster of himself wearing a little red Speedo in the wrestling ring tacked on his garage back wall. Pepper told us how he started out as a bodybuilder on Muscle Beach in LA. Today he was getting ready to wrestle Rays Stevens next weekend at the Oakland Arena, but he was also watching his three little boys who were running all over the garage. He entertained us for a few minutes on his speed bag and gave each of us a fight promotion flier that he personally autographed before we left.

For dinner that evening my Aunt Betty prepared pork chops, potatoes au Gratin and a strange vegetable called an artichoke. I had never had one before that day. While it was a lot of work to eat the inside tips of the leaves and work your way to the meaty center, they became my new favorite vegetable.

But the evening wasn't over. The real reason we were there started at seven that night. For the first time, *Walt Disney's Wonderful World of Color* was on in living color on Sunday night, followed by *Bonanza*. Betty and Cliff were the first people we knew to have a color TV, a huge, 23", Zenith color console. I know it cost over three hundred dollars.

So somehow, half asleep on the drive home, I had gotten Little Joe into my parents argument about Lyle moving out of the house. Sometime toward the end of the month, Lyle packed his clothes into his Ford Customline and moved to an apartment on South 15th Street in San Jose with Ron Maloney and Bob Ream. Our house would never be the same.

At San Jose State College, Lyle met a guy who knew cars. He made Lyle a trade, and Lyle finally got the car of his dreams. His canary yellow '55 Chevy two-door hardtop looked the part, but could only be counted on to not be counted on, and Lyle was too student-poor to do anything about it. The Chevy burned oil bad. On his fairly regular weekend visits to home, Lyle would raid the refrigerator, exchange some dirty laundry for fresh my mother had done for him during the week, and sandblast the Chevy's eight fouled spark plugs at Vierra Shell on El Camino and Kiely for ten cents a plug. When the oil gauge got too low, Lyle would get free used crankcase oil from Gil to get by another week. The ten mile trips Lyle made home were the longest trips he dared to take in the Chevy.

Lyle's Chevy looked good parked in front of the house, with a Turtle Wax shine, sparkling chrome baby moons and freshly scrubbed whitewalls, but Lyle wasn't allowed to park it on the driveway where it was bound to blacken the concrete with oil spots. When he'd go back to school, my mother would often brush some Tide onto the oil splotches on the street.

My dad wasn't happy that Lyle had traded away the problem-free Customline for what he called a "mechanical piece of crap," but he eventually lent Lyle half the cost of a rebuilt engine. Cousin Bill was going to put it in for nothing at a garage out near Alviso where he had been working for the past three months. Things were looking better.

Sunday, Roger Maris broke the Babe's home run record, and Lyle dropped off the Chevy at Bill's apartment on Benton, handed Bill the keys and sixty dollars. A week later, there was no trace of Bill, the Chevy, or the money.

I heard my mother say to my dad a few days later, "Well, you know how he is."

Lyle now drives a well-behaved but ugly old black pickup my dad bought from his buddy Spivey for him. Lyle has learned not to complain.

Winter 1961

The gates were open today. My mother and I stood at the kitchen window washing dishes when the funeral procession from Saint Lawrence the Martyr turned right down Cabrillo Avenue from the former "street to nowhere," now Lawrence Court, led by a black hurst carrying Neneh Ruffino.

"There goes Neneh making the last journey past the house that she so loved. What a shame," my mother commented to no one in particular. Then we watched in silence as the long procession of cars turned onto Cabrillo east on way to the Santa Clara Catholic Cemetery.

She'd been sick only a few months but lost her fight to a brain tumor quickly. During that time, the Ruffinos turned inward. Paul, Teddy, and Donny were never outside. The Galaxy 500 was never in the driveway.

"It's such a tragedy. You know I don't think I have ever met anyone as devoted to her husband as Neneh, and she took such good care of herself, always exercising and eating right, and she never missed mass. You just never know. I wonder who will take care of the boys and Paolo," our neighbor Emma rattled on to my mom as she applied a Tony's home permanent with her plastic gloves to my mother's sopping-wet chestnut hair. Ammonia fumes filled the house for hours.

Shortly after the funeral, Neneh's younger sister came to stay at the house with the boys. At first glance, you would think she was Neneh sweeping in the garage. She looked that much like her. She stayed and routines returned at the Ruffino house. She never left. Paul, on the other hand, enlisted in the United States Army that September. Teddy bragged that Paul was an official United States advisor in a country called Vietnam.

Carl Price was too early and Neneh Ruffino was too late. Timing is everything. It snowed Sunday morning in Santa Clara, just in time for Art's confirmation practice. Sunday, January 21, kids in the bay area awoke to a flannel-thin blanket of snow. The Kiely prune orchard was a winter wonderland. It was a miracle, and up and down Cabrillo, kids were doing their best to make a snow festival out of the scrim of snow that was quickly disappearing by the time we were all out of bed. Tennis shoe footprints and skidmarks defaced the front lawns of houses where we all tried to gather enough white powder both front and backyard to construct a snowman, even if that meant not rolling but globbing snow, slush, mud and debris to hold shape long enough to say, "I built a snowman." Those lucky enough to have a family car parked in a driveway were at an advantage and had an extra layer of pure snow they bare-handedly slid off the car's metal snow runs to add to their snow creations or to crush into snowballs. It was all very wet and so were we.

I kept expecting Art to show up, but he never did. When I finally got through to his house on the busy phone, Esther told me he was across the street at Saint Lawrence practicing in the rec hall for something called confirmation. As I stretched the white phone receiver from the kitchen wall, I could just see from the front window the back gates of Saint Lawrence facing Cabrillo were closed.

Later, Art would tell us all about it. How he and his buddies were put on the spot rehearsing responses to catechism questions a new Catholic Bishop *might* throw at them—Bishop Mitty had died in October—all the time distracted by the once-in-a-lifetime snowfall outside the gates, and practicing how to march orderly in procession indoors to impress the Bishop who would only be present at the real thing while another real thing was quickly melting away just outside. One nun told them God was testing their faith with the temptation of snow. And then he told us about Jimmy Ellis who refused to answer anymore to Sister Peter on our snow day and called her bluff, walking out of confirmation practice when she told him after he failed to pay attention one too many times that he didn't *have* to complete confirmation, ever. It reminded me of Billy Preacher refusing to take the bus to school anymore in fourth grade. Jimmy was a hero to the other kids at confirmation practice, but no one had guts enough to applaud him. He has not shown up at Saint Lawrence the Martyr since and proudly calls himself a "fallen Catholic" whenever asked about it. When we later recapped our snow stories in classes on Monday, Carl told everyone at school his only regret was not collecting used-Christmas trees for snow wars this year.

The last time we played flag football on the Owens field was in February the day after Jackie Kennedy led a tour of the White House on national TV. The White House was interesting, but most of my friends at school that Thursday talked more about the good-looking First Lady than the White House. On the Owens field we wore strips of cotton sheets for flags but there was more tackling than flag pulling in the game. And the only girl tough enough for that kind of play was Nadine Padilla. Razor thin and quick, Nadine had always been part of our block games, but she hadn't been around recently. She was Renny's current girlfriend and two years ahead of Pauly and me in school. Since last summer she had developed into more a woman than we were used to. She seemed to know it, too, and being in a pile up after a play with her in it was the object of most of the boys out there. We were silently thankful to Renny for bringing her with him. Football had taken on new dimensions, and we didn't exactly know the rules. We knew those weren't shoulder pads she was wearing. We played until the sun went down that evening.

This morning Astronaut John Glenn drank orange Tang he mixed in a Zero-G pouch for breakfast while making the first manned orbits around the earth, enjoying the view from *Friendship 7.* I mixed my tablespoon of Tang powder that morning from a gallon jar I retrieved from the bottom kitchen cabinet where we keep at least three other oversize jars of Tang that we had been drinking for many years before Tang ever orbited earth, and then I watched the traffic whiz by on Lawrence Station Road from my kitchen window. Tang is one of many random tokens of friendship my dad now and then gets from customers while driving truck.

Right after we moved to Santa Clara my dad came home with a 25-pound square tin of Carnation malted milk powder that the creamery manager gave him. My mother makes malted shakes for us using her black-handled hand crank eggbeater. Sometimes she sneaks a raw egg into her blended concoctions and tells us it's good for us. I have powdered malt on everything from chocolate ice cream to Kellogg's cornflakes. We keep the huge tin on a low kitchen shelf right by the Tang so I can serve myself with less risk of spilling sticky chalky malt. Even now it is still a challenge to remove the big screw lid from the top of the tin and scoop without spilling. I can smell the sweet malt barley just by thinking about it.

Throughout the spring, the perfume of creamy white pompon mums also sweetens our house. Mr. Shibata at Mt. Eden's Wholesale Flowers in Fremont personally readies a huge foot-long stemmed bouquet of perfect, curled petaled flowers wrapped in green waxed paper for my dad nearly every Friday for him to take home to mother.

At least once a month my dad brings home a huge chunk of fresh Precious mozzarella cheese from the California Cheese Company out on North 30th in San Jose right next to Highway 101. My dad works a couple of Sunday mornings each month loading cardboard boxes of cheese into an empty semi-trailer in the parking area for Mr. Morino and his son Angelo, who are always there dressed in tailored suits to supervise the Sabbath-Day operation. The Pontiac holds onto the pale cheese aroma for several days after dad brings the reward home.

And dad always carries stapled pairs of Wells Lamont saddle tan cowhide work gloves in his car trunk or spare tire well. He makes a dollar for every pair he sells for his friend Pete, a factory distributor. One day Pete gave dad a two-foot square box of men's and women's plastic dress belts, in various colors and sizes but all Garter snake thin, some inlaid with decorative patterned strips of silver or gold plastic and a few with studded rhinestones. At one time there were probably a hundred belts coiled and tangled up in the box. Lyle and Maloney like to wear them with their white Levi's. We have belts for life and Lyle and I are always letting our friends dig through the box in the garage for themselves. I have found many other uses for them when I need a strap or even a rhinestone for something.

Today we are going to Larson Ladder on Martin Avenue, a trip my dad makes at least four times a year. We pile the rear of the Tempest station wagon with pieces of yellow pine router-grooved steps, the scraps from three-legged orchard ladders Charlie Larson and his crew build. We will load them in the woodbin my dad built along side the house next to the chimney. Dad has taught me newspaper, walnut shells, and Larsen Ladder steps kindle a good family room fire.

The peculiar gifts of friendship and his long hours at work are most of what we know of my dad's life driving truck. I can't remember a morning when I've gotten up before my dad. Even during school months, he is gone to work before Lyle or I crawl out of bed. We can tell how close it is to having to get up by my dad's morning routine. It's all about sounds that invade sleep. First, it's his morning coughing and hacking, which sometimes goes on throughout the rest of his morning ritual. Then it's kitchen sink water filling the Pyrex glass coffee percolator. While the coffee begins to burp and bubble on the range, the shower splashes in their bathroom against flesh, tile and glass. Then it's coffee at the kitchen table with the slow rhythmic spoon clinking against his coffee cup as he stirs sugar and Carnation condensed milk into his cup, over and over again while he reads the *Mercury News*, which we hear him crease as he folds back pages. The solo conversation is always the same. "I'm tired.... I'm so tired I can hardly keep my eyes open." I think to myself in bed, *"You wouldn't be so tired if you didn't get up so early."* But if I actually said something it would mean waking to consciousness. A couple of slaps of Lectric Shave on the jaw, then comes the rising and falling buzz of the Remington as he shaves at the table. That's followed with a vigorous rub of Old Spice on the hands and several finishing pats on his face. I hear him brushing and blowing on the razor heads before he pops the razor case closed. He is almost gone. By this time my mother is up and she has bagged his lunch. It's mumbles between them before he warms the car in the garage for a long five minutes before the springs settle with the garage door closing. It's a pattern that's both annoying and comforting. In another half hour Lyle and I will begin our own routines, but at least the rest of the world will be up with us.

When I was eight, my dad came home in his bright yellow and blue Willig bobtail to stop for lunch. It is the only time I have actually seen him drive on the job outside of the trucking yard I have visited a couple of times. When lunch was over, he showed me around the truck's cab and then drove off down Lawrence Station Road. That day our cat Wally disappeared. Just last week my dad confessed that when he drove away that day the cat had been chewed up in the wheel well of the truck. I guess he told me because he was tired of my hoping Wally would return.

CHAPTER 18

S *pring 1962*
    One early May afternoon after school, Allan and I rode our bikes down to the Santa Clara A&W on Franklin Street. We had an hour and a half to kill before baseball practice at Briarwood. I had finally made it to the majors, and Allan and I were both on Grandview. The journey to A&W was at least three miles away, but worth the ride. You could now buy a paper, coned-shaped "take-home" root beer quart for two bits. A quart of root beer was just about the right amount for an eleven-year-old. We were making good use of our time. We were cruising along on our bikes up Warburton, heading for home, goofing around, one hand on the handlebars, the other on our root beers. When I had thoroughly finished off my cone, I threw the empty behind me and over my head into the street. My toss got a good laugh from Allan. My intention was to wheel back around and crush it at high speed on my bike. Just as my A&W missile went whirling into the air, the all-too-loud blare of a police siren blasted our ears. It was a Santa Clara black and white behind us, and we were busted. I composed myself as best I could, though I was on the verge of tears as I tried to explain to the uniformed officer who had us put our bikes on their kick stands and stand on the curb as he lectured us about littering and tickets and talking to our parents that *I wasn't really littering.* My dad would kill me if he found out about this. Finally, the officer relented, but first he made us answer an impossible question:

"You know I'm a cop, right?" We nodded. "So. What does the word 'cop' stand for?" Allan and I stood there with stupid expressions on our face, trying to guess what he was getting at. We figured it had to be some kind of civics lesson about how the law stands for respect or pride or some kind of adult wisdom. He could see he had us.

"Now when you go back to school tomorrow you ask your teacher the same question. Cop stands for 'constable on patrol' and you never know when one might catch you littering." He laughed at his own joke so we forced a smile to humor him. "I'll let you off this time because you seem like pretty good kids. Now go pick that up and don't you ever litter again." To this day, whenever I see someone litter I think about that Santa Clara cop, a constable on patrol.

Allan and I cut through Briarwood schoolyard and then the field on our bikes to get to Allan's house for our baseball gloves. His backyard faced Briarwood School—how convenient. Like the fence in Art's yard, his was equipped with a sliding slat. When they built the school, they had added a six-foot cyclone fence in front of all the neighborhood wooden fences, surrounding the back edges of the school. That made a lot of neighboring kids unhappy. Unlike the cyclone gate the Catholics put up that stopped me from getting to Art's back fence, there was still just enough space between the metal and wood fences at Briarwood to nimbly push through on bikes at a few openings along the field, and we quickly made that space a beaten path. Since Allan's house was just three doors down from the alley on Nobili, we had access between the two fences where the alley opened to the school grounds. We left our bikes leaning against the wood fence behind Allan's house and entered his yard the way any kid would, through the slat. Before we headed off to practice, Allan insisted I hear some of the new "First Family" album his brother Alex bought last week. A guy who sounds just like President Kennedy made the record. We were chomping on cherry Popsicles, listening to the jokes, and laughing it up when the phone rang. It was Allan's Uncle Mike. He told Allan to get to his house immediately. Something important was up, because Allan almost always had the run of the neighborhood 'til way after dark.

"I gotta go. Tell Coach Ramsey my uncle called."

" 'kay. See you later." I went to practice by myself. On my way home, from a distance, I could see Allan's bike behind the cyclone fence, still leaning against his yard fence.

Allan didn't show up for school the next day, but Sarah told me when she cut through Briarwood on the way to Monticello she didn't see his bike along the fence. Mrs. Musson read the morning bulletin as usual, and then said, "Children, I have a special announcement to make. Allan Callahan's brother Alex has had a serious car accident so Allan won't be in school for a while. Let's all have good thoughts and say a prayer for Allan and his brother."

By morning break, word was out that Alex was dead. There were rumors about drinking and drag racing. It was the talk of the school, and A-1 kids mixed more with the other kids that day than usual. The truth was Allan's dad was the tow truck driver called to the scene of the accident. Alex had lost control of his Plymouth Special Deluxe and crashed into a street pole. He died instantly.

Allan did not return to finish 6th grade with us. He was also a "no show" for little league that summer. We were all afraid to knock on his door. Little did I know I would not see him again.

Michelle McClintock had all the softness her father lacked. Her long blonde hair, soft blue eyes, and delicately shaped face made all my friends take notice. When playing out back at Michael's, we would frequently hear her lilting voice as she practiced singing to her 45's in her bedroom. She knew all of the Patsy Cline, Shelley Fabares, and Connie Frances hits. Although I never heard her perform in the choir, she was often a soloist in junior high and high school. One year she even starred in a Buchser High musical. I don't know how she ever convinced her father to let her do that. But the pinnacle of her career came the May night she debuted her song on KNTV's Record Hop, live for all of us to see and hear.

"Let's hear it for Buchser High's own Michelle McClintock and her single "Love Him."

Though the song was a little too sappy for my taste, it was a hit the next morning at school, and so was Michael. Michelle was the topic of schoolyard discussions for weeks. I looked for the record at Campi's Music at Valley Fair but never found it.

Michael told me later Michelle came home immediately after the Record Hop performance that night, escorted by her father. There was a big argument in the house, threats and ultimatums, and doors slamming. Her friends had planned a debut celebration at someone else's house, but Michelle was not allowed to attend. Too many boys, I guess. She spent the rest of the night and weekend crying in her bedroom. Her dad even pulled the pink princess phone from her room. Not too long after that, Michael's house went up for sale. His father had been re-assigned to Cape Canaveral, Florida, and just like that, Michael was no longer part of our lives.

Briarwood Little League was expanding, and teams practiced at every available field in our area. My last year of Briarwood Little League, Bennett school was added to the practice fields on the schedule. Grandview practiced there Tuesday afternoons. It didn't take us very long to take advantage of the school's location, surrounded on two sides by familiar orchards.

Everyone on the team rode bikes to practice, except of course Coach Ramsey's son David, who always arrived along with all the gear by pickup with his father. Practice was pretty routine, loosening up by jogging around the field and stretching, and then outfielders shagging fly balls hit by Assistant Coach Smith, who always wore tan Bermuda shorts and tall black socks and looked less athletic than anyone out there; infielders practiced game situations with Coach Ramsey drumming grounders from the plate before we all took hitting practice against our own pitchers.

We were a fairly good team, especially with Pauly at shortstop, Johnny at third (Johnny was moved up to first-string when Allan left), and Billy at second. Because Billy lived on the west side of

Lawrence and actually in Sunnyvale, he shouldn't have been in Briarwood Little League, but he said his dad, an engineer at Westinghouse, pulled some strings. Unfortunately, Carl was catcher for Gallenkamp and not us, and I was kinda losing touch with him. Art was now the Texaco Fire Chiefs second baseman and sometimes pitched. I played first base for Grandview most of the time, though I was definitely the weakest hitter of the infielders. At least I was left-handed. I was strong enough when I connected, I just never could figure out a curve. I wish I had had some more adult coaching like some of the kids whose dads practiced at home with them. Baseball was never a priority for my dad. Besides, he had two jobs and often wouldn't get home before nine at night, but those are just excuses for my lack of talent. Other kids like Pauly and Johnny were naturals. Billy made up for any skills he lacked with his size. When he connected, the ball was hit hard. He led in home runs hit on our team. Only Bobby Huber on the NY Sausage team had more home runs. When Billy covered second, runners thought twice about sliding into a wall of brick.

After a productive first practice at Bennett field, there was a good hour of sunlight left so about seven of us decided to do some exploring on our bikes. We waited for Coach Ramsey and Smith to leave and then discussed a proposition Billy had for us. Actually, Billy did the talking. He lived close to the school in distance, near the Corn Palace, but on the other side of farmer Jim's bing cherry orchard, northwest of the school. It was a long journey if you took the streets to his house.

Billy delivered the weekly *Santa Clara Journal* on Wednesday afternoons throughout the neighborhood. We seldom had practice on Wednesdays so I would occasionally help him stuff inserts and fold and band his papers before he went out. He had the biggest route in all of Santa Clara, with over three hundred papers to deliver. Though the paper was technically free to anyone who lived in the

Santa Clara vicinity and parts of Sunnyvale, once a month he would go to houses and apartments where he had delivered and ask for volunteer subscription fees of thirty-five cents per month. The Journal awarded him several times for his record collections with certificates—never extra money. He did get a nickel for every collection he made. Billy could talk people into things. This afternoon was to be no different. His plan was for us to raid the bing orchard, big time.

It was almost expected that kids would take a few cherries as they cut through the orchards. Even mothers would help themselves to cherries from the out-of-site trees or those closest to the roads. But farmers didn't like thieves, and more farmers were posting no trespassing signs as their orchards became surrounded by more houses, schools and shopping centers, and some farmers had shotguns ready loaded with rock salt shells they could shoot in the direction of bird or human intruders.

Since Bennett school opened, farmer Jim had made himself particularly visible to kids at the school, hoping to keep them at bay during cherry season. He had a couple of big loud brown dogs that were always in his pickup bed when he left the main house that was tucked far into the orchard, probably a hundred-fifty yards west of the schoolyard. The only real road to the house was a long gravel and dirt driveway defined by towering palm trees from El Camino. The paved road to Bennett was around the block, off Lawrence Station Road, a quarter mile north of El Camino and just up from my house. Of course every kid at Bennett had stories about the shotgun farmer Jim always carried with him, but I never knew anyone who had actually seen a gun of any kind. I am not even sure if his name was farmer Jim, but all the kids in the area knew which orchard you meant when you mentioned him.

Billy's plan was for the seven of us to spread out and quietly walk our bikes some twenty yards into the orchard at the back side of the baseball field near the street to nowhere, where the bings were visibly plentiful, deep garnet, the sweetest nearly black, and ready for picking. The hired workers would show up to pick these cherries any day.

Billy always had his canvas paper route sacks tied to his bike rack behind his seat. They were handy for many things besides a load of *Santa Clara Journals*. Today, the seven of us would load them with mouthwatering cherries. He would walk the middle of the attack and prop his bike against a tree so we could put our pickings in his bags.

"What if we get caught?" asked Pauly, considering the consequences of the perilous effort.

"How would we? Farmer Jim can't cross the orchard fast enough to catch us even if he does see us. He's not going to drive through the trees and risk hurting his cherries. He'll have to go around to the road. We'll cut through to Lawrence and be long gone." That sounded reasonable enough and so we started.

We fanned out about ten yards across, Billy in the middle, until we reached some loaded trees. We plopped our bikes down and got to work, each of us stretching our arms and picking a different tree, loading the untucked tails of our t-shirts like produce sacks or our dark blue Grandview baseball caps and then scurrying over to Billy's bags to dump our cherries. A little too much motion for the dogs gave us away, and the barking began.

"Hey, you kids get out of my orchard!" we heard in the distance. Out the corner of my eye I saw the distant silhouette of a man, who indeed had a rifle in hand. The frothing dogs were nearly to us when he reversed them in their tracks with a piercing two-fingered whistle. We heard the loud bang of the gun and several branches splintered, leaves and cherries spraying in every direction while we scrambled for our bikes. Trying to ride between rows of trees with baseball gloves dangling from our handlebars through giant clods of dirt and dust churning everywhere was no easy task, especially when you're trying to do it fast. We hadn't calculated that in our plans. At one point, Johnny went down in the dirt like a runner sliding into third, but he picked up his bike and recklessly ran toward home with it. In what seemed like hours but was probably three minutes, tops, we were on pavement on the "street to nowhere" and then raced to the edge of the highway. To the right, we could see farmer Jim's beat-up blue pickup just turning left off El Camino and heading toward us. Our only chance was to cross over the highway to my house.

I had the side redwood gate opened and closed with everybody and the seven bikes inside the garage before farmer Jim screeched around our corner. He had no idea where we went. From the gaps between the garage door and frame, we all stacked on one another, dripping sweat and catching our breath, angling in the cracks of outside light to see farmer Frank now ever-so-slowly motor down Cabrillo, looking for any sign of kids on bikes. Fearful of betraying our hideout, we needlessly whispered as he drove up and down Cabrillo at least three times before he and his dogs left in defeat. Even then he crossed the highway and scoured the "street to nowhere" that was once part of his orchard, looking for any of us at the school or among the Kielys' prune trees. I am glad his dogs weren't bloodhounds put on our sweaty scent.

We never tried that again. Not to be wasteful, we split up the cherries that survived the trip among us, but many ended up permanent red and purplish stains on Billy's bags. His mother threw the bags in the washer eventually, but he never kept the cherry stained evidence tied to his bike again any longer than it took to deliver the *Journal*.

CHAPTER 19

S*ummer 1962*

    I missed hanging out with Allan, and together we missed our last chance to see Franklin Street downtown on the last bike ride we took together. Channel 11 News cameras were there when the bulldozers started tearing down the eight-block area for the new downtown mall. Back in May we knew lots of the stores beyond Monroe were already empty, and the Santa Clara theatre hadn't been running any matinees for a long time. Art, Allan and I went to the Sunnyvale theatre on Murphy during Easter vacation. We didn't really try to get downtown before demolition began. Somehow it wouldn't really happen if we just waited until the people who decided these things came to their senses, but the film clip on Channel 11 News uprooted us from the comfort of what used to be.

The downtown storefronts and buildings were plowed over much like the orchards, bit by bit, then they were gone for good, and most of my friends and even our parents were uncomfortable about it. By December, except for the post office and city hall, downtown Santa Clara would be gone, but most of the news story on TV focused on the new Franklin Mall that was to replace downtown. It was the newness factor at work again.

• • • •

BILLY AND I HAD A SHORT time to kill before McDonald's Hamburgers opened for the day. With our pockets full of coins, we had already reached our morning destination, not thinking about the fact that it wouldn't open much before noon. Lyle knew all about the new drive-in just beyond Scott on El Camino Real. He and Maloney had already made it a regular stop in his Ford Customline. Si's drive-in was out of business and McDonald's promised to be much cheaper than any other hamburger places around here. We rode all the way to Scott on Warburton Avenue. The red and white porcelain tiled building with its bright yellow plastic arches sat nearly catty-corner from the Texaco on El Camino. Cousin Bill no longer worked at the Texaco but I told Billy about Allan and I visiting him once.

The big red and white sign out front of McDonald's now read: "Five hundred million sold." And we had yet to have even one. At 15 cents a burger we could each afford the works. Fries were only 12 cents and an "old fashioned" milkshake 22 cents. That was a real treat worth biking all this way. While we waited, we rode the sidewalks of the PW Shopping Center, right by Fosters Freeze, and then all the way to San Tomas Aquino Creek before we headed back to the Golden Arches for lunch. Along the way, I pointed out to Billy where I saw the dead guy on the road and told him about my connection to Me & Ed's across the street.

As we sat outside at a red metal table at McDonald's, slurping our thick chocolate shakes, savoring our cheap "100% pure beef burgers" and "crisp golden fries," we watched workers behind the tilted glass aquarium windows. Uniformed teens in white short-sleeved shirts, black bow ties, black slacks and white paper hats cooked thin red meat patties and toasted brown buns in rows on the grill in assembly line fashion, dropped wire baskets of raw sliced potatoes into sizzling amber vats of oil, and poured thick blended chocolate, strawberry, and vanilla milkshakes from metal to paper cups or waited for the soda machine to fill a paper cup with a Coke, root beer, or orange. Our interest in the operation quickly faded and we decided it would be boring work, but we enjoyed our food.

We could see Uncle John's Pancake House just down to the left from us across El Camino. Its oblong brown and white sign towered above all others on the street except for the green Canada Dry bottling factory sign beyond it. We made a plan we would fill up on silver dollar pancakes at Uncle John's another morning this summer. And Uncle John's was always open for breakfast. We spent the rest of the morning biking through Scott Lane School before we headed home to get back for little league practice. The morning reminded me of bike rides with Allan.

On the morning of my birthday, the Giants and Dodgers were tied for first place, each with 40 wins. I was batting number five in the Grandview lineup. I was excited more than usual before a game because my dad and Uncle Jack were going to be there to watch. It was the first time either of them had been to one of my games. Uncle Jack was visiting from LA so he had an excuse. My dad often promised to come to a game, but usually "lost track of time" while out collecting from his pen machines. I got a hit that day though they didn't see it. They didn't show up until the last inning. I struck out. They apologized for being late and took me to Baldwin Toys, where my Uncle Jack bought me a Louisville Slugger for my birthday. I didn't say it, but it felt more like a consolation prize than a birthday gift. At least my dad kept his promise and he did see me play in a little league game. What more could I ask?

Every Giants game I went to at Candlestick Park we sat in the nosebleed section. It was always foggy, cold, concrete, and windy. The team the Giants played usually won even though the Giants had the better record at the time. Today's three o'clock game was against the Houston Colt .45s, a new National League team this year. It was already hot in Santa Clara so even the weather looked promising for the game. Coach Ramsey took our Grandview team, and I was excited to see a team other than the Cubs or Pirates, which seemed to be the games where groups got cheap or free tickets.

We went in three different cars. Six of us road with Coach Smith in his dove blue '61 VW camper and he didn't fail to wear his Bermuda shorts and black socks for the day. Riding with him didn't turn out to be the best choice. We putted along Bayshore Highway a bit slower than most of the other cars on the road, and while Billie and I had talked about how neat it would be to ride in the coach's camper with its walnut trim paneling and cabinets and even a built-in ice box and sink, we didn't realize how enclosed the ride would be in the back seat of a camper. We saw very little on the way to Candlestick. The camper's small louvered windows didn't provide much air on a warm day. It was getting hotter. Jeff Bents, our left fielder, was usually the most talkative guy on the team. He sat between Pauly and me on the back seat. Somewhere after Mountain View, Jeff stopped talking. Somewhere near Burlingame, he threw up all over coach Smith's camper sink and narrowly missed our feet with the oatmeal-looking barf that splashed about. That almost caused a chain reaction from the rest of us who gagged at the lumpy soup and sour smell that had no way to escape.

Coach Smith at first thought we were clowning around and so he yelled at us to knock it off. When he realized his mistake, he pleaded with us to stay calm. Jeff traded Johnny for the short backseat behind coach so he could aim the window vents at his face. Despite the fact I was already sweating, I stuffed my head inside the bunched up jacket I had brought along so I didn't have to face the sight or stench. Coach Smith pulled off at the next exit. We ended up in the parking lot of the Burlingame Ramada Inn where we all jumped out of the camper. Coach did the best he could with paper towels he had stored in the camper to clean up the mess. He dampened the towels with a thermos of water. There was no water stored in the camper tank. I was glad I wasn't the adult in charge. I would probably have made Jeff clean up his own vomit.

When we finally got to the "Stick," it was a sunny 72 degrees. We spent twenty minutes trying to find the rest of the team. Coach Ramsay had all the tickets in his pocket. We sat in the upper deck in right-center field and fought the sun most of the afternoon. When a fly ball was hit, you determined which way it was headed strictly by the way the players reacted. We watched anxiously for Mays or McCovey to hit one out and had our mitts ready, but it didn't happen that day. Pagan did hit a double. The Colt .45s beat the Giants, 6-4, even though the Colt .45s were in seventh place at the time and the Giants were 1 1/2 games out of first behind the Dodgers. At least we got to see some of our baseball heroes. By the sixth inning the wind began to swirl and found out where we were sitting, as usual. The fog rolled in and the grey and white seagulls showed up just in time for the last inning. By then we were Candlestick cold and some of the guys had been stupid enough to leave their jackets in the car. I knew from experience at Candlestick than to make that mistake again.

When we found the camper, we tried airing it out by opening the sliding van door wide a few minutes before we left the gravel parking lot, which was slow at emptying out anyway. The camper had gotten pretty stale over three hours. I zipped my black jacket collar over my nose and sat that way most of the way home.

Just three years ago Pauly and his family moved into the redwood house on Lawrence Station Road. Now the Owens are gone. Since sixth grade I had not spent much time around Pauly except for little league practice and games. We had gone different ways and spent our time with different people so it was a shock when I found out Pauly had moved last week. He hadn't even said anything about moving when we went to the Giants game last month. His family is renting another farmhouse. This one is out on Reed Road, not far from the Lawrence train station.

I road to the new house one afternoon after practice with Pauly and Johnny to somehow make up for my own loss more than anything else. The Lawrence house looked like a ghost town out of a *Gun Smoke* episode when we rode by it. I hadn't even noticed until now, and I kept going over in my mind when I had last gone by it and wondered if it was empty then.

Their new house was much smaller than the redwood house. The paint-blistered bungalow had only two tiny bedrooms. There were blanket-laden mattresses on the floors of the living room and the back porch. Each boy kept his stuff in a tall abused cardboard box by a mattress. I don't know what happened to their dressers and I didn't ask. Pauly tossed his glove and baseball cleats into his box in one corner of the living room. I recognized his Shakespeare fishing pole amongst his other things. I said hi to his sisters who were lying on the floor busy watching TV, even as we climbed through them. Pauly and I went into the kitchen where Mrs. Owens, frying up something oniony on the stove, stopped to greet me like her lost child with a big-breasted smothering hug, complained about how I had not been around anymore, and then insisted on making the two of us peanut butter and jelly sandwiches on Sunlite bread. Pauly and I sat on the comfort of the front porch wall eating our sandwiches watching the traffic pick up along Reed as cannery and electronics workers up the road got off work.

"Thursday is demolition day," Pauly announced. I knew he was into cars so mistakenly I thought he was talking about an event at the fairgrounds. "It was a pretty good old house. I don't see why they have to tear it down."

On Thursday morning Art and I watched from Del Monte Avenue on our bicycles while one big yellow bulldozer splintered the Owens house in less than an hour. All that remained were the concrete slabs of foundation, porch and breezeway. By noon, the concrete was broken up into chunks and piled in a separate mound from the house splinters and pipes. Pauly did not show up to see the destruction.

Before school started in September, two new houses were built where the redwood house once stood, their stucco fronts facing Del Monte Avenue, just like the rest of the houses on the block. Del Monte Avenue had lost its playing field. There were now no more houses facing Lawrence Station Road along the east side all the way to Bayshore Highway.

This July AT&T put a communications satellite into space. Hopefully, Telstar will do better than Kiddie World or Wham O broadcasting events. Just a little over a year ago, Kiddie World Toys moved to Stevens Creek from their smaller store on San Carlos near the water works corner. The new two-story building is huge and the side of the parking lot displays doughboy pools and playground equipment for backyards. Two luxury items I know our family will never own. I had only been to the new store a couple of times before Alvin and Ricky told me about the big Wham O event on Saturday. I figured anything with the Wham O name on it had to be a hit. A lot of the kids at school—mostly girls—are hula-hoop experts. Lorraine's family has had a Slip 'n Slide on their from lawn for most of the year (My mother complains in the car to us every time we drive by it). I don't know anybody who doesn't have at least one scuffed up plastic Frisbee somewhere around the house, if a dog hasn't chewed it up yet. Of course wherever we have our Saturday dances there is always an official Wham O limbo party kit. The constant rhythmic thumping I heard coming from the Kellers' garage Saturday morning was kind of annoying.

I was in my driveway washing off my bike when Alvin and his brother Ricky came from inside their garage out to the street, and neither one of them missed a beat. They were playing paddle ball, with a twist. Instead of the flat wooden paddles with a stapled rubber band and red rubber ball, these paddles were Dodger blue plastic, about an inch thick and hollow. The ball and band were attached to the hollow racket, and the normal rebound of the ball on the Wham O paddle was ten times louder than a wooden paddle. As they walked over to me on the sidewalk, the rhythmical beats got louder. I could see Mr. Schlegel peeking at us from his kitchen window.

Alvin and Ricky had moved two doors down from us shortly after St. Lawrence chapel was built. They were a good Catholic family and the two most competitive kids at either Briarwood or Jefferson. Their dad had gone to Stanford University in Palo Alto, and they let everyone know it. No one doubted their story. They were both the top math and science students at their schools. For me that meant having to put up with Alvin every day in class.

Alvin always had to win in a competition or get the best grade on a test or assignment, and he always had a big smile on his face that made you think he was smirking at you. Alvin was at the top of our class but at the bottom of the picking order whenever we had to pick teams for anything, especially in P.E. Teachers would help him out by selecting him as a captain so he could do the choosing. He thought it was because he was so good, but I think some of them just felt embarrassed for him.

Alvin was never part of our Monticello clique by choice, his and ours. He was too busy doing math problems or reading to play little league. He didn't have time for girls, so he was never invited to our Saturday dances. Yet he didn't seem to mind, and the next time you spoke with him he would start bragging about something he or his dad was doing.

Mr. Keller was another suit in the neighborhood. He was a design engineer for a company called Fairchild. Alvin said his dad engineered integrated circuitry, whatever that means. It seemed a little unlike Alvin to be wasting his time on a silly paddle ball game on a Saturday, but why he was doing it became quickly clear.

"Hey, want to enter a contest with us?" Alvin asked me while still paddling and counting under his breath. I knew better than to compete with Alvin most of the time. He just wanted to beat you and rub it in. With his lower lip he kept puffing his straight black hair out of his eyes much like Hitler must have had to do when he was due for a haircut.

Suddenly, Ricky stuttered his bounces and the ball shot off out of his reach on the rubber band. "Damn it. I'll never be able to keep up with you," he said to Alvin who still hadn't missed his rhythm and was softly continuing his count under his breath. Ricky knew his limitations.

"Seven ninety-nine, eight hundred," Alvin blurted out and then grabbed the ball as if to discipline it before it hit the paddle again. "That's a record for me, but I'm going for a thousand this afternoon. How do you like our paddles?" When the noise quit, Mr. Schlegel left his window.

"I've never seen a paddle ball like that." He handed the blue plastic paddle to me to examine as I put my towel across my bike. On both sides of the paddle was the Wham O name in large white letters.

"A friend of my dad got a bunch of these from a Wham O rep the other day. The guy told him to give them to people he knew that had kids. Wham O is sponsoring a big contest this afternoon at Kiddie World to promote these things. I saw the ad in the *Mercury* this morning for the contest and they're supposedly advertising it on KYA and KLIV. They're giving away all kinds of neat stuff, just for participating. I plan to win the portable TV they're giving to the kid who paddles the most reps without a miss," explained Alvin, all the time grinning or smirking as he spoke.

I knew I wouldn't stand a chance against Alvin or Ricky or a bunch of other competitors like them, but I went over to Alvin's and he gave me a brand new paddle ball. The three of us practiced at the mind-and-ear-numbing paddles for at least an hour in their garage. With some persuasion from Alvin, I went to Kiddie World that afternoon. Alvin's dad took us. I figured he wanted to see his kids beat the competition, but I was wrong. I went just hoping I wouldn't embarrass myself.

Mr. Keller dropped us off at Kiddie World for a couple of hours. We waited for the competition, and in front of the store the Wham O people, a young guy and girl, set up a folding table full of Wham O toys from hula-hoops to Frisbees, Wham O t-shirts, a Brownie camera, a fancy transistor radio, and the first-place prize, a Philco portable TV, just as Alvin had described it. The Wham O people played music through a loudspeaker and talked to the three of us, waiting for the crowd to arrive. The young woman from Wham O did some hula-hoop tricks for us while her Wham O partner narrated her moves. Except for few shoppers who were at the store managing their excited little kids, nobody else showed up for the contest.

Alvin won a silver Philco 19" portable TV. It sells for almost $200 in the stores. Ricky won a teal Realtone Comet transistor radio, complete with leather case and ear phone. I went home with a brand new Kodak Brownie Hawkeye camera. We all got Wham O t-shirts, more paddle balls, some kind of Wham O bouncy balls the company was going to promote soon, and big smiles on our faces. I never saw the Wham O paddle ball game in any other store. I guess the 15-cent wood paddle ball was good enough for most people. Alvin was an okay guy sometimes.

• • • •

IT WASN'T LONG AGO that the Drifter's "Save the Last Dance" was number one on the music charts, and we had played that song at every one of our Saturday night record hops. Had I known then that tonight was *my* last dance, I think I would have done things differently.

This month Sharon Miller and I were a hand-holding couple. We had been so officially for two weeks. I didn't really see a future in our relationship, especially when I found out her dad was a Santa Clara cop. Too scary. Barbie Bell and I had broken up in early April.

It seemed like destiny that she and Ken Leahy should get together, anyway. "Here come Barbie and Ken. How cute," we all would say at our dance parties. Couples in our clique changed faster than the number one hit on Billboard. We were comfortable with that and each other.

Rita was as enthusiastic as ever about our record hops and more of our Saturday night dances were in her garage than in anyone else's. We took her for granted, and I had taken all of them for granted. I just didn't realize it yet. Word had gotten out quickly that I was moving away some day, and I was strangely kind of proud of the fact. I kept thinking about how Lyle had sold me on my good fortune to eventually be headed to Buchser High, not Wilcox, where all my friends were heading. I did not allow myself to think otherwise. Besides, I thought I was ready for something new. I had known all these people since second grade. We still had two months before seventh grade would begin so there was plenty of time for goodbyes. Besides, I didn't know exactly when I was moving anyhow. I figured even after I moved I could see them anytime I wanted as long as I had a bike. That night Sharon and I broke it off, but we both tried to make each other jealous throughout the evening, dancing with other people and laughing it up. We would both get over it quickly. In August, Rita went to Michigan with her family for vacation. Nobody hosted a party that month. In September *they* all went back to Jefferson. School at Jefferson and parties were over for me.

My mother knew where she wanted to move and when, but the city didn't run on my mother's schedule. Shopping for another house was vaguely familiar to me. It was about going through model homes again and again. At least this time we didn't have to make an eight hundred mile train trip to complete the search. Of course, if my mother had to move, it would be to another new house. When the city council started talking about widening Lawrence Station Road, my mother and father were not happy. We had rights, my dad would say to whoever listened. We already slept on the edge of the two-lane highway Lawrence Station Road had become.

Once city officials came up with an actual plan to widen the road, my parents' attitude changed. The new plan included removal of our house entirely for access to a newly designed expressway. My mother saw it as another chance at something new. The adult talk shifted from complaining about what rights we had to how much money the city would pay us for our house. New was good again.

Before anything from the city was in writing, my mother and father had picked out a new house that was just a red dot on a map in a showroom. Lyle no longer lived at home so it was a relief to me that we were going to move just six miles down the road off Pruneridge Avenue, not so far from Lawrence. For me that would mean the comfort of going to Buchser High, just like Lyle. Lyle would remind me every time he came home—usually with a load of laundry—how lucky I would be to go to Buchser and not Wilcox High, which just opened last year along Monroe. I didn't realize at the time but something wasn't quite right with his picture.

The recently ripped out prune orchards along Pruneridge were bought up by Killarney Farms #2, and I found donkeys Grace and Morris in their old re-built corral just like Michael had said they would be. With the Killarney salesman, we drove to a leveled prune orchard down the road to imagine our new house, but all we saw was dirt. A creek ran through the middle of the dirt fields where the orchards once stood, which was part of the same Saratoga Creek I knew on the north side of El Camino.

Back in the sales office, my mother ordered up another pink house, and the appliances she selected were again pink. She and my father put a $500 deposit down on its construction. Building went ahead on our new house along Colgate Avenue in the latest new neighborhood. It would be ready September 1.

When we came to California my dad's plan was to work full time at Willig until he got the pen vending machine business off the ground in a couple of years. Five years later, he was still working at Willig. His new pen machine business lasted four years, weekends and evenings, before stacks and stacks of vending machines and iron stands again filled our garage, eventually finding their way to the side of the house, hidden under soiled and weathered canvas drop cloths on the damp concrete before they made their last journey.

My dad seemed most content when he was tending to his machines, talking with customers, or making another sales deal with a grocery store owner or dime store manager to carry his ballpoint pens in their shops, and it would be the topic of conversation and speculation with my mom at supper every night until he made another deal. I know his business kept him away from home a lot. The handful of weekend mornings I went collecting with him are the most time I have spent with my dad.

My mom and I became experts at "rolling" the quarters into orange paper coin wrappers in the evenings. She'd sit at our Formica maple kitchen table working piles of quarters from coin-stained canvas bank bags full of loose quarters onto the tabletop and stuff and tuck the $20 rolls. I preferred the comfort of the den carpeting and the distraction of TV while I worked. Rule Number 1: Pile quarters on a cardboard box flap so as not to stain the rug. Rule number 2: "Don't put your hands to your mouth." Rule Number 3: "Wash your hands when you finish. You don't know where that money's been." My mother would repeat the rules at every coin session. She made a real cleaning session out wiping down the kitchen table area when she finished.

Another pen business task we had was putting the brass and plastic top-click pens of dozens of colors into grey cardboard tubes so they would roll out of the vending machines. When a new order of pens arrived at the house, we'd inspect them for the newest colors, perhaps a chartreuse or burgundy or puce, and I would occasionally take one or two for school. I found the five-inch long tubes particularly good spitball shooters.

One cloudy Saturday morning Lyle and I helped my dad heave the machines and their iron stands out the back of a borrowed rusty black utility trailer into a heap of garbage at the seagull-infested Alviso dump. It was a filthy job. Mother can now stop complaining about "those dirty old machines" on the side of the garage and reminding my dad he can make more money working overtime for Willig than he can selling pens. I am sure my dad appreciates that. It seems to me that more than pen machines were left at the dump that day. We drove home in silence.

Dad hasn't talked at all about the pen machine business since that day. It must be like talking about fighting in the war, and he doesn't do that either. Ballpoint pens in drawers and unexpected places around the house are our family's reminders of the new California venture my dad made real, and the reason I was in California in the first place.

Just before seventh grade started, I was rummaging around in the rafters of the garage attic and found a lone Rite Master ball point pen-dispensing machine my dad had apparently saved. It sat, already collecting dust, along side his dented army green footlocker from the war. I am sure my mother will throw out the machine and possibly the footlocker before we move to our new house.

CHAPTER 20

F*all 1962*

Saturo Avery lived most of his life in Japan, and he and I were both foreigners to Curtis Junior High. At least Saturo lived near the school he would now attend. I rode my bike every day to Curtis from Cabrillo when the city council delayed final approval to pay for the new expressway by September 1, and that meant my parents not being able to pay for the new house they had ordered at Killarney Farms.

Curtis Junior High, home of the Cougars, was a fairly new school so most of the buildings were nicer than Jefferson's, but it wasn't comfortable. Yet there were similarities I had never thought about before I arrived my first day. That morning I sat in the mostly empty cafeteria at a long fold-down table testing in booklets with a No. 2 pencil and with a handful of other "new students." The rest of the kids at Curtis were busy getting reacquainted in their new classes with their new teachers and *old friends*, just as my Jefferson Jaguar friends were doing. The newness of it all got me down.

This morning the banner headline of the *San Jose Mercury* front page announced the death of Marilyn Monroe. The obituary on Arturo's father who died of a heart attack the same night wouldn't be in the *Mercury* for another four days, which is where I found out about it. I hadn't see Arturo or any of my other old friends since school started.

Nothing seemed the same. On Sunday, September 23, I stood in line with my mother and 2,500,000 other people in the Bay Area, mostly kids, on the first SOS, Sabin Oral Sunday. I was back at Briarwood school to get my polio sugar cube. Even though I had already started seventh grade across town, we still lived on Cabrillo. As my mother and I waited in the line of kids and parents that snaked within the corridors, everything was smaller than I remembered it, even the number of old friends I expected to see.

In October, the Giants beat the Dodgers in the playoffs and were headed to the World Series. I was proud I had seen the Giants play this year. I didn't feel the same about having to move this Saturday, but riding out of my Cabrillo neighborhood to a new part of town, new school, and new faces was getting old in an unfamiliar solitary way, and the weather was making it harder. One day it rained so hard I stayed home. It wasn't like my mother was going to drive me there.

Though it was now October, we were still moving to Killarney Farms. My mother had to give up the house she had chosen. The only finished house left on Colgate Avenue ready now that the city was ready for us to leave was a more expensive model, identical to Michael McClintock's house, and my mom and dad spent the next couple of evenings discussing how they could afford it. They even talked about refusing the city's deadline. In the end, they went ahead with the purchase, and my dad got the city to give us an extra hundred dollars for the inconvenience of moving later than what was originally agreed. I could see my mother's delight in her attitude prior to the move. Another good outcome of the delay was no more pink. The completed house was yellow and the brand new pink Frigidaire that had been sitting wrapped in cardboard in our Cabrillo garage was actually hauled away to be repainted yellow to match the rest of our new kitchen. I think Killarney Farms paid for the paint job.

Thursday night my dad had a terrible coughing fit. Over the years we have grown used to his coughing spasms, usually just after bed or first thing in the morning while the coffee percolates. It seems the entire Collins family are coughers, and the ones in his family who smoke are the worst. Lyle and I tell dad again and again to stop smoking, but he ignores our pleas. He reminds us just as often that he's been smoking since he was thirteen. He usually sucks on a lemon drop or licorice button and gradually the coughing fades, but we have come to expect his daily coughing bouts.

Tonight while I lay in bed I could hear an occasional groan between some of those hacks, and then I heard my mother and dad shuffling around in their room, talking about something not looking good and seeing a doctor. By the time I got up Friday morning for school my dad had already left. Tomorrow was the big move, and he was going to borrow Chet's trailer tonight for the move. A group of friends would be over to help tomorrow. The house was a maze of cardboard boxes.

"We think your father's got a hernia. He drove to O'Connors Hospital to have it checked out," my mother told me as I sat down to eat breakfast. I had never heard of a hernia. Was it some kind of disease like cancer? I had no idea.

My mother explained about the abdominal rupture and assured me that it could be fixed so I was relieved, and then the phone rang. No hernia for my dad. He had a double hernia! He had been admitted to the hospital and was scheduled for surgery that day. Mother insisted I go to school but I could sense the anxiety in her voice. She had a lot to do, and of course the move was postponed again. She was still on the phone with friends and neighbors when I road off on my bike Friday for Curtis.

That night Lyle came home and drove us to the hospital to visit my dad. Emma had taken my mom to O'Connors and back earlier in the day. My dad looked good. He was good enough to dig around in the box of Whitman's Sampler we bought for him at Drug King to look for the caramels. I worry that someday I too will get a hernia now.

The move was on again for October 13, the day after Columbus Day. In the meantime, we shuffled around the house between boxes everywhere that cramped us like freight aboard a ship's deck. Columbus probably had an easier time landing in the New World than we were having landing in our new house and starting our next new life. The TV news called the biggest storm to ever hit the Bay Area on Columbus Day the "Big Blow." It would delay the World Series and our moving day again.

Three days later, the Giants lost to the Yankees in Game 7. That weekend the short move we made across town was my loss. Time is already making the distance greater.

Everything is new again.

Tuesday afternoon and Santa Clara schools were done for the day. The wind worked against me as I pedaled my bike to the other side of town. Lots of people were in their houses this afternoon, watching TV or listening to radio for news about the Russians and Cubans after the warning President Kennedy gave to the Reds yesterday. My teachers put on a big show in class today, with pull-down maps and wooden pointers, newspaper headlines, and radio reports on portable radios that played mostly static, attempting to explain what these events meant for us and them.

I knew I would not be seeing my friends anymore, even if the world didn't end tomorrow. I still needed to go back there. Cutting through Briarwood schoolyard felt like a history lesson of names and places of a distant past. October chilled my face, but I cuffed my jacket collar to my neck and rode above my seat, thrusting my legs and heels at the pedals as the wind resisted me. The playground was a forgotten battlefield, absent kids screaming and laughing, playing and fighting. Only clanking sounds of tetherball chains and monkey bar rings spoke in the wind that blew through the grey asphalt space.

There were other times growing up in Santa Clara when I went beyond the miles I would ride today, but how far I went this day had more to do with changes I knew were coming. I will be a teenager next year if the country doesn't blow up first. My *Warriner's* grammar book said nouns name *people, places, things and ideas.* Lots of nouns I can name have changed around here in the last five years. I have moved on from the town I knew and the friends I made there, and their memory of me will soon be lost, I am afraid.

• • • •

Weathered by neglect, a few dusty, drab pyracantha hedges clinging to a faded grey redwood fence that surrounded the back edge of our yard were all that was left when I reached what was now just another plowed up lot, a common sight in Santa Clara. I stopped my bike where the sidewalk ended abruptly at fresh dozer tracks in the disturbed dirt. Straddling my bike, I studied the exposed shadow of darker dirt in the middle of the lot where our pink tract house once stood. I was too late to see the house sawed in two and hauled away on giant trailers, but unlike acres of orchards and crops plowed over before it, the house will be plopped on another lot somewhere and hopefully get a new color in another life. Maybe I can find it someday.

When the house was new, just five years ago, it *was* change in Santa Clara, one of thousands of tract houses that replaced the orchards and farms. Everyone in the neighborhood had probably been through our house, the first model home of Lawrence Meadows that announced more change in Santa Clara. Now it too was a victim of change. So was I. The bulldozed brick, rock, dirt, patio, driveway, walkways and mangled shrubbery were shoved into an ugly pile in one corner of the lot, like an attempted cleanup following a bomb's aftermath—ground zero was limited to one house and . . . .

I looked up, just now aware there was nothing to stop the wind around me. The shelterbelt of black walnut trees that bordered Lawrence Station Road on either side were also gone. The Kiely family prune trees across the highway lay in wide splintered piles, ready for burning. For the first time since I had lived here I could see deep into Sunnyvale from this side of the roadway where exposed pale fences stood acres in the distance, boxing in more tract houses, where they had once lined the prune orchard whose trunks, limbs, buds, leaves, blossoms, and plums in seasons had hidden their view. In the grey and empty sky, Mrs. Kiely's once-white stately Victorian house stood naked, fresh plywood sheets nailed over its window casings. Bruised white pickets, uprooted hedges and rose bushes were tossed randomly into the funeral pyres of the orchard wasteland. Dismantled, twisted wrought iron lay in another heap. The ancient house stood blindfolded awaiting its reckoning, too.

Afterward

I think I actually began writing this story in the fourth grade, in 1959, and even then the events and people of those short pieces were based on things I personally witnessed. Fifty years later, I began doing research on the local history of Santa Clara, and I became obsessed with revisiting the Santa Clara I remembered from the fifties and sixties. The five years of this story were years of rapid change, especially in the Santa Clara Valley, and we were all caught up in its vortex.

Historical information is available at a touch of the screen. The bigger the event the easier the access. The records of things not so big reside mostly in our memories, though social media is changing that as well. My story is an attempt to put a few of those not-so-big events into their accurate historical settings and bring a little piece of Santa Clara's past back to life.

I have tried to share a fairly accurate map of a changing Santa Clara in the late fifties seen through a boy's eyes. I have researched bigger events and local places for that accuracy. Occasionally, I have taken small liberties with an event for the sake of the storyline, such as what month an event took place.

The people in my story are fictionalized as are most of the small events of the narrator's life, but I hope they feel familiar and real to the reader. The boy narrating the story is based to a large degree on details of my own life, but the storyteller and his friends and neighbors are fictional and serve as vehicles for telling the story of what is was like growing up in the new suburbs of the Santa Clara Valley. I hope my story captures small moments in a kid's life, maybe a life not so unlike your own.

I would like to thank the many people who have helped me in my research, from school district secretaries to personnel at the Santa Clara Planning Department to the Santa Clara librarians to people at the Sunnyvale Heritage Society for access to records, maps, directories, newspaper archives, and heritage genealogical information. Thanks also to friends and family and locals of Santa Clara who have provided me with the minutiae for me to recreate that time and place.

. . . .

". . . PARTLY TRUTH AND partly fiction."
The Author

About the Author

About the Author

Kenneth Crowther grew up in Santa Clara, California in the 1950s and 60s. He taught high school English and journalism in San Jose, California, for nearly thirty-five years. Today he resides in the Monterey Bay Area and spends a great deal of his time traveling and continuing to search for adventures on his bicycle much as he did as a young boy.